ALSO BY HUBERT L

HORROR

Under Crete
Under Snake Island
Empty Skies
Under Bethel
A Menagerie of Suffering
Pieces
The Hearth
Better Left Buried

SCI-FI DRAMA

Breath of Mars
The Last Library

DARK FANTASY

Birth of the Vampire
The Vampires of Hope's Covenant
Rage of the Vampire
War of the Vampire

BLOOD
&
SALT

HUBERT L. MULLINS

For Liam and Jess, always smiling brightly whenever I rattle off a new Titanic fact. . .

All this time there was no apprehension of any danger in the minds of passengers, and no one was in any condition of panic or hysteria; after all, it would have been strange if they had been, without any definite evidence of danger.

-Lawrence Beesley, second-class passenger

PART I

DOOMED FROM DESIGN

Southampton, England

"Too early to be sleeping, William," said Doctor Simpson as he reached across Benjamin and nudged the old man in the ribs.

"Just studyin' the backs of me eyelids," said Doctor O'Loughlin, *Titanic's* chief surgeon. He became fully alert and turned on the honest Irish charm so many aboard had come to know and love. "When you reach my age, you'll be lookin' for these sparse moments of rest. I'm the oldest crewman on the ship, ye know."

"I thought Captain Smith was the oldest," said Ben. "He told us at muster he's sixty-two."

Doctor O'Loughlin grinned, his grizzled face turned in jubilation. "And he is. And so am I. But I'm three months older." He winked at Ben and grabbed his knee in affection before standing up and smoothing his uniform.

The rest of them joined him, all wearing their finest full-dress regalia for the swarm of passengers about to embark. Today was a big day, and Ben felt out of sorts. Of the medical staff, aside from Matron

3

Wallis, he was probably the least experienced. They were good people to let him come along, even if he didn't plan on making the return trip.

The gangway door yawned open, bleeding in crystal air and golden sun. A breeze carried in something a little more sinister—the rot and ruin of a hundred unwashed Irish, Swedes, and gypsies. They sparkled all the way down the ramp, but it wasn't like those in first-class. These sparkles weren't borne of excess, these sparkles were of new beginnings. The crowd of mostly women and children was difficult to read, for half seemed content to stay in the old world while the others were nearly pushing the staff aside so they could board. They carried with them their entire lives, reduced to a few burlap sacks and frayed steamer trunks.

"Eh, better get on with it then," said O'Loughlin. "Smith says we got almost a thousand of 'em. Mostly fam'lies."

Benjamin York suspected as much. He stepped up to the gangway door and put one foot on the ramp and looked out. To his left, the ship extended for as far as he could see, a solid wall of black steel and rivets. The smell of fresh paint still lingered on the air, mixed with the sour water of the quay. He counted at least three more gangways, these filled with first- and second-class passengers who were segregated now and would remain so for the next seven days. Those ladies looked impressive in their dresses and wide hats and decadent ermine and seal coats.

He'd turned to the right, to the open harbor and *Titanic's* forward. Today was a special day for many reasons, among them his second sighting ever of an automobile. It was being lowered down to deck through the ship's hatch, its white wheels gleaming in the morning sun. Someone would partially deconstruct it for the journey across the Atlantic.

Ben must have been staring for too long, because Doctor O'Loughlin jabbed him in the ribs with something sharp. He said, "Get yer mind back here this instant. We've work to do." And then he placed a buttonhook on his palm.

Both Ben and the good doctor lined the door and checked each passenger's eyes before coming aboard. Trachoma was a nasty disease that was easily transmissible, especially in close quarters. And since Ben regularly saw as many as ten tickets for the same cabin, he knew he couldn't let a single red or pus-filled eyelid come aboard. Using the buttonhook, he flipped eyelids out, checked them for redness or swelling, then let them proceed down E deck.

Most of them had lice, but if the crew started turning away passengers over that, there'd be no steerage class at all. Ben was far more lenient than

Doctor O'Loughlin and Doctor Simpson and even Matron Wallis, who all broke up families when only one member was denied embarkment. Ben watched as the rejected turned and headed back down the gangway, dreams dashed.

In the middle of the ramp, a boy no more than eight was being escorted by his mother, a frizzy-haired girl with freckles and a nervous smile to the surrounding people. Ben's attention found them rather quickly because the boy was scraping something metal along the gangway railing. It was so obnoxious that he thought Doctor O'Loughlin was ready to part the potential passengers and address it himself.

But the boy lost his hold on the shiny piece of metal, and it tumbled off the railing. It was too noisy to hear the splash, but nonetheless, it would forever live in Berth 44, Southampton. The boy wailed and the mother looked over the gangway and Ben was certain he saw her tears chase the object into the water. And then she pulled the child into her chest and hugged him. Ben didn't understand the significance of what he'd dropped, but knew that with her crying, she was going to make her eyes red and puffy before seeing the medical staff.

Ben turned to O'Loughlin and said, "I'll be right back."

"Where d'you think yer goin'?"

"Just there. Back in a jiff."

He pushed through the third-class passengers until he reached the mother and boy. Most everyone parted around him, recognizing his White Star Line coat as something important. They also realized that this was one of the men who decided whether they sailed away. When he reached the crying duo, he knelt in front of the boy and appraised him with practiced, gentle eyes. Ben always had a knack for calming children. He'd been with many during the worst parts of their lives. His mother always said it was a gift, and that's why he should go into medicine. To calm people in the face of sickness.

"What's wrong, lad?"

He shook his head, as if saying the words were too awful.

Ben searched the mother for an explanation.

"Dropped his da's cross right over. Metal crucifix. Reid's carried it all the way from Killarney."

"You're Reid?"

The boy nodded, his big, blue eyes like dots of ocean water. He sniffed back tears, his nose dripping.

"I had a cross like that when I was a boy. Belonged to my dad, too." Ben looked past the mother—a trio of kids and an elderly lady stood waiting patiently. "Is your da here?" Families and single women were all to board via this gangway.

The boy shook his head.

"C'mon, Reid. Let's not bother this man any longer. Do I give this to you?" She pushed the boarding pass into his hands. Their cabin was number 66, down on F Deck.

"Let me see you first," he said, and without the buttonhook, did a quick inspection of their eyes and mouths. As he escorted them to the front of the line, he said, "I'll be seeing you again, Reid. And we'll see if we can't find a replacement crucifix. How's that? One that would make your da proud?"

At this, Reid's eyes lit up, and so did his mother's. He didn't know how he could fulfil that promise. Then again, there were bound to be holy men on the ship. Later, once they were all on their way to Cherbourg, he'd ask around.

Ben was about to step back through the gangway door when he turned to the cranes, hoping to spy another car being lowered into the forward hatch. He'd heard there were at least seven on the cargo manifest. But now there were no cars at all, but a long, black wooden box that creaked and rocked back and forth on its davit.

This box seemed to swallow all the light, for it was so dark and ominous that he expected it to call up a storm. The more he stared at it, the more unease he felt, and he quickly averted his eyes just before his stomach churned. He didn't understand this at all—it was only a box. *Titanic* was full of them. The next influx of passengers rushed forward. Families of Hungarians, Swedes, a couple of Italians, and a lot of English were among those ready to start their new lives. And the next time Ben looked back toward the crane, the box was gone, lowered onto the ship it would share with him for the next week.

Boiler Room 6

He missed the coal mines.

More than that, he missed the cool air, the repetitious mattocks as they bit into the tough ground. Down in the boilers of the world's grandest ship wasn't where he thought life would take him. The heat was enough to drive him mad, and if not for the lax dress code of firemen and trimmers, the job would've been unbearable.

Normally the lead fireman would make sure they were in pants, but this morning was especially hot in the boilers, so they'd all stripped down to shorts and thin shirts. They hadn't lit so many boilers since the sea trials, and in a couple of hours, they'd be steaming away. Right now, that wasn't John Coffey's priority.

A fire had been burning in the Number 10 bunker for almost two weeks. No one noticed it at first, but a little nugget of red coal had blossomed into something that was now uncontrollable. John, along with a dozen other firemen and trimmers, were moving the coal out of the starboard bunker and into one on the port side.

This presented a precarious problem. Burning coal couldn't go back into the bunker, else they were simply creating the same problem on the other side of the ship. So any coal with excessive heat went right into the furnace—wasted, if someone were to ask John, for all it could do was turn to idle steam while the folks above boarded and became situated. With the coal strikes plaguing Southampton, he couldn't believe the White Star Line had enough money to let their precious fuel burn for nothing.

Coal jobs were the only jobs he could do. And in another few years, his spine and knees wouldn't let him do even that. He wanted off the ship—he wanted off ships for good. This would be his last one, for sure. Maybe back home he'd pick up painting or something in textiles. Somewhere the air didn't choke him when he breathed. He always thought he was a good enough talker to sell something. Maybe shoes or umbrellas.

The more he sweat, the more the coal dust stuck to his face. When it got in his nose and mouth, he pulled out his handkerchief and coughed into it. The smear of black probably wasn't good for one's health.

He stared up at the three-story bunker, the unending supply of coal trickling down for the trimmers to break into manageable chunks. At this pace, which was surprisingly efficient, they wouldn't have this bunker cleared until they arrived in New York.

The stokers resembled sleepwalkers as they toiled. Strong men of every nationality covered in soot and grime—the Black Foot Brigade, as they'd been called. In the dim light, all John saw were the whites of their eyes. They were shadow people, slaves of industry earning six pounds a month for their services.

Right now, it was calm. The coal dust was settled, the boiler room quiet. It was all because the engines were idle. Once they started up, this place would be abuzz with activity, noise, and squalls of soot that would blind them if they weren't careful.

And also the heat. With over a hundred and fifty furnaces fed around the clock, it would feel like a walk across the sun.

"John? John Coffey? Who here's seen John Coffey?" He recognized the voice and almost wanted to throw himself in the bunker out of sheer embarrassment. He turned toward the starboard-side staircase and saw a man coming down, set apart by his dress. He was wearing the trousers and jacket of upper crewmen, and it wouldn't take long for his clothes to look like everyone else's in the boiler room. Ernest was going to get them both in trouble.

John pushed his way through the firemen and the trimmers who were trundling along with their heavy barrows of coal. He grabbed Ernest by the collar and pulled him beneath the staircase, hoping to avoid Lead Fireman Barrett's watchful gaze.

"I told you I'd find you at noon," said John, cupping his hand and screaming in his friend's ear. When he separated, Ernest was left with a half-circle of black soot on his cheek.

"I know, I know, but I was excited to tell ya so I had to come on down. We got somethin' special up there."

Ernest was one of *Titanic's* cargo loaders. He'd spent the entire morning in the nice sunshine and cool air, loading passenger baggage and freight onto the Orlop Deck.

"Yeah?" said John, slightly interested. They had a lucrative plan, one that could go wrong rather quickly if Lady Luck did not kiss them.

"Someone's shippin' treasure. Gold, jewels, and what have you."

John didn't believe it. Ernest—a fellow Irishman—had grown up down the street from John. And he'd been a liar back then as sure as he was here, crouched beneath the stairwell.

"How do you know that?"

"Seen the manifest."

"Ernest, chap . . . you can't read."

He took offense to this jab, but ended up laughing anyway, his stark white—if sparse—teeth, shining against the furnace fires. "True, true. But it was read to me, Johnny. We're movin' stuff from the big museum in London. They have one of them . . . what do you call it? Ex . . .exhab . . ."

"Exhibition?"

"Right, that's what I said. They're movin' a bunch of it to America. Now listen: Those riches, along with whatever those silk and taffeta wearin' sticks upstairs brung with 'em, are all just a deck above our heads. We can take it and we can get out of here, and what have you."

They'd always planned to jump ship in Queenstown. Neither liked the job they'd signed up for on *Titanic*, and John knew Ireland had far more prospects for a man of his limited intelligence than Southampton. And his flat here was too expensive, considering he only used it for a bed. All of his worldly possessions were in a bag down in his cabin.

"What'dya say, Johnny? Hey, if we find enough good stuff, you won't have to work at eight tonight! Start your desertion early, my friend."

"Don't say that word. I hate it. And we'll have a look, yeah? But if we see anyone, anyone at all, I'm turning around and coming back down."

"That's good enough for me!" said Ernest, smacking his hands together. "Noon?"

He shook his head. "After lunch. I'll meet you on the stairs, okay?"

He smacked his hands together again and hugged John, pulling the man so hard he bit his tongue. When they separated, Ernest was covered in coal dust. He brushed the front of his shirt, but it only made the mess worse.

"It's alright. I got another one in me steamer, and what have you. Bye, Johnny Boy! See you after lunch!"

He bounded up the steps and disappeared around the corner. John stayed there for a moment, long enough to see lead fireman Barrett walking by with a cigarette dangling from his lips so he was probably heading to grab a bite to eat—which meant John had a few minutes to steal a breath of fresh air.

He headed the opposite way, moving across deck, through Boiler Room 5 all the way through 1. The first room was lit, but only because it was used to maintain portside functions. When the ship was in motion, the captain wouldn't relight it. The darkness of the few fires kept the tall boiler hidden in shadows. Right now, it was just a dark maze of steel catwalks and platforms above his head.

The third-class promenade at the stern of the ship was empty now, but sure to be full later when the passengers were acclimated to their cabins and as-sembly areas. The air was cool and crisp, but it al-ways was whenever one came from the bowels of the ship. Above him, the blue White Star Line pennant slapped in the wind.

Passengers continued to linger on the quayside and fill the gangways. Most of the cargo seemed already loaded, so once the medical checks were done, they'd put Southampton to their rudder. John expected to be underway as soon as his shift was over. And it would be the last shift he'd work on the vessel, for tomorrow he'd hitch a ride on one of the tender ships back to Queenstown.

John's attention snapped up to the Boat Deck where a pair of officers were lowering a lifeboat into the water. Once it was settled on the calm waves, they pulled it right back up. A drill, mandatory in these days of maritime regulation.

It was silly, he thought. Why even have lifeboats on a ship that couldn't sink?

F DECK

10:40 A.M.

IT WAS THE SMALLEST space she'd ever occupied. Fiona wasn't a large lady—on the contrary, she was quite thin. Reid was no wider. But the two of them could barely stand up at the same time inside their cabin, all the way down on F deck. They were lucky enough to have a single with a pair of bunk beds. She wasn't sure how Reid would've been sharing space with two other people.

It bothered her they had no toilet facilities for themselves. The lavatories were on the starboard side of the ship, or at least that's what she heard the matron telling a group of clueless Chinamen.

The ship was abuzz with passengers, all looking for the place they'd call home for the next week. These ships all had a pecking order. Although she shared the deck with some of the crew, she and Reid were still considered steerage class. But steerage on *Titanic* was the best steerage of all.

Reid sat on the edge of the bed with his book, barely looking up, barely acknowledging the ruckus in the cabin next door. It sounded like a hundred children, all excited to start their new life. If Fiona listened closely, she could hear a man's voice in the mix, although she didn't understand his words.

"It's not so bad, is it?" she said, folding out the single chair at the head of the cabin. All of their things were divided between two large sacks. That's all she wanted to take to America. It was nasty business, this trip, but one couldn't start over if one carried lots of bags from the old life.

Reid shook his head and stuck his nose back into his book. Fiona put her hand on the spine—something called *The Tale of Mrs. Tittlemouse*—and pushed it down until he looked at his mother.

"Are you hungry?"

He nodded and wrestled her hand off his book. Reid didn't talk much these days. Not at all, actually, but at least there were moments when he was still excited. He saw a brightly colored finch in one of the cherry blossoms on the way to Southampton's pier. The way his eyes lit up made her heart sing. He'd already been handed so much sadness, and a boy of only eight years shouldn't be concerned with so many adult problems.

"I've still got the cornmeal cakes from yesterday," she said, unrolling one and placing it on the bed next to him. It had already crumbled into many small pieces. She packed little food. Why would they even need it? Food was included with a boarding pass even for steerage passengers.

"You wanted the gingerbread, didn't you? Down on Simnell Street?"

He smiled and nodded.

They'd passed a throng of costermongers on the way to the pier. The smell of their wares was so good, but Fiona had to make their money stretch. America was going to be a challenge, one that she knew she wasn't possibly prepared to meet head-on.

"C'mon," she said, and stood. He looked at her quizzically. "There's bound to be food ready. Let's go explore this grand ole ship, shall we?"

At first, he didn't want to go. His eyes fell back on his pages, but then they both heard a rumble in his belly and he brought his elbows into his stomach to hide the sound. Neither of them had eaten all day. He grinned and stood and she said, "Are you goin' to leave the book?"

He shook his head.

Their cabin was tucked away on the forward end of the ship, on the portside. *Titanic* was still loading, so the corridors were lined with people, from the steerage class passengers to the crewmen and stewards. She held Reid's hand and pulled him along. He never looked up from his book.

There were maps on the ship, apparently printed with *Titanic's* own printing press, but she still had trouble reading and understanding them. Most of the ship, F deck especially, was labyrinthine in its design. She followed signs as best she could, only to be turned around by a steward or come to a locked lattice gate. She smelled food, but was clueless to which direction.

Finally, she arrived at a gate where a man on the other side in a White Star Line apron said, "Sorry, miss. This is the squash court."

"What's that?" she asked.

"Rich people's game. You wouldn't understand it."

She knew she shouldn't take offense to that, but the casual way the man said it, devoid of any kind of malice, made her realize her place in society now. Instead of becoming combative, she smiled and turned around just as he locked the gate and disappeared down the hall.

A pretty, middle-aged lady stood in the hallway just in front of them. Her hair was red, like Fiona's, and she had enough freckles to tell that she was certainly Irish. She smiled at the two of them with such a genuine happiness that Fiona thought for sure she was about to ask for money.

Instead, she said, "Are you two lookin' for a bite?"

Both of them nodded. Still, Reid didn't look up from his book.

"They'll be havin' food ready soon. C'mon and I'll show ye where we dine. It's a fair bit tricky to get to."

Rather than continue down the F deck hallway, their new friend took them up a set of stairs to the right side of the squash court. On E deck, she held her hands wide, as if she'd finally come home.

"They call this Scotland Road," she said. "Not sure why. I don't see no Scots and it sure as hell ain't a road."

But it was a long, uninterrupted hallway. Fiona couldn't believe the width and distance—it must have run the length of the entire ship. Currently, it was clogged with more passengers and crewmen, all darting to get settled in their cabins before the ship started to move.

"I'm Fiona. This is Reid."

"Pleasure to meet a fellow greengirl. Name's Matilda. But you can call me Tilda. Or Til. Whatever's to yer likin.'"

In the time they walked the length of Scotland Road, Fiona had learned that Matilda was traveling with her husband Erik and their four children, Micky, Jack, Molly, and Colin—who was around the same age as Reid and who he would love to play with, she was sure. Matilda talked about growing up in Antrim, about how her da owned the most plots of land in the county but lost them all in a card game and how her husband didn't speak the same language, but it was his burden to learn English, not hers to learn Swedish.

From E deck, they descended back down to F where she led them into a large dining room. The walls were steel, covered in white enamel paint. Between the portholes hung posters displaying all the colossal ships in the White Star Line fleet. Long rows of tables, mostly empty until lunch was called, dominated the free space. She would've never guessed that steerage passengers would have such nice chairs rather than long benches.

A pregnant black and white cat encircled a few passengers' legs, begging for scraps. When Fiona entered, the cat looked at her, sneezed, and trotted over.

Reid kept his thumb in his book long enough to pet it as Fiona took a seat in the middle of the room with Matilda just across. There was no food on the tables, not yet anyway, but the victualling staff would serve lunch soon enough. Matilda pointed to Reid and said, "You don't see many boys his age with a book. Only thing mine do with books is light 'em on fire."

"Yeah," said Fiona, running her fingers through his hair. "He's always escaped into books."

Matilda watched them for a moment and said, "Where's his father? You're all travelin' together?"

Reid's body tensed, and he gripped the book tighter. Fiona's hand moved down to his back and rubbed. She said, "No. He's in America."

The boy relaxed, but only a little. With his face hidden behind the book, Matilda couldn't see how his lip twitched.

But she smiled warmly and nodded. "I'm sure you're both excited to be reunited."

Reid looked up at her, then bounced back to his book. Fiona said, "Yes. We will be."

Before their light conversation turned uncomfortable, a baker in a stark white uniform came down the steps with a tray twice as wide as his body. Atop it were small loaves of bread, still smoking from the oven. It was the best thing Fiona had ever smelled in her life, and it was aromatic enough for Reid to look up—and close his book.

The baker said, "Sorry ladies and gents, but Titanic's first meals won't be for another hour. But I won't tell cap'in if you won't." He was met with laughs as he picked up loaves of bread and started tossing them to the groups of people. They caught them and eased them onto the tables, for they were still hot.

He hand-delivered Fiona's group their bread, as they were seated closest to the staircase. She snatched the book from Reid's hand because she wanted him to give this nice man his full attention. The baker dropped the loaf of bread on the table in front of the boy and said, "Careful, lad. That's just out of the oven." He smiled at the ladies, gave them each their own loaf, and then finished his rounds across the room. He paused once to pull something out of his pocket—some tiny sliver of meat—and feed the cat. She snatched it and raced off toward the kitchen.

The bread was so hot, but she risked a burn by stuffing a piece into her mouth. It was the greatest bread she'd ever had, and Fiona came from a long line of skilled bakers. No Irish soda bread ever came close to the quality of the bread that was now melting against her tongue. If third-class passengers had food this nice, what were they eating upstairs?

They finished the bread and then Reid tugged on Fiona's shirt, meaning he needed to be led to the lavatory.

"It was nice to meet you, Tilda," said Fiona. "We'll find you again, I'm sure."

"'Tis a big ship, but not that big. I'll be seein' ye!"

The good thing about ships with multiple classes was they were divided within those classes, or at least they were in steerage. Fiona didn't have to worry about meeting strange men in the corridors, and if she did, those strange men came with a family. Single men had their own facilities—their own washrooms, their own cabins, and their own spots in the dining saloons.

She helped Reid find the toilets and made sure he put the book away so that he could find his way back to their cabin on his own, should he need it.

They were just about to go in when they found Matilda standing in the hall, next to the door. Fiona first thought she was waiting for them, but when their eyes met, the Irishwoman's face lit up in surprise.

"Golly me, is that yer cabin?" she asked, pointing to their door. Fiona nodded. "Blimey!" She turned to the opened cabin next to it, the one that had been the source of all the commotion, and said, "Get out here, the lot of ye! I want ye to meet these nice people!"

And from a cabin as small as the one Fiona and Reid were sharing, came a man with long features, a nose that hooked and a chin that pointed. And behind him, a throng of children: an older boy who was almost a man, perhaps fourteen or fifteen, then a boy who half-walked, half-crawled, followed by another girl and boy, both around Reid's age.

Matilda introduced them all, but Fiona already knew their names. Colin acted as if he wanted to talk to Reid, but the book was always there to provide a wall.

After presenting her family, she shooed them away, a long string of orders to prepare for lunch that came out as a hybrid of English and Swedish words, none of which Fiona understood. Matilda kissed Colin and whispered something in his ear before disappearing inside the cabin.

"Told 'em to get dressed proper before lunch. We're to be seein' family, I'm sure."

Fiona hardly thought such things mattered. Her own family was spread across Ireland and England, and she was certain none of them were onboard the ship. But before she said anything, they each felt a sudden rumble beneath their feet. Reid looked up at her with confusion, curious he'd missed something while reading.

"Engines," said Matilda. "Bet we're about to—"

A loud whistle, several decks above, silenced her words. It was so tremendous that the walls shook.

Matilda's cabin door nearly sprung from the hinges as the torrent of her family came rushing out with Erik in the rear. He turned back and spouted something in Swedish, but Fiona didn't understand.

Matilda turned and said, "we're leaving! Titanic is leaving!" before following her family up the steps.

Fiona took Reid's hand and followed their earlier path up, then along Scotland Road where they joined several others trying to get up on deck. He wasn't reading now—he was laughing. She turned to see her sweet boy's tiny legs struggling to keep up, but he was happy and that's all that mattered.

It was easy to cross the ship and head up to the third-class promenade where John Coffey stood not two hours before while thinking of his plan to rob the rich and directly disembark.

There were so many people crowding the promenade, and it was difficult to wrestle through and find a place at the railing. Matilda spotted them and shoved her family aside so they could join. Micky was tall enough to see for himself while Matilda held little Jack high above her. Both Molly and Colin stood atop the railing, perched precariously.

Erik took a knee before Reid and tapped his own shoulder, offering to lift him up. Fiona knew her boy and knew he'd refuse, but much to her surprise, Reid passed her the book and held his arms up. Erik knelt to the ground so that Reid could straddle his shoulders and then the big Swede was on his feet again, with Reid's head above all the rest.

Titanic lurched, almost hitting another smaller vessel in the suction brought on by its massive propellers. It was called the *SS New York*, and unknown to all the passengers and the world, it was the closest the ocean liner would ever get to such a thing.

But in no time at all, they were off, waving to those on the quayside. The White Star Line offices loomed in the background, their glittering windows coasting by.

Fiona stared up at the Boat Deck to the passengers there who also waved and watched as Southampton drifted away. The class divide was so prominent here—her people in all their rags and with their unwashed bodies, and those up there with their dog leashes and frilly hats and parasols. In the middle of the high-class group she spied the doctor, the same one who'd comforted Reid after he'd lost Emmet's crucifix.

For a moment, he looked down at the promenade and she thought he saw her, so she waved. But then he reached out and touched the railing again and looked toward the water.

They were all so different, yet all so alike. Different walks of life, everyone, but all ready for a change. That was the beauty of *Titanic*; it afforded everyone, from the crumb grabbers to the stockbrokers, an opportunity to find change a world away from home.

First-Class Dining Saloon

1:15 P.M.

BEN HATED DINING WITH the elites, but perhaps this would be the only time. There was no denying the beauty and grandeur of the sprawling first-class dining saloon, and he was gifted a rare opportunity to see it before most of the guests. With the Cherbourg and Queenstown embarkments still before them, the saloon was nearly empty.

Seated beside him was Doctor O'Loughlin, dressed in his finest uniform, befitting of the highest naval officers. In front of him sat a platter of the finest English and French cheeses.

Across the table, a man who seemed to dwell on a hundred things at once. His mind lingered here in the dining saloon and all over the ship at the same time. His dress was formal, but no less fancy than the doctor. A nearly perfect tie hung down his stark white shirt. His hair was oiled and slicked back, moustache thick and tapered to curly points.

This was J. Bruce Ismay, the chairman for the White Star Line, and for all purposes, the owner of *Titanic*. A cigar hung from his lips as he pored over

31

O'Loughlin's paperwork. Ismay didn't care about the health of the passenger so much as he cared about the health of the ship.

"You only turned away eight?" he said in his usual haughty tone. "Seems a tad bit low."

Doctor O'Loughlin cleared his throat and said, "It is, but they were first screened on the quay. My guess is many more were turned away there. But Doctor York, Doctor Simpson, and myself are a bit more stringent at the bulkhead."

"Good men," said Ismay, and he folded the top sheet of paper and placed it in his jacket pocket. "Is there anything else I should know? Are there pregnancies onboard? Anyone overly frail?"

Ben looked at O'Loughlin, waiting for him to answer this odd yet predictable question. The only thing Ismay concerned himself with was the image of *Titanic*, and through extension, the White Star Line and himself. If someone died while aboard, the papers would forget all about this Unsinkable Ship of Dreams.

"Pregnancies, I'm sure," said O'Loughlin. "But you've got the best team o' doctors on the best ship in the world. Nothing to worry about, sir."

"And you?" said Ismay, beady eyes on Benjamin. "I'm still not sure why Smith allowed you to join the crew on such short notice. It's not how White Star Line takes on doctors and—"

"Doctor York is an esteemed physician," said O'Loughlin. "He comes highly recommended from Samaritan Cross Hospital. We were lucky to add him."

Nevermind that Ben left that post in quite a hurry, but if Doctor O'Loughlin knew that, he would not tell Ismay.

"And what's your plans with the White Star Line, Doctor York?" asked the chairman, putting out his cigar in one of the fancy napkins. "Will you take over when Billy here retires?"

O'Loughlin laughed. "I ain't going nowhere until me legs give out." It was nice to see his upbringing rise to the surface when he relaxed. But he sobered quickly and added, "But I'll surely welcome Benjamin to my staff."

Ismay's attention left the table just as a group of men entered. All were dressed nicely, although they didn't seem like first-class passengers other than the lead man, a tall and gaunt fellow with a pencil mustache and a notepad in his hand. He spotted Ismay and walked over.

"Bruce, good to see ye!" said the man in an Irish accent as thick as O'Loughlin's. "Excuse me, gentlemen," he said to the doctors. His smile was gentle and genuine.

"I see a lot of scribbles on that paper," Ismay said, rolling his eyes.

"I've already found a problem with some of the hot presses and it's nary past noon." This was met with a smile from Ismay, who forgot lighting another cigar and stood.

"Gentlemen, keep us healthy and safe. We're counting on you." He left, followed by the note-book-toting man and his entourage.

"Who's that?" asked Ben.

"That . . . is Thomas Andrews and the Guarantee Group. He built the damned ship. Designed her. And they're all here to make sure she stays seaworthy."

"Oh. Seems White Star Line is taking all the necessary precautions to make sure the trip is a smooth one."

"Ismay always sails on the maiden voyage. But not Andrews. Isn't it bad luck to have the ship's designer onboard for the maiden voyage? I swear, me ma always said something like that." He pulled his glasses off his face and cleaned them on his shirt.

"I don't think that's true," Ben laughed. "But your ma sounds like a wise lady."

"Aye, she died when I was but a lad, but I think so, too. Anyway, I suppose we're leaving a lot of rounds for poor Doctor Simpson, so we should at least walk the ship and stretch our legs."

"Yes, doctor." Ben stood and said his goodbyes. They would meet again that evening when *Titanic* dropped anchor at Cherbourg.

Titanic's medical facilities and team were a secret. Passengers didn't need to know about the hospital, the surgical suite, the isolation room for infectious disease, nor the coffins brought aboard per standard protocol. To the White Star Line, it didn't need to enter their paying heads that they could get sick. So Ben and his colleagues were to remain as invisible as possible throughout the trip.

While all the stewards handled minor ailments of the passengers, six people made up *Titanic's* medical team. The chief surgeon, O'Loughlin, and his assistants, Simpson and York. Then there was Matron Wallis, their hospital steward Mr. Dunford, and finally Mrs. Evelyn Marsden, who tended only to first-class passengers. This group cared for the well-being of over two-thousand souls. It was daunting, to say the least.

From the dining saloon, he went up on deck. It was the first time in many years that he saw the open sea. They were headed south and would see the coast of France in a couple of hours. The wind was pleasant and the doors to the first-class entrance were open, revealing the magnificent grand staircase beyond. Right now, it was choked full of people either arriving for a late lunch or heading off to the smoking lounge for brandy and cigars.

As a doctor, Ben had full run of the ship, except for a few crew areas. But as he began his first walk about the decks, he noticed the stark differences in class. He didn't like to consider himself as any sort of class, but White Star Line did, and that class was second-class. That's where he was to take his meals and enjoy leisure, although there was no guarantee he'd find it. Unlike the rest of the crew, doctors were considered to be on duty at all times.

On the Boat Deck, he passed a gentleman taking photos with a camera. *Titanic* was rather grand, although it had a pair of sister ships that most considered equally majestic. The photographer offered him a warm smile, then continued rolling his camera, capturing a young boy kicking a ball across the deck.

Ben disappeared down below, heading to the aft end of the ship. The first-class cabins were quiet and calm, but the steerage folk were anything but silent. From two decks up, he could hear music playing, a piano's low bass chords rolling out a jaunty tune. Most of the third-class passengers assembled either on their promenade deck or the general area below it.

By now, they'd all had lunch and were in their cabins or drinking in the lounges. The general assembly area was full of passengers, at least sixty of them. Ben felt out of place as he approached. He leaned against a support beam and listened to the piano music, wondering if such a big instrument was nailed down to keep it in place during rough waves.

None of them seemed to notice him. There were lots of children, probably twice as many here as on the decks above. The first-class, and to a lesser extent, the second-class passengers, were vacationing or heading to America to visit family. But those in third-class were uprooting their lives. Entire families emptied out of shanties, flats, and group homes. The average family size in third-class was four, and *Titanic* was yet to pick up the rest of her passengers.

A trio of children played a game on the floor, something with two sticks and three dice. One boy kept his knees tucked up to his body while another tried to explain the rules. It took Ben a moment to realize it was the same boy from the gangway, the one who'd dropped his crucifix.

And I told him I'd find him a replacement.

He scanned the room, looking for a specific red-headed lady amongst of sea of Irishwomen. At the same moment he found her, she found him, and their eyes locked. She threw up a hand and smiled. Ben pushed his way through the crowd, sidestepping the game on the floor, and stood over the pretty lady.

"Are you getting yourself acquainted, miss?" said Ben.

"I am, thank you," she said. "Reid, look. It's the nice doctor from before."

He looked up from the game, relieved to have a moment away from listening to long-winded rules.

He smiled but said nothing. This was a shy one, for sure.

"I don't believe I got your name," said Ben.

"Nor did I get yours," she said back.

He grinned. "Benjamin York. Call me Ben."

"Ben? Not Doctor?"

He shook his head. "Titles don't mean much to me. Ben is fine."

She seemed so busy digesting what he'd said that she forgot to reciprocate. He raised an eyebrow and smiled until she caught on.

"Blimey, I'm not for thinking today. I'm Fiona. Fiona Lynch."

"Pleasure to meet you, Mrs. Lynch."

"Fiona is fine. I don't need a fancy title, either. Just Fiona."

Ben looked around at the other passengers, all engaged with each other, their music, or their drinks. A lady sat on the bench next to Fiona, invested in the game the children were playing. Next to her was a tall man with a hooked nose. Perhaps they were the parents of the other children.

Ben said, "So . . . just the two of you, is it?"

"Just the two of us," she said, and didn't elaborate. But perhaps sensing the dead-ended statement was hanging too heavily in the air, she said, "Will I see more of you? Is this your part o' the ship?"

"The entire ship is my part of the ship. But yes, I prefer to tend to the third-class passengers."

"You mean the poor folk?" Ben was at a loss for words, and when she saw him struggling to say something, she threw her head back and laughed. "It's okay, dear. We all know our place."

"That we do, deary," said the woman next to Fiona, leaning over to join the conversation. "What was we talkin' about?"

Fiona smiled. "That we're all lucky to be on this grand ole ship. Isn't that right, Doctor York?"

He felt as if he'd overstepped, or perhaps he'd cornered a third-class passenger in a reality she'd hoped to escape. His smile faltered, but it was so fast that no one noticed.

"That's right, Mrs. Lynch. We're lucky to be here. We have good food, grand music, and calm seas. What more could we possibly want?"

CARGO HOLD

2:35 P.M.

THE ORLOP DECK'S FORWARD end was packed so tightly that both men had to turn sideways to navigate
it. Once the crew stacked and secured it all and
the engines purred to life, no one had a reason to
enter the hold. John's nose filled with strange, exotic
scents that he would never smell again in his life.
This place was awash with wealth—fancy birdcages,
pricy books, aged bottles of wine and spirits. And
then there were the cars—at least three automobiles
in various states of assembly. John wasn't sure how
anyone afforded a horse, much less a car.

"Look'a this!" said Ernest, prying the wooden lid
off a small box on a shelf to his right. "Bloody wal-
nuts. You ever had a walnut?" He put one on the
ground and John smashed it with his boot, coal dust
spreading all over the place. Ernest plucked the
center goodie from the shell and stuffed it into his
mouth. "Not bad, not bad. C'mon, let's find better!"

John followed toward the bow, glancing at the
shelves of perfectly stacked goods and wondering
how they kept track of it all. He knew little outside of

shoveling coal into a furnace and shoveling ash back out of it.

Ernest paused every few feet to inspect boxes, and those with fancy lids or embroideries, he wedged in the claw-end of his hammer. They were looking for small baubles and trinkets—anything to shove into their pockets or hide in their cabins until tomorrow when they deserted. If the stewards—or worse, the officers, caught them stealing, they'd never leave the ship in Queenstown.

They passed short boxes and long boxes and tall boxes containing rolls of expensive linoleum. Stacks of rugs to the ceiling and exotic tapestries and furs that made the piles look like stout, hairy animals. Ivory, silver, gold, herringbone, velvet, and silk, all held in place by rope netting. Most of it was too large to hide.

It all paled compared to the long, ornate box at the end of the hold, right against the sloped wall.

"What'dya think's in *there*?" asked Ernest. He lifted the cargo tag, a thin rope tied around one of the embroideries at the foot of the box. "I'm not . . . I'm not good with words. What's it say?" He squinted his eyes as if that were the only reason he couldn't read.

John lifted it and said, "New York, Pier 54. Care of: British Museum, London. Handle with exceptional care."

"Is that all it says?"

"No," said John, for he had paused because once he read the rest of the tag, there would be no going back. This wasn't petty theft. This was big. And if they were caught, it would be severe.

"Well, what's it say?"

"First King of Ulster."

"Irish?"

"Yes."Ernest laughed and slapped his knee. "Bloody hell! They're shippin' a damned Irish *king* to America? That's rich!" He rubbed his hand across the box. "And I bet he *was* rich, too. Probably buried with the lot of it and what have you." "Maybe," said John. He looked over Ernest's head and said, "I see a jewelry box up there. Let's go have a look."

He started to walk off but Ernest gripped him tightly. The man's eyes never left the box. He said, "Imagine it, John. In here's a dead bloke from back home. Probably dressed in his finest and what have you. Wearing all his rings and baubles. Probably even took some of his gold with him. You know how people used to believe. Thought it would serve 'em in the next life and what have you."

"Yeah," John said, feeling a queasy knot in his stomach. "I thought I heard something." He didn't, but turned around and pretended just the same.

"Bah, we'll only be a minute. If anyone asks, this dead fella tipped over and I called you up from the boilers to help me lift 'im and what have you."

43

"Just hurry," said John, and now he really was worried someone would happen upon them while they were pilfering the rich folks' belongings. Ernest wedged his hammer between the box and its lid, wrenching it back and forth. A line of darkness appeared between the wood and a foul stench filled their nostrils.

"Bloody hell," said John, pulling his handkerchief from his pants pocket and covering his mouth and nose. "What *is* that?"

"Hell if I know," said Ernest, working the opposite side. "Smells like rot and decay. This ole boy's been sealed up for a long time."

"But should it smell like that? This smells . . . like it just died."

That stopped Ernest for a moment as he considered it, but the lure of trinkets and gold were too much to change his course. He slipped the hammer in a third time, at the top of the box, and then the lid tilted sideways. The smell continued to billow out, nauseating in the confines of the cargo hold.

"Let's feck it all and get out of here, eh?" said Ernest, and he hung his hammer through his belt loop and shoved the lid onto the floor. John wasn't sure what he was expecting, but it surely wasn't as lackluster as what they actually saw.

It was a person, although they couldn't tell if it had been a man or woman. The body was so old and rotten that the robes—and flesh—had merged with the insides of the wooden box. A face—if that's what it could be called—wasn't complete, as there was no jaw, just rocks stuffed beneath a row of fangs. Empty, sunken eye sockets saw nothing. Skin, like an old drum, stretched across the face and neck. Its hands were gnarled like twigs, both wrapping around a thick wooden post that was jammed right into the corpse's chest.

But there were no pretty gems, no money, and certainly no crown upon this dead Irish king's head. Ernest was caught somewhere between anger and confusion. The box . . . the box had been so pretty and ornate.

"What the hell happened to 'im?" asked Ernest. He reached out, as if he were going to stroke the thing's face but John snatched his hand.

"Looks . . . wet. Like it hasn't finished drying out. That's the smell, I'm guessin'." That had to be it, thought John. This thing, probably a thousand years old, had been sealed so tightly that the decay slowed to a crawl.

"Maybe there's something under 'im," said Ernest. "You know, maybe he's layin' on his treasure and what have you."

"No, Ernie, it's done. He's got nothing. Let's get out of here before this gets back to Captain Smith and he throws us overboard."

"Just wait. Look at his hands. He might have somethin' under there."

"His hands are grippin' the stake," John said. "Someone stabbed this bloke through the heart. Musta been a bad fella."

"Well he can't hurt us now," Ernest said. "Just keep a watch out. I'm gonna check under his hands. Who know? Might have on a pretty necklace and what have you."

"Ernest . . ." John trailed off because he was curious about what was beneath the stake as well.

Ernest grabbed the wood with both hands and slowly lifted, but the whole body rose with it. At first, both men startled and jumped back, sure this decrepit pile of bones was only sleeping and was now angry they'd disturbed him. But it was only because he was stuck to the stake. Ernest placed one hand on the tattered robe and another on the stake and pulled. He winced in effort, but as the stake pulled out, John realized it was far longer than he'd imagined. There was only a tiny, twisted knub of yew sticking out, but two feet of it pierced inside the body.

Ernest held the end of the stake up for John to see—it was pointed and dripping dark, nearly black blood.

"Christ, it's still wet?"

46

And against his better judgement, Ernest dabbed his finger in it, then rubbed it against his thumb. "And it's cold too."

"It's time to go," said John, but their attention was drawn to the body and how the spot where the stake had been was knitting over. Little tendrils of flesh tugged across the gaping hole, lacing it up as if it were a boot. In a total of two heartbeats, the wound was gone. The box filled with thick, choking smoke.

Both men fell away, but it was a godsend for John that Ernest collapsed first. John reached to grab him, but instead of finding his arm, he snatched the yew stake. It was heavy for something so slender.

A low growl erupted from the box as the figure moved. It didn't stand, nor wince from old age or disrepair. It glided upward until its whole body was concealed by thick, billowing smoke that lingered in place like a cloak. Only the head was visible atop this nine-foot-tall figure, and what a horrible head it was—the eyes were sunken, but they were no longer empty. Now, they were little flickering flames of red light. The jaw was missing, but that was because it would've been impossible to accommodate the upper teeth. There were eight of them in a row, each long and slender like roofing nails.

The creature—for that's all it could be called—did not move. It let out a yawn, the black smoke swirling around its mouth as if it were taking a breath after

47

a long sleep. And then, the red flames flickered and found Ernest on the floor. In the blink of an eye, the head descended, the teeth glinted, and then it was biting into the side of the man's neck. It lifted itself back up to its nine-foot height while spindly fingers gripped Ernest's shoulders. Blood spurted from the wound as the creature drank ravenously. Ernest was dead before his feet even lifted off the floor.

Without even thinking, John was up, rushing away, tripping over boxes, toppling shelves, and throwing anything in his path to slow the creature's chase. But he felt a hand swipe across his back—it wasn't forceful, but it was enough of a surprise to stagger his step. He crashed against the Renault's shiny white wheel and rolled onto his back.

John crab-crawled away, the billowing smoke approaching. It formed the shape of voluminous black robes, the popped collar flanking the creature's head. It was creeping along, as if studying John, or perhaps making sure his blood was pumping fast enough before going in for the kill.

"Back!" he said, and for the first time since running off, he realized he was still holding the stake and that's what gave the creature pause. He swung it to the left, nowhere near the smoking form. Somehow, just as the creature floated forward, he found his footing and took off running, expecting it to rend his entire backside.

An ear-piercing wail, like the ship's metal plating coming apart, staggered him to the ground. The creature's long, bony fingers covered its face as the light from the half-closed hatch bled inside.

It screamed, black eyes full of malice and rage—the eight long teeth flicking spittle into the air. The creature refused to cross the sliver of light . . .

Again, John rushed to his feet and ran off, determined to reach the steps up to E deck where he could enter Scotland Road and run at a full gait—away from this dead Irish king.

At the large sliding partition that marked midship, he turned back and saw it one last time. Its red eyes. Its quivering fangs. Its long, clenching fingers. The creature hissed at the light, then became a black vortex of smoke and disappeared through a vent along the ceiling.

CHERBOURG, FRANCE

7:30 P.M.

"THIS ENTIRE SHIP'LL BE Irishmen once we leave Queenstown tomorrow," said Matilda. Fiona figured she was correct.

They'd finished dinner and when Reid refused chocolate pudding, she knew the boy had eaten his fill. Just as Matilda believed, he got along nicely with Colin, although the conversation was one-sided. Reid only offered acknowledgement, and that was the best anyone could hope for since the night of the fire.

They sat on the third-class promenade, now less crowded than before. All classes shared one commonality—they enjoyed the sea and the salt air by day, but once the sun dipped beyond the horizon, they enjoyed their comforts of drink and smoke and conversation indoors. Even now, Fiona could feel the deck vibrating beneath her feet as the passengers below enjoyed this temporary life at sea.

For the last hour and a half, they watched the boarding of passengers. Cherbourg lay to the south, but *Titanic* was too big to enter the port, so tender ships brought the passengers to where she lay at anchor. These were among the wealthiest people in the world, thought Fiona.

Reid, standing at the rail, began clapping his hands and motioned for his mother to come over. She joined him, gently pinning him to the railing with her body, feeling his heat, and wrapped her hands around him. His heart beat so fast.

"What is it?" she asked, eying the gangway full of pretty dresses and fancy, expensive suits. The sun was falling, speckling the water with flakes of gold. He pointed again, this time more vehemently. "Oh," she said at last.

A pair of passengers, a regal-looking man in spectacles and a small, waif of a woman, were walking a short, hairy dog on a leash. She'd never considered the idea that people would bring their pets, but then again, *Titanic* was only a one-way trip for some. It certainly was for Fiona and Reid.

"Nothing quite so pure as a love between a mama and her boy," said Matilda, watching them. Her daughter Molly stopped her game of chase with her father long enough to cast a questioning glance at her mother. Matilda shrugged. "Our love is just as pure." And when Molly looked away, Matilda shook her head.

"How long have you and Erik been married?" asked Fiona. This was a diplomatic question to figure out if all four kids belonged to the Swede. None of them seemed close to him, although Colin and Micky did speak a bit of his language.

"Goin' on eleven years, I suppose. Doesn't seem as long. Lots of movin'. Lots of fightin' Lots of growin' up."

"Yeah. Reid and I have lived in a few places, too."

"So the father . . ."

"Is in America."

"Right," said Matilda, just before standing up to snap at her husband. "You can't hold Jack that close to the railing! Blimey, are you gonna go in the water after 'im once ye drop 'im in?" He looked at her curiously, so she pantomimed swimming and floundering. He laughed and shook his head.

Colin seemed like a sweet child, perfect for Fiona's boy. He was quite animated, so Reid simply watched and listened, the same as he always did.

"I seen that cat again," said Colin. "I wonder if she knows she's gotta have them kittens on a ship?"

Reid shrugged.

"I bet they'll all turn out black and white. Guess so, unless the da is somethin' else. You like cats?"

He nodded.

"You don't talk a lot, do you?"

Reid shook his head. Fiona just smiled. Interactions between her boy and others were as rare as sailing on a majestic, world-class ocean liner.

The sun continued to dip until the only light that touched the sea was provided by *Titanic*. She wasn't sure how electricity worked as she'd never lived in a house that had it, but she found it marvelous, just the same. They saw through the portholes from where they sat, down into the general assembly area. Across the well deck, they watched the first-class passengers, those just coming aboard, walk the promenade.

After a lengthy game of chase across the stairways connecting the promenade and well deck, Reid approached his mother and sat down on the bench. He tapped her leg and she smiled, then handed over the book, now something called *Old Mother West Wind*. At this rate, he'd read through all of them before they even reached America.

He started off to the opposite end of the bench where more of the hanging light fell across his book, when she grabbed him gently and pulled him close. She made sure their eyes were constant before asking, "Are you okay?"

He nodded solemnly.

"Is there anything you'd like to talk about?"

He shook his head.

"You don't have to keep it all inside you, Reid. We both share the burden, yeah?"

He nodded.

"I love you."

He nodded.

She put her arms around him and gave him a hug, and he stiffened almost immediately. Confused, she pulled away to see what made him tense. He was staring into the sky, over her shoulder. She stood and followed his gaze, putting herself behind him so she could find his line of sight.

From the promenade, they could see to the top of the fourth funnel, the one that barely sputtered smoke. And through the billowing exhaust, she spotted a pair of floating, red lights. It made her shiver. She couldn't be sure, but she thought those lights . . . were watching the passengers. They twinkled out, then appeared once more.

Reid was shaking. She didn't understand it, only that she felt the same unease.

"Hey, it's nothing," she said. Her mind reasoned that it was a pair of stars, changed by the filter of smoke in front of them. But her heart knew something was wrong. Still, she didn't want to worry her boy. "It's a pair of God's angels. Watching over the ship to make sure we have safe passage."

He turned around and looked at her, brow furrowed in confusion. Fiona wasn't sure if he accepted that answer, but at least he'd stopped shaking. And when they fixed their eyes on the spot above the funnel again, the red lights were gone.

BOILER ROOM 3

11:15 P.M.

HE WASN'T SURE HOW long he'd been asleep. His body had rotted from time and the elements before they threw him in a box and hid him from the world. And somehow, after they learned the King was truly dead, they paraded him around like some simple court jester. They even stuffed rocks in his mouth.

But the yew was gone, purged from his heart by the unluckiest of seamen. Even after so many years, his parched lips reveled in the taste. The man was a Bitterblood, but one couldn't be choosy when one was dying of thirst.

As he hovered at the ceiling of the massive boiler room, hidden amongst the darkness and the smoke, he marveled at how the world had changed. There was no way for him to know how long he'd been asleep. But no one from his time could've built something like this. Those who'd stabbed him through the heart were from a village that probably no longer existed. The village, the country, the island—it was all gone, for time had stood still for him

57

while it marched on for everyone else. How long did he slumber? A hundred years? A thousand?

When he left the world, it was mostly stone and wood. Now it was metal. Blood. Salt. He'd been on a boat or two, but nothing so grand as this marvelous vessel. The entirety of his village would occupy a single deck of this . . . *Titanic*.

The King wasn't completely out of sorts. When he drank the Bitterblood, he learned all about Ernest Burr and his twenty-one awful years on the Earth—the *bitus*—and how he'd joined the crew of the most famous ship in all the world because he didn't 'have two pennies to rub together.' The King also knew the ship would enter a new land in a few days, but Ernest had never planned to make it that far. He was going back to Queenstown, a place the King had never heard of before, but the images in the dolt's head looked familiar.

So because he absorbed all that Ernest Burr knew, he learned much that would help him survive. The biggest font of information was the layout of the ship, or at least the bowels of it. The King cared little for how coal made such a big ship move, nor where each parcel was placed in the cargo hold. That was the extent of Ernest's mind, but it was enough. The King's awakening could've been so much worse. They brought from his slumber during the day, after all.

After feeding, he fled, fearful the bloodlust would leave him vulnerable. The King could drink every drop of blood on the ship, but that would leave him with a problem. He didn't know how far they were from land. Sure, he moved as swiftly as any bird in the sky. But it didn't matter if he couldn't rest during the day atop the desecrated earth from his box—the same loam the villagers buried him in without even knowing its importance.

Whether he liked it or not, he was still a prisoner. At least for the next few days. When he saw this new world, this America, he would put down new roots. He missed the old world, but longevity came at a price. One had to keep moving forward, rebuilding and restocking the coterie.

And that was tonight's goal. He'd survived the day, he'd fed on a Bitterblood, enough to keep his wits about him, enough to stay hidden. As he hovered there in the boiler, he attuned his mind to all the beating hearts above and below. There were so many Bitterbloods onboard, but there were also a lot of Sweetbloods, too.

It seemed as if the class system had remained the same since his time, given the way they were segregated on the ship. There were the poor, the vagrants, the sodden waifs at the bottom of society. They lived on mealworms and potato mash and bog beer and their blood tasted foul because of it.

But the nobility was always healthy. Their wealth afforded them opportunities to exercise, eat well, drink well, stay well rested. And this made them delicious. Their blood was as sweet as any nectar. Feeding from nobility came with a risk, though—ailments given to them by the King were noticed quicker because they were important, and made his survivability more difficult. Back in his day, there were hunters for his kind. Hopefully, they'd all died of old age by now.

The King turned to vapor and followed the steam out of the funnel until he was sitting atop it, his second time of the night. This spot afforded him a view of the complete ship, although at this late hour it was mostly seamen and officers who walked the upper decks. He spied a pair of ladies at the stern of the ship, talking and watching the flag snap in the wind. An officer exited the bridge with a cup of tea, looked up at the stars, then tossed the dregs over the railing.

He smelled the fresh air, tasting his homeland on his rotten tongue. They split the ocean toward it, although the red dots in his eyes saw nothing but an explosion of stars meeting the faraway line of horizon. But he could *smell* it. The sod fires and the yellow furze and the mills and the dung piles. It was probably all gone by now, reduced to ashes and kindling by man's wars and God's curses. But he would still remember it, even if he never stepped on that hallowed ground ever again.

He descended back into the funnel, reaching the boiler room once again. Nothing more than black smoke, he trailed through the Tank Deck, passing unsuspecting engineers, firemen, and trimmers. He moved back up until he was at his box with the dead man lying in front of it. Ernest had been delicious, but he wanted *more*. A part of him thought it would be best to settle back in for the night, as he was still building strength. Right now, there were but a few weapons that could kill him, although he wasn't sure if the humans could figure them out.

The King stared longingly into the bed of the box, spindly fingers sifting through the earth of his homeland. It was much too early to sleep. He looked above his head, attuned his mind to the beating hearts, and found a thousand of them. Surely, he could have a taste without arousing anyone who mattered . . .

Bearing eight fangs, he rushed upward, through the steam pipes, looking for easy blood. It didn't matter if it was bitter or if it was sweet.

Tonight, his coterie began.

E DECK

THE SUN HAD GONE down on *Titanic* and risen again. And twenty-one hours he'd been awake. He wasn't sure he could ever close his eyes again, not after seeing the creature bite into his poor friend like a turkey drumstick.

John Coffey was beyond tired, but the rush of adrenaline was keeping him awake. There was no way he would rest while something like that was loose on the ship. He'd not seen another person since, as he'd completely forgotten about his cabin and instead found a tiny crawlspace behind the stairway between E and F decks.

No one bothered him there. Early that morning, he saw shadows, but figured those belonged to stewards. He expected to hear screams, expected to feel the ship shudder as the captain ordered the engines to a full stop. But none of that happened. Life aboard *Titanic* coasted along, only poor Ernest and John privy to the monster down in the cargo hold.

The only possession he held was the stake. In his inability to sleep, he used the bloody tip to draw

63

the creature on the wall. He wasn't sure why, per-haps so someone else wouldn't think he was crazy when he later recounted his story. Its face tormented him—the sunken eyes, the red pits, and those eight, almost symmetrical, fangs.

Although he couldn't see a clock, he knew it was just past eleven. The smell of food had wafted up hours ago, and now the kitchens were preparing lunch for the passengers, both those already on-board and those they'd be picking up shortly.

Once the drone of the engines died away, he knew they'd stopped at Roches Point, the outer anchorage by Queenstown. The tender ships would come soon, ready to ferry passengers and cargo to *Titanic*. But more importantly, they'd be ferrying passengers and cargo *back* to Queenstown.

He was finished passing time. John had a decision to make. He either jumped ship now as intended, or waited another six days and left in America. The thought of spending more sleepless nights and days made his skin crawl, so John stood on his stiff legs and squeezed his way from beneath the stairs. And perhaps his best contribution to the ship, he left the yew stake behind.

It wasn't just the creature he had to worry about—he was a fireman, in fireman clothes, so if any officers or stewards saw him, he'd be asked to leave immediately. There was a reason the engine crew had their own mess and cabins. They were to always stay separated from the passengers. And John wasn't about to go back down, closer to the creature, in order to clean up and change clothes.

But he was lucky because there were lots of preparations for the newest arrivals to embark. Stewards were all either working in rooms or helping prepare lunch. Officers were all up on deck or minding the gangways, ready to receive their last load of passengers and cargo.

He wasn't sure how he'd get off the ship. If anyone of importance labeled him a deserter, he'd be thrown in cuffs. John wasn't about to be captive prey for whatever had killed Ernest.

He peered around the corner and saw a crewman carrying a large bag across the hall with the letters *RMS* stitched on the side. John waited for him to drop his load and then rushed into the mail room, unsure of what to do next. On hooks in the corner was a trio of white jackets, so he quickly pulled off his dirty shirt and put one of them on, buttoning to the top so no one saw his dirty, hairy chest.

John ran his fingers through his hair, thankful the sweat kept it pushed back, rather than wild and unkempt. He certainly couldn't pass for a mail clerk, but hopefully at a distance no one would notice. He grabbed one of the mail sacks in the corner, which was thankfully large enough to cover most of his body, and carried it out of the room.

But as soon as he stepped into the hall, his mail bag hit another, held there by a tall, gruff-looking man who eyed him skeptically. John figured the postal workers were a small group, so this gentleman no doubt assumed he was up to no good. John held his breath, waiting for the chastising, or at the very worst, a call for the quartermaster.

"You're supposed to stay with your tender, mate," he said, annoyance thick in his voice.

"What?"

"You're from the tender, right? We'll bring the mail bags to you. Now run along."

"Right," he said, slowly understanding. Normally he'd be quicker to play along, but he'd been without sleep for so many hours.

The man stepped aside and when John failed to acknowledge, he motioned for the corridor behind him and said, "Off you go then."

John nodded and hurried through, ascended a deck and immediately felt the slap of wind and salt. The gangway door was open. He stepped up to the ramp and looked out, spotting a man coming toward him with a bag of mail. John stepped back into the ship and waited, holding the bag over his face. When the man started down the steps, John darted past him, racing across the gangway as fast as he could.

It was a busy ship, but most of its passengers were already aboard *Titanic*. A man carried a mail bag down a set of steps to the cargo hold. John followed.

Down below was a wide space filled from floor to ceiling with bags and crates, the cargo that was bound for Queenstown. John had a single porthole, and through it he saw the black steel of the vessel in which he'd just disembarked.

Those poor people, he thought. None of them knew what they were facing. This was perhaps the smartest decision John had ever made. That ship, along with all two-thousand souls aboard, was most certainly doomed.

He settled into a pile of mailbags and pulled a few of them on top of him. He closed his eyes, tried to master his breathing, and prayed to God above, thanking him for sparing him the horror on that ship

. . .

Part II

Across the Sea on Gilded Eggshells

Boat Deck

Noon

Checking the third-class passengers at Queenstown didn't take long because less than a hundred embarked. But it was here that Ben sent the most away. These poor Irish and their large, sprawling family trees. They moved the entirety of their household at once. Most lived in hovels no bigger than the cabin they hoped to occupy on *Titanic*, so if one caught an infectious disease, they all did.

These families were inseparable, so if only one member was denied travel, the whole lot of them turned around and marched back down the gangway with their shoulders slumped. Ben felt bad for the ones who continued on, those who would be split apart by an ocean.

While the ships exchanged passengers and mail, venders from Queenstown boarded *Titanic* and sold their wares from little trollies. Most of it was handmade crafts or food prepared beforehand, and it was all catered to the wealthy class who saw such baubles as novelties. Ben found the Irish merchants to be nice people, even if they were a little insistent.

One woman with three emaciated children sat on the deck outside the gymnasium with her wares strewn across a patchwork quilt. The little ones looked at him with wide, pleading eyes, as if they'd rehearsed it beforehand. Although Ben was sure this lady's troubles ran deep, he was also certain the children played upon the wealthy's philanthropy.

"Hello there, good sir," said a man to Ben's left. A throng of passengers exited from the first-class entrance by the grand staircase. Standing directly in front of him was a man holding a cane in one hand and a dog leash in the other—the mutt was an Airedale Terrier, almost like the one his resident doctor had back at Samaritan Cross. Behind him was a string of others in his party, most likely his daughter, his valet, and perhaps a manservant.

"Afternoon to you, sir."

"Are you a doctor aboard this ship?" he said, looking at Ben's perfectly pressed uniform.

He nodded. "Yessir."

"Marvelous," said the man. He put the cane beneath his arm so he could extend his hand. "John Astor."

"Benjamin York."

"So nice to meet you. This is a fine ship you have, Doctor York."

"Thank you, sir," said Ben, but it felt odd hearing it because he couldn't be anymore detached from *Titanic* or the White Star Line.

He crept close so the ladies behind him couldn't hear. "Say, that's my wife, you see? She has a . . . delicate condition. We've brought along our nurse, but may I call upon you if we encounter problems that the good Miss Endres cannot handle?"

Ben looked past him, to the wife that he spoke of—a real beauty, probably half Astor's age. By the way she held her stomach, he could probably guess the nature of her delicate condition.

Ben nodded. "Of course, sir."

"Good man," said Astor, tossing his cane vertically and catching it. He tapped it on the ground. "And good day to you. A fine day for sailing!" He started off toward the next vender before Ben said anything, but Astor called for his wife and said, "Look, darling. Isn't this the most beautiful lace you've ever seen?"

Ben was about to walk off in the opposite direction when the sun glinted off something on the vender's blanket. Between two of her kids sat a metal crucifix with a wooden Savior tied to it with hemp rope.

"How much for that?" he asked her.

She picked it up and stared at it, as if she didn't even know it was part of her wares. Finally, she said, "Two pennies?"

He thought this was quite underpriced, as the lady was afraid to make too high a markup in case he decided against the purchase. Ben gave her six pennies for the cross and said his thanks. He tucked it into his pocket, covering it with his jacket flap.

For most of the afternoon, he remained on deck, watching the tenders sway idly in the water and the merchants peddle their wares. The rich moved in small groups across the deck, mingling with fellow passengers who ran in the same circles. These were landowners and railroad owners, bank owners and department store owners. Most of them were insufferable, but they still gave Ben a laugh. He longed to have the problems they considered serious.

He saw a woman on the Boat Deck counting lifeboats. Another had a long-stemmed cigarette in one hand and a martini in the other. An older man and woman were both eating cheesecake from small silver platters as they lounged on deck chairs.

Through his rounds, Ben saw Mr. Andrews again, as well as Ismay, Second Officer Lightoller and even Captain Smith who watched the new passengers from the doorway of the bridge. Benjamin caught his eye, and the gentlemen shared a curt nod before going their separate ways.

On D deck, he tried to remember the cabin number of the mother and boy because he wanted to drop off the crucifix. He knew it was on F deck but was unsure of the room number. The second-class purser's office would know . . .

As he started down the steps to E deck, a young steward darted up and came rushing right toward him. Ben braced himself, suddenly caught off-guard by this frantic man. His face was pale, his eyes glazing over.

"Doctor? You're a doctor?"

"That's right. What's wrong?"

"I think . . . I think . . ."

He bent at his knees and took a deep breath, then wobbled as if he might fall over.

"Catch your breath," said Ben, easing him against the wall. A stewardess crossed the intersection up ahead and stared a moment before moving on. "Tell me, are you hurt? Sick?"

"Not me, sir. But you're gonna want to come with me down to the cargo hold."

This was bad.

Ben held his handkerchief over his mouth and nose. A body sprawled across the floor at the forward end, just in front of the Renault automobile. At least

Ben thought it was a body. It was so mangled that it could've been anything. A splash of blood reached across a large box and up the wall behind it. He couldn't understand the scene before him.

There was no use in checking for signs of life because half the man's insides were hanging down his shirt. His neck was ripped open like a flower. Although his blood painted half the wall of the cargo hold, there was very little on the ground. With wounds like this, they should've been walking in it.

"What do we do, sir?"

Ben ignored him and stared at the box. He felt a cold shiver race down his spine. It was the same one he'd seen yesterday morning, the same one being lowered onto the ship. The blood was across the side and above on the wall—but not on the top. He inspected it closer, noticing the splatter ended at the gap where the sides met the lid. When the blood hit the walls, the lid wasn't on the box.

"Who else knows about this?"

"No one, sir."

"Let's keep it that way until I can talk with our chief surgeon."

"Yessir."

"Find something to cover the body until I get back."

"Yessir."

Ben tried to remain calm as he searched the ship for O'Loughlin. He followed direction from at least four people who claimed 'he was just here a moment ago,' and finally tracked him down in the first-class smoking room. He approached him and said, "We have a problem."

But he didn't see the other gentleman seated in the high-backed chair until he was upon it. Bruce Ismay stood and faced Ben, puffing cigar smoke to the side. They'd been discussing the third-class passengers who'd just come aboard.

In his usual haughty tone, he said, "What sort of problem?"

THIRD-CLASS DINING ROOM

12:35 P.M.

LUNCH WAS FAR MORE crowded that afternoon. After the influx of passengers from Queenstown, Fiona decided they must have all been steerage class. It made sense—Ireland was a poor country with lots of poor little towns set up along the coast. She couldn't imagine anyone who could've come aboard there, garbed in delicate dresses or suits. As Matilda had said yesterday, the entire ship would be Irishmen after the last embarkment.

Seeing all the red hair and freckles and patchwork clothes, and hearing the uilleann pipes in the corner, Fiona thought her correct. There were a lot more children here, as nearly every table was occupied. They were probably experiencing the best meal of their lives. The best of many things. This was certainly an adventure, as Fiona just that morning overheard a stewardess explaining how the flush toilets worked. Some of them had never seen such a thing.

Her attention turned to a family of three, just past a post on the opposite side of the dining room. They were young, dirty, but overwhelmingly happy. She saw the sparkle in the young girl's eye as the man ran his fingers along the table, tracing some fantasy—a dream house, a plot of land, perhaps. The young boy at the mother's side was more interested in the pudding in front of him.

The way the man looked back at his young wife—it was the way Emmet looked at Fiona when they first met all those years ago. She twisted her ring, tight as it was these days, and thought of him. Those young people, that young love, that promise of a future not yet earned—she longed for that feeling, and knew her time to experience it again had passed.

Reid tugged at her sleeve, shaking her from her thoughts. He was pointing across the crowded dining room to Colin and his siblings, all seated alone with large plates of food in front of them.

"You want to go play with him?"

Reid nodded.

"Show me our cabin number."

He held up one finger straight, then two across it from his other hand, forming the letter F. Then he put up six fingers and six again. She nodded and said, "Go on, sweetie."

As he bounded away, she was left with a momentary pang of regret in her stomach, but it quickly dissipated. It was tough letting him out of her sight. In the beginning, it had been tough for him, too. She figured he would always be at her side, but moving on was easier for him. Children were remarkable, she always thought. They could absorb the brunt of trauma and somehow recover faster than anyone else.

After eating, she thought to ask him if he'd like to come up on deck, as the air was fine and they would pull away from Roches Point soon. He so loved the boats and she figured the tenders might still be coasting alongside the ship. But then she just as quickly dismissed the idea. In America, there'd be no family, no friends. She wasn't sure when he'd get the opportunity to 'talk' to another child, so she left him with Matilda's brood.

When she stepped toward the stairwell, she found Erik frantically attempting to speak to a steward but having no luck. He was terrified as he clutched his tiny journal of translated words. The steward, unable to move past the language barrier, was growing impatient.

But as Fiona neared, Erik caught sight of her from the corner of his eye and he forgot all about the steward and rushed toward her. The look on his face broke her heart because she knew something had happened.

And after a glance back at Reid and the children, she noticed Matilda wasn't with them.

"What is it?" Fiona asked him. "Tilda?"

His face lit up and he nodded, then he put his hands together and lay his head on them with his eyes closed. He sputtered a string of foreign words that she didn't understand, which propelled anger at his own inability. His shaky fingers reached up and tugged at his hair before snatching her wrist and pulling her along. The steward took a step forward as if to intervene, but Fiona shook her head and allowed Erik to lead her on.

Just as she suspected, they ended up back at the cabin. The sun was positioned in the middle of the sky, so it absorbed completely through the tiny port-hole, casting light across the bunks and the middle of the floor. There were only two beds, but the ground was covered in blankets where she guessed the chil-dren slept. A large mound lay upon the bottom bunk.

Erik continued to sputter words she didn't know, but he waited by the door and allowed her to pass by. She'd seen a few dead bodies in her time, but she wasn't prepared to see this one, for that's surely what he was showing her. Fiona looked back into the hallway as she stepped into the room. He was staring at his feet, eyes full of tears. Perhaps he just wanted Fiona to confirm.

She knelt by the blanket—Matilda's entire body was covered. It was unclear if that's how she slept or if Erik, hoping to spare the children, had covered her. She peeled back the blanket away from her face and for just a moment, there was no question this was a dead woman. Her sun-beaten skin was pale. Eyes were clamped shut, lips blue. Fiona placed a hand over the girl's mouth and rejoiced when she felt a tiny puff of air.

"She's alive!" Fiona said. Erik didn't register her excitement. He tapped at his throat, then pointed to Matilda.

Slowly, Fiona pulled the blanket away from her neck and then recoiled. She wasn't expecting this.

Matilda's shirt had been ripped away and a small trickle of blood ran from her neck, just below her jawbone, down to her exposed breast. But more alarming was the reddish, almost black veins that popped out along her neck and cheek. They all centered around a nub on her throat that looked swollen and infected, like a walnut beneath the skin.

Fiona reached up and stroked it, just long enough to feel that it was hard, and that's when Matilda snarled, sounding like a feral cat. It was loud and unsettling enough for Fiona to back into the wall. Matilda's eyes never opened, and once Fiona's fingers were no longer there, her face returned to peaceful.

Erik came into the room and pointed to the bottom of the bed.

"What is it? You want to show me something else?" She could only guess.

He pulled back the blanket from his wife's feet, revealing her dark, dirty soles and a length of her pale calf. Erik took Fiona by the shoulders and eased her to the side until she was no longer blocking the porthole.

And when the light fell across Matilda's leg, her skin hissed and smoked until she turned to the side and pulled it back into the shadow of the top bunk. The room filled with the smell of charred flesh.

"Christ Almighty!" said Fiona, pressing herself as far against the wall as possible. Erik looked as if he might cry, and now she understood why he'd been so frantic—this was curiouser than death. "Matilda? Tilda, sweetheart, wake up." Fiona pulled at her, but she wouldn't move. Now that she was on her side, the network of bloodshot veins could be seen wrapping around her shoulder and going down her back, where it disappeared into her mangled shirt.

Fiona stood, turned to Erik and said, "stay with her, I'm going to find a doctor," without even waiting to see if he understood.

CARGO HOLD

1:00 P.M.

"WHAT THE BLOODY HELL happened to him?" asked Ismay through his handkerchief. "And *who* the bloody hell is it?"

The body now lay beneath a green tarpaulin, small and shriveled. Golden light from the electrical lamps made it look like a giant smudge in front of the box.

The crewman shrugged. "Not sure." Ben had learned his name was Edward Bessant. "Hard to tell being mangled and all. Looks like a bear got a hold of 'im."

Edward had come down at the request of a first-class passenger to retrieve a bottle of exotic rum when he discovered the poor man's body. He ran off to tell someone, and that's when he found Ben in the hallway.

"Could another crewman have done this?" asked Ismay, eyes wide and horrified.

Ben shook his head. "I doubt it, sir. There're viscera so high on the wall, as if the crane had pulled him up. Then there's the viciousness of the attack . . . His neck, the way it's broken. I don't think someone could do that with their bare hands, nor wielding any weapon. And then there's the blood."

"The blood?"

The doctor nodded. "Yessir. There isn't much of it. His blood is . . .well, it's mostly missing."

Edward shook his head. "Probably just dripped down between the slats. Dried up in the firemen's mess, I'm wagerin'."

Ben scraped his foot along the floor, noticing that it was all solid wood. *Titanic* was a stout ship, built strong. He didn't buy Edward's theory, nor did he suggest otherwise.

"Christ in heaven!" Ismay said, taking a step back and turning a circle so he could inspect the entire scene. "Who else knows about this?"

"No one but us," said Edward. "I took the tarp from my quarters."

"Good, good," said Ismay, and then as if an after-thought he reached into his pocket and pulled out a five-pound note. "For your service. And your silence."

"Yessir." Edward seemed a little embarrassed and perhaps a little guilty, but he took the money and stuffed it in his pocket anyway.

"Get rid of it. Carry it down to the furnaces or put it into the ash injectors."

"Sir?" said Ben. "You want us to dispose of him out to sea? Like rubbish?"

"Is that a problem?" he said, dropping his handkerchief so the doctor could see, without question, that it had been a serious request.

Ben had encountered men like Ismay before. He knew all about the White Star Line's chairman but this put it clearly the measures the man would go to in order to keep *Titanic's* name unsullied. It would be impossible to appeal to his humanity, so Ben tried a pragmatic approach.

"If this is discovered, it will be in all the papers."

Edward nodded. "Doctor's right, sir. We need to store him, not dump him."

Ben said, "We have coffins. They come along for this very reason. We can put the poor chap in one of them."

"I know there's coffins here!" Ismay snapped. "I own the bloody ship!" He paced in a circle before adding, "You'll never get him up to the surgery without being seen."

The doctor shrugged, conceding the point. "We may. But you have to consider what happens if we're seen throwing a body into the furnaces, sir. Right now, you're only dealing with a death onboard. You can take care of that when we arrive in New York. But if we're seen dumping him . . . Well, then you have to answer for the dead body *and* why we're in a rush to get rid of it."

The man's eyes glazed over and finally he said, "Fine, in a coffin then!" He started to walk off, but grabbed Ben's hand and raised it so he could slap a wad of money in it. "And tell O'Loughlin to embalm the bastard! Maybe we can cut down on any . . . unpleasant odor."

He stormed off, shaking out a cigar from his breast pocket.

Edward and Ben looked at one another across the tarp. The doctor said, "C'mon, let's wrap him a little better."

This was nothing out of the ordinary for Ben. He'd seen many horrific things in his tenure as a doctor. Mostly with children—poor little things with lungs full of gunk who struggled for each breath. If he could see those atrocities, a mangled corpse wasn't so bad.

Edward allowed him to do most of the repacking. They rolled up the dead man and placed him on his back, then tucked the ends into the center. Since there was little blood, there was also little mess once they contained it inside the tarp. When they lifted him, Edward made a grunt that was purely out of instinct.

"It's light, innit?"

"Too light," said Ben. "He's got no blood at all."

The trip up wasn't as awkward as they thought it would be. Since they were already on the cargo deck, the three crewmen they passed paid little attention. Once they got to C deck and to the surgery, they found Mr. Dunford sitting at the desk cleaning his shoes.

"Where's O'Loughlin?" asked Ben. He glanced down the stairway, but the hospital room on D deck was empty.

Mr. Dunford saw their cargo and said, "What's in there?"

Ben gave him a scolding look, as if he should keep quiet. Mr. Dunford's mouth and eyes widened and he leaned back in his chair.

Edward helped to maneuver the body back to the partition and placed it on the gurney. Then Ben pulled the curtain and thanked the man for his help. He left the surgery, pale-faced but at least five pounds richer.

"The chief surgeon?" Ben said.

"Right," said Mr. Dunford. "He's making his rounds, as is Doctor Simpson. They were both summoned. I imagine they'll be here soo—"

His words were cut off when the ship began to hum. The engines had started. They were leaving Queenstown, off to their final destination, America.

A Deck Cabins

While Benjamin York and Edward Bessant pleaded with Ismay seven decks below, Evelyn Marsden was treating Edith Rosenbaum for a hangover. Such was the case for most first-class passengers. Some of them didn't know how to mind their spirits, and once they were out on the water with inhibitions fraying with each nautical mile from shore, they drank themselves sick.

Edith was lying on her back with stacks of pillows beneath her head and shoulders so that she could be elevated enough to see out the window and onto the promenade. Right now, she was grimacing from the light. Her eyes were rimmed red as she drank the magic elixir that Evelyn poured from her cart.

"This tastes foul," said Edith, pinching her nose and closing her eyes before taking another sip. "What's in it?"

"Who knows?" said Evelyn. But she did know—she just didn't want to say it was an old recipe her mother had brewed for her father on many drunken nights. It was a combination of myrrh, chamomile, honey, and rhubarb. She learned from her time on *Olympic* that it was best to come prepared when there would be lots of drinking involved. And these Americans like Edith sure loved the bottle.

"It was just cards and brandy," she lamented, as if she needed to explain herself. "I'll go easy tonight."

"Smart gal," said Evelyn. She stood and noticed the strange—and somewhat horrifying—stuffed pig on the armoire. "What's that, miss?"

"That's my lucky pig. Twist his tail."

Evelyn did as she said, fearing that she would destroy this toy if she weren't careful. It was merely papier mâché covered in fur. When she twisted the tail, it straightened and snapped back, now playing a beautiful song from within.

"That's just lovely," said Evelyn.

Edith nodded and said, "It was a gift from my mother after the accident."

Evelyn was about to ask the nature of the accident when her friend Mary Sloan, a first-class stewardess, appeared at the door and knocked. Her face was ashen, eyes blank.

"Drink the rest of that down and I'll check on you later."

"Thank you, dear," said Edith. "By the way, I love the ribbon in your hair. We should talk fashion sometime."

Evelyn didn't hear any of it, for she was too concerned by Mary's face. Out in the hall, the girl said, "You need to follow me this instant." She turned and walked off toward the port side of the ship.

They passed few passengers but the victualling crew was in full force. Mary led her to a stateroom at the far end of the narrow hallway. The door was open and she immediately saw an arm hanging from the covers—the skin pale and bluish.

Evelyn prided herself on knowing many of the passengers under her care, so it didn't take long to come up with the name of Minnie Pembroke, a hotel heiress who was traveling alone to see her brother in America.

"What's happened?" asked Evelyn.

"Found her this way. I haven't . . . gone to check. Just thought it strange that a proper lady would have her door open and all. Right when she's asleep, yeah?"

"It is strange," Evelyn said, and she entered the room, knocking first and announcing herself. The woman on the bed didn't stir. The curtains were pulled, and the stateroom was dim. Evelyn waited to see if there was a rise and fall of her chest, but there was none. Either she was dead or breathing so shallow that it was impossible to tell.

She circled around and pulled the sheet back, horrified by her appearance.

"Is she . . . is she gone?" Mary asked from the doorway, her skin taking on a similar pallor.

"I don't know. Mind the doorway, will you?" Mary nodded and stepped back into the hall with her arms folded over her apron.

Evelyn knelt back down for a closer look. Minnie looked horrible—her long shock of blond hair was all a matted mess, as if she'd been beaten to death. But there were no bruises, only a bead of dried blood from her chin to her breast. Little veins popped out along her flesh, circling a fleshy nub in the center. This was all beyond Evelyn's talent, so she pulled the blanket back over the girl's head and stepped back into the hall.

"Well?" said Mary.

"We need to find a doctor at once."

SURGERY ROOM

DOCTOR SIMPSON WAS LEFT with the entire ship for hours following *Titanic's* departure from Queenstown. Ben found Doctor O'Loughlin and Matron Wallis on the Bridge Deck, together on the way to see about a pair of unresponsive sisters on C deck, and told them to return to the surgery at once.

"Is it important?" O'Loughlin asked, but upon seeing Ben's stern expression, nodded. The old man turned to Matron Wallis and said, "Find Doctor Simpson and have him give the Shelter Deck a look-sie."

"Yes, Doctor," she said, then hurried down the steps.

Back in the surgery, they closed the hatch to the hospital steps and locked the door leading out to the C deck hallway. They gave Mr. Dunford the order that no one was to bother them until they pulled back the partition.

"Christ above!" said O'Loughlin when they peeled away the tarp. "Did this fella get caught in the engines?"

"No idea," said Ben, and he explained the circumstances that led to *Titanic's* chief surgeon having to perform an embalming on the ship's maiden voyage.

"Are there exotic animals down there?"

"Not that I'm aware of. We have a few dogs onboard, but nothing capable of this."

"See the neck?" O'Loughlin said, tilting the head. It was barely connected, only hanging on by a few pink strands of sinew. The doctor cradled it in one hand so he could point with the other. "Look at the marks. These are *bite* marks. See the curve?"

Ben *could* see it. Whatever had bit into him left semi-circle cuts at the top before clamping down and mangling the flesh. He counted them—eight.

"What kind of animal has eight teeth like this?" Ben said. "Most meat eaters have incisors at the sides, but these teeth go right across, all in a row."

O'Loughlin shook his head. "Stop callin' them teeth, Benjamin. These were done by fangs. And it wasn't an animal. I don't know of any animal on God's Great Pasture that could do somethin' like this. Do you?"

"No," Ben said, and now that they saw the extent of the damage, it was clear.

"This keeps getting more upsetting," said O'Loughlin after cutting the shirt down the middle. The shoulder and arm on his left side were ripped off—dangling from a strip of meat at his hip. The right side was intact, but it was crushed and punctured.

"One wound in the front and four in the back," said Ben.

"A thumb and fingers," said the older doctor.

"You can't be serious. You think a *person* did this?"

O'Loughlin squared himself with the body and held his hands out as if they were claws. He lined it up with the shoulder that still existed and showed Ben how a thumb could poke through the front while four fingers could do the same on the back.

"Someone grabbed this poor bloke by the shoulders, dug into him and bit him at the same time. This someone also got a little aggressive and ripped his left side clean off. Then he dropped him and scurried right off."

"But where? And you're talking nonsense, old man."

O'Loughlin gave him a reprimanding glare.

"Sorry."

His smile returned and he threw up his hands. "I've seen a lot of things in my day, Benjamin. I'm no longer surprised by the evil of men. They're capable of anything."

"So you really think a man did this?"

The old doctor shrugged. "It isn't our job to know, lad. But I'll say this: There's a lot o' men on this ship. This killing took place yesterday. It stands to reason that it was done by a man, rather than some giant, crazed animal. Such a creature would've turned up by now."

Ben nodded, but he couldn't help thinking that perhaps such a monster was just adept at not getting caught.

The embalming took most of the day, as O'Loughlin was precise in his work. They placed the aspirator on the floor and barely pumped out half a pint of blood before the glass bottle and tube hissed hungrily. O'Loughlin couldn't save the mangled shoulder and arm, nor the head. So, faced with an awful decision, he used his Liston knife to remove them. He wrapped them—along with most of the bloodless organs—in butcher paper and used hot glue to seal it all. It wouldn't be a permanent fix, but it would do until they arrived in America.

After that, it was merely the tedious job of treating the body with preservation chemicals and finally stitching up the holes. Without a head or left shoulder, the threads weren't perfect, but at least the bloke wouldn't rot so quickly. Ben helped O'Loughlin lay one of the three coffins flat, then lifted the dead man into it, along with his wrapped innards and head. They nailed it shut and moved it as far away from the beds as possible.

When it was over, O'Loughlin pulled a bottle of scotch from one of the medicine cabinets and poured himself and Ben a glass. Ben didn't want it—his stomach was in knots—but he took it anyway as not to be rude.

"Lovely way to start the voyage, yeah?" said the old man, throwing back his glass.

Ben nodded. "Let's hope the worst is behind us."

"Doctor Simpson needs the two of you downstairs," said Mr. Dunford as soon as they stepped out of the surgery. O'Loughlin nodded and pulled open the hatch, then descended the steps.

Ben followed, nearly bumping into the old man's back because he'd stopped to assess the room. They were in the infectious partition of the hospital. *Titanic* came equipped with twelve beds for isolation—a truly worst-case scenario that O'Loughlin had probably never seen in his career. But right now, *Titanic* had four patients, all women, all unconscious upon the beds.

"What's wrong with them?" Ben asked Doctor Simpson, who was listening to a woman's heartbeat—she was first-class, no doubt about it. Her finger and toenails were clean and well-maintained.

"I don't know," he said. "But it's the same with all four of them. They won't wake up and they have these weird markings on their necks."

Weird markings on the necks.

It was too much of a coincidence. Ben inspected the nearest girl, a red-headed lady with lots of freckles. There was a blanket across her because her shirt had been ripped to shreds.

He touched the skin at her neck, feeling the little nub and immediately she hissed, as if agitated.

Doctor Simpson said, "They seem sensitive to touch, especially that spot on their necks."

"What *is* that?" Doctor O'Loughlin said, putting on his bifocals and inspecting a tall, auburn-haired lady who held a striking resemblance to the girl lying across from her. He put on his gloves again and touched the nub on her neck and she hissed and rolled away onto her side. Her breathing increased for a moment, but quickly settled back down.

"Is this some sort of contagion?" asked Ben, taking a step back.

"It's something blood-borne," O'Loughlin said. "Look at them. They all have a dried trickle of blood from the hard place on their necks."

"A wound," Simpson said.

"Aye, that's what it looks like," O'Loughlin agreed. He turned to Ben. "Almost like somethin' bit them. We need to flush the blood, get the infections out."

"What decks were they found?" asked Ben.

Doctor Simpson pointed to the girl by his side. "This is Minnie Pembroke, she was found on A deck. Those two ladies across the room are sisters, Catherine and Elizabeth Campbell. They were on C deck. And that red-headed lass over there is Miss Matilda Olsson. F deck."

"Makes no bloody sense," said O'Loughlin. "If this is a bite, how did it happen to four ladies spread across three decks?"

Ben felt a shiver. Maybe their mystery creature could not only stay hidden, but could also *move about* hidden. The implications of that troubled him greatly.

"That's not all, gentlemen," said Doctor Simpson. "Miss Pembroke here had a lot of trouble on the way down to the ward." He threw the blanket back, revealing her pale leg with a large, red splotch across it. He stared at it quizzically. "Quite curious, indeed. This wound was much worse an hour ago."

"What wound?" Ben asked.

"Observe." He pulled out a shaving mirror from a nearby desk and walked over to the porthole. The sun was low in the sky—it would be dark in a few hours. But he was able to use the mirror to direct a ball of light until it touched Miss Pembroke's knee.

And the flesh hissed and popped and smoked until she screamed out and rolled over. She fell right off the bed and landed on her face, but she didn't wake up. All the men rushed to lift her back onto the cot. Her leg was bright red, the skin charred. They smelled it in the air.

"This is the devil at work, men," said Doctor Simpson once the lady was still. "What do we do?"

"Keep them out of the light, for starters," said Ben. "We need to check the wounds. There's something in there."

He pointed to Matilda's throat, to the dark bulge that was now a little bigger than it had been that morning.

"Not now," said O'Loughlin. "We need to search the ship up and down and make sure no one else is infected."

"Right," Ben said. "I'll take the lower decks. It'll be dark soon. I'd like to trouble people before they're off to bed."

Doctor Simpson laughed. "Have ye been down there? They don't sleep. They're Irish."

"Right," Ben said again.

O'Loughlin stared at the girl's burn spot, then shook his head in disbelief. "I need to tell the cap'n."

"We need to keep this quiet," Doctor Simpson said.

Ben nodded. "Normally I wouldn't agree, but the last thing we need is a panic. Let's assess first. See how bad the situation is, and then we'll have more information to report."

Reluctantly, O'Loughlin nodded. "Okay, boys. I'll meet you back here after supper. Stay safe." He turned and headed back up the steps to the surgery.

Ben unlocked the door to the D deck hallway and stepped out. Sitting outside was Fiona and another man who looked Ben up and down with worried eyes. He started into a barrage of foreign words, so Ben looked to Fiona for answers.

"That lady in there? Matilda? That's his wife."

"Oh," Ben said, sighing heavily. The man read his expression as purely grim and he sank back down on the bench and put his hands in his hair. "She's alive." He pinched his eyelids and pulled them open, unsure of how else to explain to a foreigner her condition.

"What's wrong with her? The sunlight . . . did you know that . . ."

"We know. We don't understand it. None of us have seen anything like it. Have you come across anyone else like her?"

"No," she said. "Do you think there's more?"

He glanced nervously over his shoulder. Instead of answering, he asked, "How would you like to help with something?"

"What with?"

"Ask around? See if anyone else is . . . unable to wake?"

"Yeah. I can do tha—"

The bugler let out a long, cheery retort, signaling that everyone should make their way to the dining rooms. Ben nodded and said, "See you soon. Oh, and I have something for Reid."

She beamed at him, and it was the first time he'd noticed just how young she truly was—probably only twenty-two or twenty-three. Her husband was probably waiting with great anticipation for her to arrive next week.

"For Reid? That's . . . that's very kind."

He stepped back into the doorway so he could go up to C deck to his cabin, but first he turned back to her and said, "Save me a seat."

THIRD-CLASS DINING ROOM

ERIK STAYED UP ON D deck, insistent on remaining near his wife. By the way the children played, Fiona wondered if they even realized the severity of her condition. While their father was dealing with the hopelessness and confusion, the eldest boy, Micky, stepped up and made sure his siblings were eating dinner.

Reid was quieter than normal, a strange phenomenon for a boy who hadn't spoken in two years. Fiona always knew when something was troubling him, and today it was probably empathy for the Olsson kids. Reid remembered what it was like when Emmet suddenly wasn't there. That was a pain no child should have to bear.

"Potato soup, eh?" said Ben, appearing just next to her. A few of the unruly passengers hushed at his approach and turned nearly mute when he sat down. They didn't understand why this fancy doctor in his nice, pressed suit would sully himself by dining with the steerage class.

"It's good," she said, and she pushed his food—already retrieved from the window—in front of him. Before Ben took the first bite, he turned to Reid and placed something on the table, wrapped in a thin, white napkin with the White Star Line logo embroidered on it.

Reid closed his book and gingerly unwrapped the cross. His eyes lit up as he traced a finger across the metal, and then across the wooden figure of the Savior. He held the crucifix in his hand, as if testing the weight.

"Will you thank the nice man?" asked Fiona.

Reid looked up at Ben, eyes beaming, almost teary. And then he returned to his book.

"You're quite welcome, Reid," he said, for the exchange was good enough for him.

Fiona grinned warmly and reached across her boy and squeezed Ben's hand before going back to her food. They ate in silence for a little while, listening to the conversations of the surrounding passengers. Third-class was a non-stop celebration of cultures, for everyone in Europe was thrust together. Her life seemed far less interesting than the lads and lasses here who would start dancing at the drop of a hat. It made Fiona sad to think her youth was gone, but who would've known the turn her life would've taken?

She rolled up a piece of bread in a napkin and stuffed it into her pocket. After dinner, she'd deliver it to Erik. Life was going to be different for him once he got off the ship. This was a given before boarding, but circumstances had changed with Matilda's illness.

Ben watched the other passengers, specifically their necks. Right now, they only knew of four potential victims.

"Did you . . . get a chance to talk to anyone?"

"I did," Fiona said. "There's many people laid out drunk, but that's it. I asked about marks on the neck, hatin' the sunlight, and all that. Nothin'."

"Good," said Ben. "Then perhaps it's contained."

"What's contained?"

Ben glanced around the room before whispering, "We think it's some sort of contagious disease."

"Could we . . . be sick?" she asked, then subconsciously rubbed her throat.

Ben shook his head. "Not unless something has bitten you. That seems to be how it's spreading."

"Like a rat?"

"Yeah, like a rat," he said, although she didn't think he sounded certain.

"What can you do for them?"

Ben said, "We will keep them comfortable and try to flush the wounds, but other than that, not much. Titanic can deal with a lot of medical problems, but this isn't among them. Hopefully, they'll remain stable until we get to New York."

"I've never seen this in all my years. Ben, Matilda's leg was catching fire . . ."

Reid glanced up, as if to make sure he heard correctly, then dropped his nose back in the book.

Ben shrugged because *no one* had ever encountered anything like this. "If I were home, I'd have my volumes of medical anomalies to verify if this has been seen before. But I'm guessing in none of my books would I find a condition where sunlight sets flesh afire."

Again, Reid looked up and returned to his book.

"So where are you headed?" Ben asked, wiping his chin. "Staying in New York, or going beyond?"

"Oh, um . . . Philadelphia."

"I see. And what's in Philadelphia for Fiona and Reid?"

"A brewery."

That answer seemed to catch him off-guard. He took a drink of water and nodded. "Interesting. I wouldn't have taken you for much of a drinker." He waved his hand around the energetic room. "Or else you'd have probably joined in by now."

"I don't drink at all," she said. "My husband . . . he had quite the problem with it."

At the mention of Emmet, Reid looked up uneasily, then dropped his head again.

"Say no more," said Ben graciously. He noticed the shift in them both.

"What about you?" she asked. "Do you get leave in New York? Or is it right back on the ship for you?"

He shrugged. "I'll be getting off in New York, for sure. And hopefully I'll never get back on a ship again."

She nodded, for it was understandable. Lots of people hated to travel by sea. It certainly wasn't enjoyable to her, but what choice did one have for crossing enormous bodies of water?

"I'm sure New York has plenty o' good hospitals for someone as qualified as yourself."

He smiled and nodded, accepting the compliment. Then said, "I don't want to be a doctor anymore, either."

Both Fiona and Reid looked at him curiously. She said, "Why ever not?"

He shrugged, as if he'd not pondered the reasoning behind this dramatic decision until now. "It's a tough job, yeah? I worked at a place called Samaritan's Cross. We primarily treated children and our hospital specialized in breathing issues. Respiratory. In a mining town like Southampton, we only fought against tuberculosis."

"Did you see lots of . . ."

"Death? More than my life's fair share. Our ability to fight this dreadful disease . . . it's not good.

And one day I realized I wasn't helping anyone. I was merely facilitating children into the ground." He picked up the crucifix and rubbed his thumb across the Savior's feet. "On the morning we received seventeen children who were all gone by the afternoon, I decided I was done. This isn't the job for me."

"So you left?"

He nodded. "I tendered my resignation and took the first job to come open outside of Southampton. My resident doctor remembered an old friend from Trinity College and wrote to him immediately. Doctor O'Loughlin sent for me at once with the agreement I would sail with the White Star Line for at least six months—a contract I have no plans on fulfilling."

"You don't?"

He shook his head. "America is about starting over, right? And that's what I plan to do."

"I see. So . . . what *will* you do?" Fiona asked. "For work, I mean."

"I don't know. I've always wanted to farm."

"Farm?" she said, and giggled.

"What's so funny? Can't see me farming?"

"Not at all, doctor."

He shrugged. "Me either, but I've always wanted to try my hand at it. Plant something and see it take off. It has to be rewarding to watch something come of all your hard work."

She nodded. "I think you'd make a fine farmer, Doctor York."

He grinned, lost in the fantasy. She could tell he'd thought about it quite a bit.

They talked into the night, losing track of time until the dining room began to empty because everyone had finished dinner. Fiona—and Reid—enjoyed Ben's company. Tragedy had marred this entire voyage, so it was nice to speak of other things, even if they couldn't escape what was happening.

Fiona fanned herself and slid her chair out from the table. She said, "I need some air. Would you like to join me?"

"Sure," he said.

"Reid?"

He closed his book and handed it to Fiona, then pointed to Matilda's clan who was banging out a horrible string of notes from the piano. She nodded as he slithered out of his chair and joined them.

Ben escorted her up to the well deck and into the chilly night. They tasted the salt in the air. The evenings were much cooler lately with the wind biting at their noses. A cloudless sky full of stars hung above them. Both third-class decks were crowded, but they could feel the muffled beats of music already starting below them.

"The sea is so vast," said Fiona, staring off from the port side. They saw no light beyond what *Titanic* provided, just the tiny thimblefuls of starlight in the water. Fiona had always found the ocean frightful, especially this far away from land. Water for miles in every direction but upward.

"How about a better view?" Ben said, and he held out his arm, instructing her to lock with it.

She felt her cheeks turn rosy, but she nodded and took it. This served a practical purpose as they ascended the steps out of the well deck and he unfastened a rope across the stairway. She felt like she was breaking the law but Ben didn't seem troubled, so she relaxed—but only until they climbed a little higher.

The promenade ahead was packed with fancy people enjoying the crisp night. The Café Parisien was mostly empty this late after dinner, but she still took a moment to appreciate the space—white trellises, English ivy, and beautiful wicker tables and chairs. Soft fiddle music filled her ears. Wine glasses clinked together. Fiona didn't like to stare—but that's certainly what *they* were doing.

Two women garbed in heavy fur coats reclined on lounge chairs just before the café door. They gave a quick perusal of Fiona and grinned. One turned to the other and pulled at her own hair and both snickered. Fiona smoothed down her red mane with her free hand.

She didn't want to walk past all these people and their cold, cruel eyes, but luckily she wouldn't have to—Ben took her up the second-class stairway until they reached the Boat Deck, mostly clear of haughty first-class passengers. At this hour, they'd already retreated into their smoking lounges and staterooms.

A few men from the deck crew lingered about, but here on the aft end of the ship, no one seemed to care about the doctor and the lady he invited up. Far to the other end, she was amazed by the size of the windows. She was accustomed to tiny portholes, but the ones that looked into the gymnasium and the grand staircase she'd heard so much about were large enough to climb through.

"It's quiet up here," said Fiona, taking a seat on a nearby bench.

"It isn't in the daytime," he assured, and joined her. The wind whipped across both of them and disappeared out to sea.

The lifeboats in front of them swayed and creaked on their ropes. Fiona said, "How many people are on this ship?"

"Over two-thousand, I should think. Not nearly as many as she can carry."

"It doesn't seem like there's enough lifeboats."

He laughed and nodded. "No, but Titanic is its own lifeboat."

"What do you mean?"

"I don't know the specifics of it, but these big ocean liners aren't meant to sink."

"No boats are meant to sink," she countered.

"Right, but Titanic is too big to sink. I don't know the . . . design behind it, but that's what we were told at the end of the sea trials."

"Right," said Fiona. "But why have any lifeboats at all?" She pointed directly ahead. "That one there blocks my view of the ocean."

"Some are needed. We don't have enough for every passenger on the ship but we don't need that many."

"Why?"

"Titanic travels a well-worn path. Lots of ships use this same shipping lane. There's never one more than a few hours away from us. The lifeboats aren't meant to save us. They're meant to ferry us from an inoperable ship to a rescue ship."

"But what if time is short?" she ventured.

Ben laughed. "You worry far too much, Fiona."

"That I do. It's kept me alive this long."

"I'm sure you've had your battles."

She smiled because there was no way this nice man could know. And then she said, "Yes. I have."

He looked at her, the light twinkling in his eyes. He was such a good man. Would there ever be someone in her life like Ben? She didn't think so, not anymore.

Men like this good doctor knew better than to get mixed up in her troubles.

"So tell me about your battles," he whispered.

And she had softened right along with him and was about to lay herself bare when someone came up the steps behind them. Ben turned and stood immediately, straightening his uniform. Fiona expected to see the captain addressing him, but according to the man's blue coat, he was a 'hospital attendant.'

"Mr. Dunford?" said Ben. The man's face was pale, his fingers shaky as he tried to put a cigarette into his mouth. He looked once to Fiona, then back to the doctor, as if to tell him this was confidential.

But Ben said, "Go on, Mr. Dunford. What is it?"

After a few seconds of deliberation, he stepped forward, and in a tiny voice said, "They've died, sir."

Fiona's nose stung with tears. She felt a great weight suddenly rest upon her chest. Poor Erik. Those poor kids.

"Which ones?" asked Ben.

Mr. Dunford dropped his head and said, "All of them, sir. Every last one of them."

C DECK

"I'VE LOCKED ALL THE doors," said Mr. Dunford as they walked through the second-class promenade toward the surgery. "As well as the hatch down to the isolation room."

"Go on, Mr. Dunford. I'll be right along. No need to wake Doctors O'Loughlin and Simpson." The hospital steward nodded, cast a final, dismissive glance at Fiona, then continued down the hall.

Ben and Fiona stood next to the second-class entrance, the staircase not nearly as grand as the one on the forward end of the ship. He said, "I'd like you to go on down to D deck and be with Mr. Olsson. As far as I can tell, Matilda was the only one sailing with a family. He's going to need someone to help him through this."

She nodded reverently. Then she lifted herself on her tiptoes and wrapped her arms around him. At first he didn't know what to do—he wasn't one for affection, but he rested his hand on her back and let out a sigh. After no longer than three heartbeats, they separated and she exited through the door to the staircase. Ben took a breath to steady his nerves, then continued on toward the surgery.

He locked the door behind him and then the hatch at the top of the steps. At the bottom, he found Mr. Dunford standing at the row of beds, hand on his cheek, sweat beading on his forehead.

All the beds were empty.

"What . . . where did they go, Mr. Dunford?"

He looked at Ben with wild, confused eyes, and that's when the doctor realized the hospital steward was just as confused. His voice was pleading, almost child-like. "I don't know, sir. They were all here. I checked them over and over and over until I was sure. I didn't want to disturb any of you until I knew they were gone."

"They didn't die, then," said Ben. "They got up and left."

"They *did* die, sir! I would stake my profession on it!"

"Tell me what happened." Ben inspected the cots. They were cold, all of them. There was nothing hiding behind the partition, only a coffin with a headless body.

"I was at my desk there, reading, when I heard one of the Campbell sisters choking. I rushed over, attempted to get her calmed down, but then the other three started. One by one, they gurgled and fell back."

"You're saying they . . . died all at once?"

"That's how it seemed, yessir."

"This can't be right."

"It can't be," agreed the hospital steward. "But it happened."

"So where are they now?" Ben asked, more to hear himself say it than for Mr. Dunford to provide an answer.

"Haven't the slightest. The door up in the surgery was locked, as was the hatch." He pointed to the last door straight ahead. "And that one is still locked."

Ben knew no passengers could get into the hospital, nor the infectious disease room, without a key or at least without breaking down the door. He wasn't sure how four, very sick—comatose—women, could disappear.

He unlocked the door and stepped out, already forgetting that Erik and Fiona would be in the hall. The man was crying, as somehow she'd expressed what they feared had happened. Now Ben wasn't even sure what to tell him.

Fiona stood—she'd been crying too, as her eyes were glassy under the electric lights. "Can he . . . can he come see her?"

"She's not here."

Fiona stared at him and Erik stared at her, curious about what the doctor said.

"I don't understand."

"And neither do we. All four of them just . . . vanished into thin air."

Erik said something that neither of them understood and Fiona did her best to explain that his wife was no longer on the other side of the door where he'd been waiting for an entire day. There was no way he could understand, but Ben stepped back into the room and allowed him to stand in the doorway and see for himself. The doctor pointed to the cot where his wife had been, and lacking any other form of communication, he shrugged. It wasn't the best way to deliver this unlikely news, but he was out of ideas.

Erik looked once at Fiona, then turned and darted down the hallway.

She said, "He probably thinks she's gone back to their cabin."

And maybe she had, thought Ben. Although he didn't believe she'd made such a quick recovery. Those girls were dead, he thought. There was no reason to think Mr. Dunford had been incorrect.

"I'm sorry. We have to deal with this," he told her.

She nodded. "I understand. Well . . . thank you for the tour of the Boat Deck."

Ben turned around—Mr. Dunford had already gone upstairs to wake the doctors. He faced Fiona again and whispered. "Find Reid. Go into your cabin and lock the door until the sun comes up again."

"Benjamin?"

"Do it. Please?"

"Alright. I will."

"Thank you."

And then he closed the door and locked it. He sat on the edge of the cot and waited to see what they would do next.

"We have to tell Ismay," said O'Loughlin. "He's going to be madder than a wet hen when he wakes up! Christ Almighty, Will."

"I'm sorry, sir," said Mr. Dunford. "But as I've explained to Doctor York, the doors were locked."

Ben approached the porthole and swung it on its hinges.

O'Loughlin laughed. "What is it, Ben? Do you think they all slipped through there? Like four sausage links?"

Ben smiled politely and shook his head.

The entire medical team had been called to the infectious room, including Mrs. Marsden and Matron Wallis. They were all needed to quell this emergency before it became an even bigger problem.

"We have to find those ladies," O'Loughlin said. "They'll turn up. They're probably weak, stumbling around. It'll be on everyone's tongue by morning. The important thing is they don't spread . . . whatever it is."

A virus that makes someone burn up in the sun, thought Ben. It sounded ridiculous just thinking it.

Evelyn Marsden said, "I'll check Miss Pembroke's stateroom. Maybe she returned there."

Matron Wallis said, "I'll check on the sisters up on the Shelter Deck."

"I'll go with you," said Doctor Simpson.

Ben said, "I suppose that leaves F deck. I'll check on it."

"You'll go with me first to wake Ismay," Doctor O'Loughlin said. "Best he hears it from us before he hears it from a screaming passenger through the night."

Ben nodded. He didn't like the idea of presenting this news, but O'Loughlin was correct.

The old doctor turned to Mr. Dunford and said, "And for crissakes, man, keep an eye on the room in case they'd wander back."

Mr. Dunford dropped his head and nodded.

Ben and O'Loughlin stepped into the hallway. As the old man locked the door, he said, "What's on yer mind, Ben? I haven't known you long, but I can tell when a man wants to say somethin'."

"Doctor . . . you and I know better than anyone on this ship that something foul is going on. Something . . . unexplainable."

"Aye, you're right."

"We need to warn everyone. I have a bad feeling . . . about those ladies."

"Why's that?" They headed off toward the second-class stairway.

"We both know those ladies died tonight. Mr. Dunford wouldn't make that error. And four times? No, he's better than that."

"I believe Mr. Dunford believes the girls are dead. But I have forty years of training telling me otherwise. Dead girls don't get up and prance about."

"Then maybe they're not just girls now."

O'Loughlin paused at this, then said, "C'mon. Let's go wake that rich, limey bastard and get an earful."

B DECK

NATURALLY, BRUCE ISMAY'S PARLOUR suite was one of the best rooms on the ship. There were only four of them—two on B deck and two on C deck, each just aft of the grand staircase landing.

When the door opened, it wasn't Ismay, but his valet Richard, who stared at the pair of doctors with wide, curious eyes. There was no good reason for these men to visit so late in the evening.

"What is it now?" asked Ismay, pushing past Richard. He was holding a drink in his hand and was wearing his pajamas and slippers. After peering down the hall and toward the staircase, he ushered the men into his suite.

The sitting room alone was larger than Ben's flat in Southampton. A roaring fire snapped and crackled, flanked by a pair of thick, comfortable armchairs.

"We have another problem," said Ben.

"Those seem to be compounding," said Ismay, throwing back his head and draining his glass. He turned to Richard and said, "Put on tea for us, please."

Ismay instructed them to sit. He joined them, plopping down on a sofa next to the black windows that looked out to his private promenade. Doctor O'Loughlin shifted nervously in the chair.

"We have a rather unusual illness onboard," said the doctor. "It seems to be blood-borne."

"And that means what, doctor?"

Ben said, "It means the illness is spread through the blood. Bites and scrapes. That sort of thing."

"Go on."

O'Loughlin continued. "We have seen this in four passengers so far. We're . . . unsure of how it has spread, but it has done so rather quickly."

"These steerage people," he said, and shook his head as if that was the only thing he needed to say. He fished a cigar from his metal case and placed it between his thin lips.

Ben said, "We're not sure where it started. But it hasn't been contained only to third-class. Of the four victims, two were second-class and one was first-class."

Ismay pulled the cigar out of his mouth and pointed at Ben. "You mean to say this infection has already claimed one of our affluent passengers?"

Ben hated that the man framed the question this way, but he nodded anyway.

"How bad is it?" Ismay asked. "You said there are four . . . those four are contained in the isolation room, correct?"

Ben and O'Loughlin shared an uneasy look, but it was the older doctor who said, "We don't know where they are, sir."

Richard interrupted Ismay's train of thought as he walked in, pushing a service cart with a teakettle, cups, saucers, spoons, and sugar. This probably wasn't part of the man's job, but people rarely told Bruce Ismay no.

"What do you mean?" Ismay said. "Were they unruly?"

"They were unconscious," Ben said.

"I don't understand."

O'Loughlin shook his head. "Neither do we, sir."

"Why the hell are you not out there looking for them?" Ismay said, his voice rising. Richard quickly finished the tea, handed each man a cup and saucer, then dutifully left through the door, back into the hall.

"We are, sir," O'Loughlin said. "I assure you, we are. But we needed to tell you first. We need you to understand the . . . peculiarity of it all."

"Go on."

Ben and O'Loughlin took turns explaining all that had happened, from the vicious wounds of the unidentified crewman to the odd symptoms of their four patients. Ben avoided using the word 'super-natural' because it would be in that moment that Ismay would forget all about what was happening. He was a man of reason—as were Ben and O'Loughlin—only the doctors had been privy to strange things since sailing.

"So you think this mystery beast that's stowed away on my ship has something to do with those four women?"

"Aye, we do," said O'Loughlin.

Ismay grinned and shook his head, then finally lit his cigar. He leaned his head back on the sofa and blew a puff of smoke straight in the air, ruminating over the men's words.

"Let's say I believe there's a beast aboard this ship. Why would it demolish one man, but show such restraint with the others? It clearly could devour *them* just the same."

O'Loughlin cast Ben a questioning glance, as if he hadn't considered that yet. The logic of it made sense, but Ben had dwelled on this question ever since he connected their mystery beast to the women.

"Because it was hungry when it tore into the crewman. But the women . . . they weren't for food. They were something else."

"Something else? Like what?"

Ben shrugged. "If it had wanted to kill them, it would have. We don't know why, but it kept them alive for a purpose."

Ismay rubbed his eyes and shook his head. "I don't know what to make of all this, gentlemen. I really don't. What I do know is that we have four very sick women stumbling around on my ship. Find them, get them back to isolation. I don't need to remind you all that this voyage is very important for the White Star Line. I'll not have us arriving in New York with half the bloody ship sick!"

"Yessir," said O'Loughlin.

"We don't have the power to keep this from spreading," said Ben.

"Excuse me?" said Ismay with pure disdain. Even O'Loughlin grew quiet.

"You need to order all passengers to stay in their rooms until we arrive in New York. Have meals delivered, minimize contact with one another."

Ismay chuckled. He pointed through the wall, toward his bedroom and said, "On the other end of this deck is Benjamin Guggenheim, one of the wealthiest, most prominent people aboard this ship. And you suggest I go tell him that his next week's activities are cancelled? That the kitchen staff will bring his every meal, as if he's some sort of prisoner?"

"No sir," said Ben, realizing it was an outrageous request, even if it was the necessary one.

"Of course not. That would be stupid. And the last thing I want on my ship is stupid doctors." He let this insult simmer for a moment. "But I will talk to the captain in the morning and suggest we increase speed. We will need to hasten our arrival in case this . . . illness . . . were to spiral out of control."

"That may be best, sir," said O'Loughlin, although he was feeling just like Ben—that they'd wasted an hour talking rather than searching for the missing girls.

"Do either of you gentlemen have contacts at any of the hospitals in New York?"

"I do, sir," said O'Loughlin. "My old college-mate's brother is the head of St. Vincent's."

"Good. As soon as you can, please see Mr. Bride and Mr. Phillips and have them send a Marconigram before our arrival." Ismay took another puff of his cigar and blew the smoke out. "It'll look good in the papers. Let people see that the White Star Line got ahead of its outbreak, should there be one."

"I'll do it, sir," said O'Loughlin, and he shifted his body toward Ben because he was ready to go.

"If there's nothing else," said Ismay.

The doctors stood, thanked Ismay for his tea, and left. At the door, the chairman said, "Doctor York?"

Ben turned before heading through the Baize door by the staircase. "Yes, Mr. Ismay?"

"Find those girls before they turn up dead."

And then he shut the door.

Ben followed O'Loughlin off B deck and thought: *That's a problem because the girls were already dead . . .*

F DECK

CLARENCE CLARKE LOVED EXTRAVAGANT ships. He'd worked on them for most of his adult life, but this was the first time he'd signed up for bedroom steward. It was an easier job, much easier than a greaser, and here he got to keep his fingernails clean. Sure, it was less pay, but he figured he'd make up the difference in tips. He preferred the second-class passengers but his friends told him first-class tipped much better.

He was about to turn in for the night, as his shift just ended. He'd be awake to help with the linens bright and early, a job he loved because that's when he got to see Violet and hear about her stories from first-class.

Dogs barked and cages rattled in the nearby kennel of the midship's intersecting hall. The sudden sound in the otherwise silent space made him drop his load of fresh towels. He must have walked this same corridor a hundred times a day, yet this was the first time they'd ever so much as made a sound. Clarence faced the wall of cages—he didn't know breeds, but could count them. There were five in all: three big, pristine beauties, a medium-sized one, and a tiny, ugly pup that might've been a rat with a collar. And they were all barking wildly, snarling, or throwing themselves at the bars. The small one blazed circles across its linen bedding.

"What's wrong, boys? Or is it girls?" he said. The sound of his voice did little to calm them. They continued to bark, their cries turning so chaotic and loud that he backed out of the hallway with the towels pressed over one ear and his palm over the other.

The lights above him flickered.

Again, Clarence dropped the towels and did a full circle. An odd sensation crept into his bones—as if someone were standing very close, but there was no one else in the hallway. He was about to bend and retrieve the towels when the lights flickered out again, this time long enough for total darkness to surround him. He threw his back against the wall, the cacophony of barks even louder in the dark.

"Shut up! Good gracious, shut up!" he said, but they didn't listen.

At the far end of the hallway, he spied a pair of red dots. Clarence blinked, then rubbed his palms into his eyes, sure that he was seeing things, but they remained—in fact, they were getting closer, gliding along as if they were riding one of the linen trollies.

Another flicker and the lights came on. The dogs were barking just as voraciously, but now he saw the two dots of light were eyes—and the eyes belonged to a woman. She was probably first-class, given the quality of her nightgown, but it was difficult to say with her hair so matted and the length of dried blood stretching from her neck to her chest.

"Darling, are you hurt?" Clarence said, and he took one step toward her before realizing this was a mistake. She was still twenty feet away, but in the dimness of the recovering lights, he saw there were no eyes at all, but little red orbs floating where they should've been. A snarl curled upon her lips, anger as sure as the barking dogs.

But most of all, he saw the white, gleaming fangs hanging over her bottom lip. The closer she came, the more agitated she appeared. Her lip pulled back and she hissed, a spray of spittle rolling off her tongue.

In half a heartbeat, she was standing close enough for him to see her strange, otherworldly beauty, as if the things that made her pretty were the absences of all that were normal. She made no sound, had no smell. For a moment, she was as substantial as a mirage, and then it all changed.

She lunged at him, one hand grabbing his shoulder and the other his forehead. Her hands were so cold, like blocks of ice. Clarence managed the first notes of a scream, but she sank her teeth right into the side of his neck and squelched any further sounds he might have made. He pulled away from her but it was only because she let him go—she was lost in some sort of fascinated trance.

And then Clarence was running, racing away from the woman and the dogs and any responsibility he had. His hand was gripping the jagged bite on his throat, blood gushing between his fingers. His heart was pounding in his ears and he looked back long enough to lose his balance and go crashing down, but the woman was in the same spot as before, licking her fingertips as if she'd dipped them in chocolate sauce.

Still, Clarence wasn't waiting for her to catch up. He reached E deck, certain he'd find someone on Scotland Road, but there were a few engineers at the far side, standing in the doorway to the boilers and enjoying the cool air of the upper decks. He tried to scream for help, but all that came out was a torrent of pain and a wet gurgle.

One of the doors to the boiler room was open to his right and he darted toward it, stopping immediately when another woman stepped out, her eyes the same flickering red of death. Clarence would've said something, he would've pleaded for his life if only he could've spoken. His options were running out.

There was no way he'd reach the crewmen at the other end of the Road.

So, he turned around, sure to meet the woman who'd taken a chunk out of his neck but found the stairway down to F deck clear. Clarence was feeling weak in the legs. Losing this much blood couldn't be good for anyone. The more he walked, the heavier his feet felt. At the top of the D deck stairway, he pulled across the sliding lattice gate. Normally, it wasn't even used, for steerage class was allowed to go this way to reach their promenade, but he was glad it was here.

He took a step back just as another woman—this one with red hair and freckles, appeared on the other side of the gate. He risked unfettered blood pouring from his neck to find the key in his pocket—nearly dropping it because of his slippery fingers—and turned it in the lock.

After crashing against the steps, he needed both hands to get back on his feet, and he could feel his warm blood soaking through the collar of his shirt.

The woman who'd bit him appeared behind the first, a large splatter across her chin and nightgown. Her eyes burned with a brighter intensity, like fresh coals in a furnace, than those of the redheaded lady.

"Come on, Clarence," she purred. "Give us another taste."

He continued to backpedal, and just when he thought the gate was enough of a deterrent to keep them at bay, both girls turned insubstantial, becoming nothing more than grey fog that floated through the bars and became women once again.

With the last of his energy, he raced up the steps, knowing that he'd never get away from them. Clarence thought to run down into the steerage general assembly area, but another girl—one he'd not seen thus far—blocked him from advancing. When he tried to rush down C deck, they were there to keep him on the stairway. Whether Clarence wanted to admit it or not, these creatures were corralling him . . .

From the third-class well deck, he finally saw someone up on the promenade. He rushed toward them—a pair of men who'd been playing cards on the bench beneath the electric light. When they saw him, they stood and came to his aid, but it didn't matter.

Both men went flying in opposite directions, landing on the deck with ravenous women on top of them. Like Clarence, their voices were cut out so quickly that they didn't alert the bevy of officers who were no doubt on the other, more important end of the ship. Clarence counted four of them—two women tearing into each man.

He continued on, his vision darkening, his balance faltering. He was three steps from the stern of the ship, gazing out at the blackness of the departing Atlantic. A cool wind rustled his hair. Clarence put his back to the railing and watched the men—now unmoving—become the latest victims of this ravenous horde. And in that moment, he thought that jumping overboard and freezing in the water was preferable to being the prey of giant, beautiful leeches.

By the time he made his decision—the decision that he'd never see his daughter again, never see his home in Dover, nor his two cats and parrot—Clarence was so lightheaded that the decision was made *for* him. He leaned back and fell over the railing as the stars in his mind joined with the stars in the sky.

But he didn't fall far . . .

A gnarled hand was holding his ankle. Clarence's blood dripped upward now, across his cheek, along his forehead, and off his scalp. He was returned to the deck where the four women had finished their meals and a tall, cloaked figure stood in front of him. Surely, it was his eyes. They were failing, just like the rest of him.

Clarence slumped against the railing and looked up into its horrible face. It was like a skeleton with decaying skin pulled across. No lower jaw, but from the top hung four long teeth and four short ones that looked as if they'd been snapped off.

It came in close, smelling of blood and death. Clarence thought for sure it would bite his whole head off with those long, piercing fangs, but it didn't. Instead, it angled its head so that only one of the long teeth punctured his neck.

If Clarence could have screamed, he would have. It was like boiling water pouring into his throat. The creature kept pushing the tooth in—three inches, four inches, five inches. And finally, once its thin upper lip was resting on Clarence's face, it bent its neck and snapped the tooth right off. Clarence felt it in his throat as he looked up at the creature—now with only three full fangs. He clawed at his neck, feeling the tooth sink deeper into his throat as the wound quickly scabbed over.

Deeper . . . deeper . . . deeper still. And then the world became cold and quiet and for a little while—Clarence Clarke didn't exist.

The King turned to face his coterie as they each took a knee.

His mind had expanded but only a little. The passengers paid little attention to the world they inhabited, so it was mostly useless information. The best survival knowledge came from the poorest of society—Matilda Olsson knew more about the world than either of the second-class ladies, and most certainly Minnie Pembroke, the hotel heiress.

Ernest Burr and Clarence Clarke knew enough about the workings of the ship and what he had to do in order to assure a quiet passage to the new world. This America—or more precisely, New York—sounded large enough to slip away and set up a permanent hive. For now, that was good enough.

"What do you wish of us now?" said his coterie—all four women spoke in unison, their sated lips cracking with each word.

"Feast, but only the Bitterbloods on the lower decks. Too many Sweetbloods may ruin our chance of prosperity."

"But the Bitterbloods are so rank!"

"You will dine *only* on Bitterbloods!" he said, his voice rising in their minds, for the humans wouldn't see them upon the deck because the King didn't want it.

"We exalt you, Abhartach!"

A name he'd not heard in a long time.

"I will keep our numbers low, for the sake of the hunt," he said, and he swiped a fingernail across his broken teeth. They'd all grow back by tomorrow night. "Feast, and be wary of the humans. Do not assume they are all stupid."

"But the ship isn't safe," said his coterie. "The humans are everywhere. They love the sun and their weapons."

The King looked above their heads toward the forward end of the ship. He smiled, his upper teeth forming a semi-circle of points.

"I will keep us safe," he said. "Now begone."

CAPTAIN'S QUARTERS

2:20 A.M.

CAPTAIN SMITH WAS UNDER a great deal of stress.

He was at the helm of the world's most luxurious ocean liner but that wasn't the problem. In fact, he loved sailing, and the bigger the ship, the better the challenge. Smith worried about what came after *Titanic's* maiden voyage. It was no secret he flirted with the idea of retirement, but could he actually do it? Could he actually fill his days with hobbies, rather than work?

This kept sleep away for the past two nights. A part of him wished for an emergency so he could get dressed and meet his men on the bridge. That sort of thing made sense. Birdhouses, oil painting, and archery—all ventures suggested by his wife, Sarah—did *not* make sense.

Smith tossed back and forth in his bed, listening to the silence of the ship. From the Boat Deck, he was as far above the water as possible, save for the crow's nest. There was a clock on his wall that ticked relentlessly, but as he struggled to fall asleep, he noticed there was no tick, there were no sounds at all.

Until he turned over and heard a creak from his rocking chair. There in the darkness sat a figure, big enough for its head to rest high above the back and its knees to tuck close to its chest. If Smith had his wits about him, he would've realized that no human had red eyes, nor did they have long, odd-shaped fangs hanging down a jawless face.

But Smith was tired and stressed and easily persuaded, so he didn't see this strange figure—he saw his boyhood friend, Michael Finnigan.

"Is that . . . really you?" asked Smith, sitting up in bed.

"Sure it's me," said the voice. The smoke wafting off its body and the darkness of the room kept Smith from getting a good look. But surely it was Michael. Who else would it be?

"What . . . why are you here?"

"This is a fine boat you have here, Edward," he said. "You're going to steer her true, right?"

"Of course. I'm the best captain in the White Star Line."

"I know you are!" said the voice.

"Michael . . ."

"Yeah, Edward?"

"Aren't you dead?" Somewhere in the back of Smith's brain he made the connection that Michael

Finnigan had perished after the cliffside gave out beneath his bicycle and he went over the ravine.

"How can I be dead if I'm sittin' here talkin' to you?" The red eyes flashed for a moment, but Smith wasn't thinking straight—did Michael always have red eyes? Yes, he thought that he did.

"That's true."

"So I need a favor, Edward."

"Whatever you need, Michael," he said, already drifting back off to sleep.

"Good, good. Now listen. Right now, Boiler Room One is cold. It needs to remain that way."

"But what if we need to light it?"

"You don't need to light Boiler Room One."

"We don't need to light Boiler Room One."

"You're making excellent time."

"We're making excellent time."

"Good, good."

"My mother used to love when we'd play together. So did *your* mother. We spent so much time at the bakery near our house. Do you remember it? The one with the cinnamon sweet rolls?" Smith's voice was wistful, barely above a whisper.

"The one with the sweet rolls, of course. Say, I need you to do one more thing for me."

"What's that?"

"Chief Officer Wilde has just gone for a smoke. I need you to take care of something in his cabin while he's out."

Smith knew this was an odd request, but his boyhood friend Michael Finnigan—who'd been dead at least forty years—was requesting it. Smith saw nothing peculiar, certainly not a nine-foot-tall Irish king with a hand on his shoulder.

And when Smith woke the next morning, he would never remember the conversation. He wouldn't remember trudging across the deserted wheelhouse in his pajamas, nor waiting at the corner while the King kept a hand across his head so that Officers Pittman and Lowe could pass and enter the smoke room.

And he certainly wouldn't remember unlocking the gun cabinet by Wilde's bed, removing the seven pistols, and then throwing them overboard. Smith didn't notice that three were already missing, probably hidden amongst the officers' things, but the King noticed, and thought three pistols aboard this entire ship were nice odds.

When Smith settled back into bed, Michael said, "It's been really nice to see you, Edward. Say hello to your mother for me." And he rolled over and promptly started to snore. It was the most sleep he'd had since departing—and it would be the most sleep he'd get for the rest of his days.

F DECK

DINNER HAD BEEN A somber affair. Erik ate alongside his children, none of them speaking to one another. Colin had lots of energy to burn off, constantly tugging his father's hand to go look for Matilda.

After dinner, Reid lay awake, listening to Erik sob through the walls of the cabin. Little Jack, needing soothed by his mother, also wailed throughout the night. The only chance Reid was given to fall asleep was when the oldest son, Micky, took the baby for a walk.

And he'd just fallen asleep when there was a peck at the door. Reid held his breath, listening to the gentle tug of the engines, of his mother's steady snores in the bunk below him. Since he was so thin, he was also light as a feather, and he jumped down to the floor without making a peep of noise.

He creaked the door open and there stood Colin, a half-eaten apple in his hand. Reid grimaced at the golden lights of the hallway behind him.

"Were you sleepin'?" he said.

Reid yawned and nodded.

"C'mon, I wanna show you somethin'. It's important."

Reid did not know the hour, but he assumed it was late, maybe even closer to morning than midnight. He looked back into the room to check his mother, who was now on her side, snoring gently.

"We won't be long, I promise," said Colin. "But grab a jacket. These halls is cold."

Reid nodded and held up a finger, then quietly moved his books from his jacket. As he put it on, the light from the hallway cast a silvery glint on the crucifix the nice doctor had given him. And perhaps he was afraid, or perhaps he was just sentimental and thinking about his da, but Reid picked it up and carried it with him.

"Why'd you have that?" asked Colin, as Reid eased the door shut.

He shrugged, for he really didn't know for sure. After reading a hundred pages in his latest book, he found a new appreciation for crosses.

F deck was quiet, save for a handful of bedroom stewards who prowled the hallway. The boys went upstairs, entering Scotland Road, and then Colin took off running, laughing and jumping.

Reid gave chase, feeling his smile was stiff around his lips—he didn't do much of it. The more he tried, the more it felt like his skin didn't know how to crease properly. But he enjoyed this friend, even if he knew he'd never see him again after this week.

They passed a few engineers and a steward who paid them no attention. The ship was oddly quiet at this hour, even though the hum of machinery was just beneath them. All the doors were closed now, deadening a bit of the noise. On the far-end they spied the black and white cat licking its paw, then disappearing around the corner.

Reid thought Colin was going to take him back down to the third-class dining room, but he carried on until they were past Scotland Road and into a part of the ship that he was sure they weren't allowed. This was the section where a lot of the food staff slept, as well as a few of the second-class passengers who wanted a room middeck.

But at the staircase leading up to D deck, Colin stopped long enough to squat over a large, red stain on the tile. Reid looked over his shoulder—in the golden glow of the electric lights, it still looked wet.

"That's blood, innit?"

Reid nodded.

The boys followed it up the steps, finding little splatters here and there. Once they made it to C deck and heard the revelry down at the general assembly area, Colin said, "This is as far as I went. I think this blood is my mama's."

Reid shook his head, clearly unable to be sure, but wanting to convince Colin otherwise. Now that they'd been following the trail, Reid was sure it was still wet—he smelled it on the air—a coppery scent mingling with the salt.

They continued toward the well deck and the closer they got to hushed voices, the more afraid Reid became. Before going outside, he tugged at Colin's arm, eyes pleading that they turn around and go back.

"What's wrong with ya?" said Colin. "This might be my mama. You want me to turn around and go back to bed when my mama might be bleedin' out?"

Reid felt awful for even suggesting such a thing, so he dropped the arm, dropped his head, and continued on.

From the well deck, they saw a group of people standing atop the third-class promenade. Reid and Colin ascended the steps and stood behind a crowd of passengers—as well as a trio of officers. He pushed through them, foot landing solidly in a congealing puddle of blood. He fully expected to see the dead body of Matilda. But when they circled around the men and stood on the benches, they saw *two* bodies.

A pair of officers had covered them in nice White Star Line linens. Judging by the legs, they were both men. Another officer knelt at the stern railing, dabbing his fingers in a puddle of blood—but the body who spilled it was gone.

Playing cards had blown across the deck, mostly out to sea, but a few of them were stuck in the blood. Reid wanted to retch just looking at the scene.

"You saw nothing?" said one officer to a pair of men who were clearly too drunk to even stand.

One of them slumped onto the bench next to Reid and said, "I told ye. I came out to piss over the rail and I seen the bodies. I didn't do nothing wrong."

"No one thinks that," said the officer. "But this is a damned massacre. You didn't see anyone . . . flee the scene?"

The other drunk man laughed. "Flee where? We're on a bloody ship, mate." It was a silly question, thought Reid.

Two of the officers convened in the middle of the deck, their eyes flashing to the pair of boys watching this awful business. One of them said, "You kids need to be off now. Go on. No good can come of seeing this."

The other officer nodded. "C'mon, we need to go tell the captain."

The first one shook his head. "Not tonight. Let 'im sleep. We'll tell him at first bell. Go fetch a few crewmen and a doctor. They need to get these men off the deck before breakfast."

As the men dispersed, Reid walked over to the splatter by the railing. The men probably didn't see it, but *he* did—a thin line of blood leading away. Reid was certain that a third body lay here. And someone had dragged it off.

"C'mon," said Colin. "Blimey, I hope this wasn't my mama. I better tell Erik."

Reid thought it was unusual that he didn't call him father. But then again, they didn't all have relationships like Reid and his own da. That thought suddenly filled him with sadness and he carried on, following his friend off the promenade and down the second-class steps toward their own deck.

Back on Scotland Road, Reid felt an odd sensation, like someone breathing across the back of his neck. Colin seemed oblivious to it but that was probably because the boy had a lot on his mind. His mother was missing—and the last anyone saw her, she was bloody. Tonight's discoveries did not bode well for her.

When they were nearly upon the turnoff for the third-class dining room, one of the doors to the boiler room crept open. The boys were so startled that they threw their backs against the wall, fearful they were about to be reprimanded for being out so late. Beyond the door was nothing but blackness—a soul-clenching dark that was half bred of industry and half of wickedness.

In the darkness shone a pair of red orbs, floating forward as they were hanging by string. And when the figure stepped into the hallway, Colin's face went slack.

"Mama!" he said, just before launching himself toward her.

Reid, in a move of pure instinct, snatched his arm and pulled him back.

"What? What is it?" he asked, trying to wrench his hand free. Reid was crying, tears streaming down his face because he'd gotten a much better look at Matilda than her son had—and now that Reid had slowed the boy's steps—he also looked into the horrible face that once belonged to his mother.

Her eyes were gone, replaced by little red lights. If she weren't so terrifying, Reid would have wondered if all the blood belonged to her—it soaked her entire front, from her lips down to her exposed breast. Along her neck was a large lump—green and red and black.

"Come to me, Colin," said Matilda in a voice that didn't sound like her own. She stood up straighter, arms out as if to hug him, but her fingers were bent into claws. Reid looked past her and in the boiler room's darkness stood three more figures—their eyes floating like disembodied flames.

"Mama?" he said, unable to align what he knew with what he was seeing. "Are you . . . okay?"

153

"I'm fine, *leanbh*. I'm so light. So strong. Don't be afraid. You can bring your friend, too." When she spoke, the light reflected off two gleaming fangs at the corners of her mouth.

She looked left and right, assessing the hallway, and that's when Reid knew she was about to pounce. He was standing behind his friend, and for some reason, he leaned up and wrapped his arms around him like he would protect him from this . . . thing that was not Matilda.

And at the same moment his arms came up, Matilda was rushing forward with speed that shouldn't have belonged to any human—and it didn't, for she was no longer the boy's mother.

Her fingers scraped against him, ready to pull him into the darkness with the others but something curious happened. Reid's arm was draped around his friend, and in that hand, he was holding the crucifix. The moment Matilda's fingertips stroked it, they caught on fire and she recoiled, screaming maniacally. The others beyond the doorway also cried out, as if they all shared the pain.

Reid wasted no time thrusting the cross forward, lining up the crucifix with her face. She stared for only a moment, the flames of her eyes going out, replaced by little bags of milk that ran down her cheeks. Matilda sank to her knees and threw her hand over her face. Reid grabbed a fistful of Colin's shirt and dragged him on until he ran on his own power.

"That's not mama! That's *not mama!*" he said, and when Reid thought he was falling behind, he grabbed his hand and pulled him.

He stole a quick look behind him, and now there were four of them in the hallway. Two of them were racing along the floor while the others were on the ceiling, crawling across the pipes and zigzagging through the low-hanging lights. Reid screamed, but nothing came out but a startled wheeze.

A man stepped into the hall just in front of them—his face and hands covered in soot. He was about to ask if they were okay because they were running so frantically, but his attention turned to the four creatures chasing after them. Reid looked back long enough to see the man try to step back into the doorway, but one—a snow-haired lady in a nightgown—was upon him, pulling him down to the floor and sinking her fangs into him.

And now he understood those bodies up on deck

. . .

He wasn't sure who was chasing them now, if any of them. That poor man—he sacrificed himself, and the thought of what they were doing to him made Reid's nose burn. But he couldn't cry—not yet. He needed clear eyes to lead his friend to safety.

They were near the end of Scotland Road when Reid worried they'd missed the stairway down to F deck. This ship was so labyrinthine that he had trouble navigating it while content, much less when he was being chased by a pack of ravenous monsters.

He read the signs, happy to discover they could reach F deck just ahead. They'd made it just past the officer's lavatory when he jerked back suddenly. Reid smacked his face on the tile and tasted blood in his mouth. Quickly, he rolled over, sensing a fast-moving shape from the corner of his eye. The cross came up and the creatures weren't expecting it.

The ladies all hissed and backed away. But one of them lunged forward, her eyes full of madness and hate. She pushed against Reid's chest and sent him flying. The cross clattered down the stairway and came to rest where he couldn't see it. Three of the ladies turned to vapor and rose into the ceiling and disappeared. But Matilda remained, her eyes regaining the red flicker—but it was weak.

The lights blinked and snuffed out, and far down the hallway the glowing eyes watched. Colin and Reid backed away while Matilda stalked closer, knowing she had easy prey in sight. That's when Reid saw the cubby—a tight, darkened alcove where they could hopefully escape.

Without a word, he pointed and raced for it, dropping to his hands and knees and crawling back. Colin was right behind him, gasping, crying out, his arms and legs pumping as fast as possible.

Reid could barely see in the darkness of the alcove and then his fingers wrapped around something that he didn't understand—it was wood, a stick as thin as a broom and half as long.

The alcove dead-ended, and Reid turned back around just as Colin grabbed his ankle and held on. Something was pulling him out—he wasn't sure which of the creatures had come for them. All he saw were the red eyes and the bent scowl of an angry face. Colin adjusted himself and grabbed the stick and Reid tried to pull it back—hopefully with his friend attached.

But then his fingers let go, Colin gave a panicked scream, and then he clawed at the tile as he was pulled into the darkness. The boy—and the red eyes—were gone.

ASSISTANT DOCTORS' CABINS

7:44 A.M.

AFTER SPEAKING WITH ISMAY, Doctors York and O'Loughlin toured the ship, although they found little evidence of the missing women. All was quiet, like the big yawn before a storm. When the old doctor started to slow, Ben suggested they go on to bed and start fresh in the morning.

But later, when a frantic knocking at his door woke him from a dead sleep, he knew something was wrong. He sat up and quickly threw on a shirt. It was difficult to tell how long he'd slept because his cabin was in the center of the ship—smashed right between O'Loughlin's and Simpson's, so there was no porthole.

He cracked open the door just enough to hide the sliver of skin down the middle of his chest as he buttoned his shirt. There in the hall stood a pale Mr. Dunford. The light behind him momentarily blinded Ben—it was morning.

"You're needed in the Infectious Room right away, Doctor." And then Mr. Dunford turned and trotted off, as if he were in a great hurry. Ben made himself presentable and followed him.

He entered the surgery and then down the steps, fully expecting to see their four women back on the tables, ready for embalming. There were only three bodies, and none of them were women. These men looked ghastly in appearance as their skin had taken on the pallor of someone who'd been dead for a while. However, this wasn't the case.

"What happened?" Ben asked.

"Killed, I should think," said Doctor Simpson. Ben had been so engrossed with the corpses that he didn't even see him standing in the corner.

"Where's O'Loughlin?"

"Gone to speak with Ismay and the captain."

Ben put on a pair of gloves from Mr. Dunford's table and said, "What have you learned?"

"They were discovered early this morning." He pointed to the men closest to Ben. "Those two were found on the third-class promenade deck. That one by the door there was on Scotland Road."

Ben approached him. He was a crewman, for sure. Most likely a trimmer or a greaser by the soot on his clothes. He pulled back his collar and found two circular wounds on his neck, but nothing like the trauma upon the necks of the women.

Simpson said, "They're almost bloodless, but those wounds would facilitate an easy and quick blood loss."

Ben studied the two found on the promenade, both dressed in the threadbare rags of steerage class. They had the same wounds—bite marks, if he had to guess.

"Whatever mutilated the victim down in the cargo hold didn't kill *these* men," said Ben.

Simpson nodded. "I agree. The teeth surely don't match up. It also doesn't match the sickness of the girls. Their wounds inflamed the veins around the knub on their neck."

"And there are no knubs here. These puncture wounds are different. And look at this," said Ben, pointing to the steerage class duo. He turned one head to the side, then did the same for the other. Both had two sets of bite marks.

Simpson seemed confused. "So something bit him . . . and then bit him again on the other side?"

Ben shrugged. "Or two things bit him at once. Do you have a ruler and a protractor?"

Simpson found them locked away in one of the desks. Ben used them to measure the distance between the fangs. After that, he used the protractor to find the curvature in relation to one another. What he discovered was troubling indeed.

"We have four different attackers."

"What? Are you sure?"

"I'm certain. Two of them have rather straight upper jaws while the other two have a slight curve in their teeth. And then the distance is mildly different. The incisors, if that's what we're dealing with here, range from four centimeters to five and three-quarter centimeters. Four different sets of teeth. Four attackers."

"And four missing women," said Simpson.

"You don't think . . ."

He shrugged. "At this point, I would believe anything."

Ben was about to follow that thread when the door opened and in walked Doctor O'Loughlin. He was missing his cheery, jubilant vigor, but who could blame him for not being upbeat? He probably hadn't been to sleep at all, and he'd just returned from the awful business of informing Ismay and the captain about what was happening.

"How did it go?" asked Ben.

O'Loughlin pulled a flask from his jacket pocket and took a swig, then plopped down in a chair by the door. He breathed a heavy sigh and said, "Captain was almost in a daze. I think he was so wrought about it that he didn't know how to react. Ismay . . . well, Ismay wasn't as upset as I thought he'd be."

"I bet I can wager why," said Simpson.

Ben said, "Because it all happened below deck. The wealthy folk up above didn't see it."

"That's about the truth of it," O'Loughlin said. "But he was more upset the ladies continue to elude us."

Simpson said, "Ben made a discovery. It could be related."

"Oh?"

He explained to O'Loughlin the theory that four different attackers killed the three men. And like Simpson, O'Loughlin suggested it was the work of the women.

Ben said, "Just so we're clear . . . we are working with the theory that four women—"

"Four *dead* women," Simpson interjected.

"Right, four dead women got up and terrorized the ship? Took their blood, no less?"

O'Loughlin laughed and sipped his flask. "It makes no sense, boy. But I would believe it. Those ladies were unnatural. And this here . . . in this room, is unnatural."

Ben thought the logistics of it made sense as well. Two victims were on the promenade at night and these women had an adverse reaction to the sun. At least that worked in Ismay's favor—there was a greater chance that if there were more victims, they wouldn't be upper class where there was far more natural light.

"So what do we do now?" asked Simpson.

O'Loughlin stood, his knees popping like fire-crackers. "Now we see if we have enough embalming fluid for three men."

And for the next few hours, Ben helped the doctor embalm *Titanic's* second, third, and fourth victim. They barely had enough supplies but it didn't matter, anyway. The organs were so dry, the blood nearly drained, that the stench would hold out until they arrived in New York. Still, they only had two additional coffins, which meant one of the victims was wrapped in a sheet and placed atop the stack of boxes.

They had just finished cleaning up when Matron Wallis walked in and clasped her hands in front of her. The doctors exchanged glances because they knew something was wrong. Ben said, "Yes, Mrs. Wallis?"

"You're going to want to come with me, Doctor York. We've . . . found something."

F Deck

FIONA SLEPT RIGHT THROUGH breakfast. When she finally sat up in bed, her bladder full and her stomach empty, she first noticed that Reid wasn't in the bunk above her. It didn't bother her much—she knew he was probably with Colin next door, or at least surrounded by a few dozen Irishmen in the general assembly area under the promenade.

After dressing and stepping into the hall to read the clock on the wall, she figured they had at least half an hour to get to the dining room and eat. She threw on her overcoat because it was cold this morning, and then knocked on Erik's door.

Immediately she heard the wail of a baby and she felt awful for disturbing them. Before she reconsidered, the door flew open and she smelled the baby's filth, but Micky was tending to it on the floor of the cabin. In the bed was a sleeping Molly, her back to the world.

"Mornin'," said Fiona. "Where're the boys?"

Micky said, "Da don't know where Colin is. He left last night and ne'er came back."

165

Fiona's heart sank. "You can't find him? Was Reid with him?"

Micky shrugged. "Probably tucked in the corner of the dining room somewhere. They had oat porridge. It was thick."

Fiona nodded, then backed out of the room and headed up to Scotland Road, intent on checking the dining room first. But as she made her way down that unusually long and wide hallway, she knew something was wrong—that something bad had happened.

There was a stewardess on her hands and knees, scrubbing the floor in front of the closed boiler room door. Fiona approached her—a tiny, wispy girl with strands of hair flying out of her bonnet.

"What happened here, deary?" asked Fiona.

The girl looked up, eyed the officers walking their way, and waited for them to pass. She said, "Somethin' bad, lady. Somethin' real bad. I'm not sure . . . I didn't start my shift until eight, but they're sayin' someone died on the ship. There was blood all over. I'm still searchin' for it all. Can't leave no blood, that's what Rattenbury said."

Fiona sprinted down the hall, nearly tripping on the steps to the third-class dining room. It was half full, as breakfast started almost two hours ago. But she didn't see anyone she recognized, and certainly not Reid or Colin. She took a moment to steady her nerves, realizing there was only so many places on a ship he could be.

And then it occurred that she'd had a similar thought about Matilda.

Not knowing she was tracing the same path as the boys earlier that morning—and the same path as Clarence Clarke even earlier the night before—she headed up to the deck. Most of the blood had been cleared away and once she reached the promenade deck, she found no evidence of the feeding frenzy that had taken place just six hours before.

Once she checked the general assembly area, she began to panic. Reid wasn't one to stay away for long. Sure, he'd severed the dependence on Fiona, but that had been in small doses. There was no reason the boy would stay away for this many hours unless something was wrong.

Twice she attempted to get up on the Boat Deck and was reminded of the ticket she held. Reid was curious and he loved books and she knew there was a library somewhere on the ship that was off-limits to steerage class. But would they turn away an eight-year-old boy? It maddened her the ship had places she couldn't search on her own.

From the well deck, she stared up at the first- and second-class passengers enjoying the pleasant morning with their tall-stemmed glasses and plates of pie. They were oblivious to the troubles on the ship. She felt anger toward them but also sadness—it had to be a quiet pocket of hell to be so self-unaware.

After searching the decks, she returned to Scotland Road. Along this route, one could access the boilers, which were another three decks down, past a network of catwalks and metal stairs. On the forward end, the door leading to Boiler Rooms 5 and 6 wafted enough heat to make Fiona's eyes water. It was black through the doorway, the orange glow of the furnaces far below.

On the aft end of the ship, there wasn't as much heat coming from Boiler Room 1, as Fiona didn't think it was lit. It was however, the noisiest. This was close to the engine room. She stepped in and looked around. It was so dark that she couldn't even see her hand in front of her face. If not for the light coming in from Scotland Road, she would've walked right off the edge of the catwalk and landed upon the cold boiler. But something felt wrong inside that room . . . something unexplainable. Fiona prayed her boy wasn't in there as she backed out.

There was one place left to turn. She hated to bother Ben with her troubles, especially with all that was happening on the ship. She was certain he had his hands full. But without anyplace else to go, she turned and went back up the steps to D deck.

SURGERY ROOM

THE MAN, A BEDROOM steward named Clarence Clarke, had been discovered in an unlocked and unused cabin on D deck by another steward, a Mr. Sidney Barton. Mr. Barton noticed the door was ajar, and figuring he'd stumbled upon a stowaway, entered the room, only to find Clarence Clarke asleep on the bed and unable to wake up. Even before Ben arrived on scene, Matron Wallis had told him the news—he had a large knub on the side of his neck.

The first thing Ben did when he knelt by Clarence was lift his upper lip. Sure enough, there was a pair of pointy incisors—fangs, although he didn't think this man was a culprit in the murders.

You're still forming, aren't you? thought Ben. *When it gets dark, you'll kill, as will your friends.*

"Let's get him to the surgery then," said Ben, and he sent for Doctor Simpson.

By the time he arrived, Ben had already used the sheet that Clarence was lying on to cover his body. They would pass the wide windows on C deck. The secrets on the ship were dangerously close to be-

169

ing exposed and Ben didn't want everyone to see a smoking, sizzling patient.

The trip down was fraught with nosey passengers, for it was easy to assume what they were carrying. And word had already spread like wildfire that at least one passenger had died aboard—as many as eight if the rumors were believed. Ben would be glad to be off this ship in a few days, and put the awfulness aboard *Titanic* behind him.

Doctor O'Loughlin, fresh from his daily reprimand by Ismay, was already waiting for them. Ben noticed a distinct chemical smell when he entered the surgery. They placed Clarence on the operating gurney and peeled back the blanket. He was alive, for now. His breathing was labored and his skin was pale. He'd sweat right through the blanket.

"Same as the ladies," O'Loughlin confirmed, giving his face and neck an examination. When Clarence uttered a tiny, irritated hiss, Ben directed the old doctor's attention to the fangs.

"Have you ever seen anything like this?" Ben asked.

"Never. But I suppose this confirms it. Those infected, those who have these strange bloodshot veins and knubs on their necks—they eventually wake up and take the blood of others."

"C'mon now, William," said Simpson. "We know what's happening here. They aren't taking the blood. They're *drinking* it."

O'Loughlin looked to Ben. "You believe that?"

He shrugged. "If not drinking, where does it go? They're biting people and sucking them dry."

O'Loughlin nodded and said, "So what do we do now? Eventually, he'll wake up and disappear. And eventually he'll do what the girls did last night." His eyes widened, for he'd just considered the ramifications. "Bloody hell, and they'll do it again tonight. Once it's dark."

"That's what we think," said Ben. "We need to know more."

The old doctor nodded. "What are ye suggestin'?"

Ben put his hand on Clarence's jaw and tilted his head to the side. The knub was red and dark—almost throbbing. He reached up and turned on the overhead light and pulled it down by its wire until it was nearly sitting against the man's skin.

"My God," said O'Loughlin, coming closer for a better look.

Through the light, they saw the shadow of something in Clarence's neck—it was deep and dark and thin, but it exploded with little tendrils, as if the man had morning glories treating his neck bones like a trellis.

"What do you think's in there?" O'Loughlin said, and when his fingers traced Clarence's knub, the man peeled back his lips and hissed, although he never opened his eyes.

"Is it a boil?" Simpson asked.

Doctor O'Loughlin snorted. "You ever seen a boil like this, doctor?"

Simpson shook his head.

But O'Loughlin relented and sighed. "Maybe it's infection. Maybe we drain that and the fella will start to feel like hisself."

"We need to cut him open then," said Ben. "Are we equipped for that?"

"Aye," said the old doctor, turning to a cabinet with glass doors. He ran his finger across the assortment of bottles until he found the one he needed. It was small and blue and it would certainly get the job done.

"Ether?" said Doctor Simpson.

"You got a better idea?"

The assistant doctors both shook their heads. All three of them covered their noses with surgical masks. Simpson closed the hatch while Ben opened the door to the medical suite, hoping that no passengers took a wrong turn and headed down the hall toward the surgery. Then he opened all the portholes. A cool, salty breeze rushed in.

"Should we restrain him?" asked Ben.

"Restrain? He's about to fall into an even deeper sleep," said Doctor O'Loughlin. He moved to the sink and doused a thin cloth with the ether. Even across the room, Ben smelled it. He stepped into the hallway and kept a watch while O'Loughlin placed the cloth across Clarence's nose and mouth.

The man shifted on the gurney, his hands drawing up into fists. He writhed for a moment before settling down so still that Ben took a step forward to make sure the man hadn't breathed his last.

"He's fine," said Doctor Simpson, lifting Clarence's hand and checking his pulse. "That should do it, William."

Doctor O'Loughlin quickly pulled the cloth away and stuffed it into the waiting glass jar in Simpson's hands. He tightened the lid and set it aside. Now, the prone man looked peaceful, his breathing rhythmic, slow, and shallow.

Doctor Simpson laid out the surgical tools on a metal tray. This job was usually relegated to Mr. Dunford, but all three doctors had an unspoken agreement that no one would know about Clarence's condition. While Simpson handed O'Loughlin a scalpel, Ben pulled the light down so the old doctor could see his work.

"Watch the jitters, old man," said Simpson. "You and I should trade spots."

Doctor O'Loughlin looked back at him as if he'd been wounded. "My boy, I have the steadiest hands this side of Tralee."

They had a good snicker, but the room turned serious once the doctor rested the scalpel across the knub. He was trying to decide whether to cut through it or around it. Either way, Ben had a towel at the ready—the wound would likely ooze blood and infection.

O'Loughlin pushed the blade in and that's when Clarence rose from the table, hissing and kicking his legs. Ben let go of the light and it swung on its wire while the scalpel and all the instruments clattered to the floor. Simpson quickly knelt down to collect them all. Clarence settled back on the table, his breathing returning to normal.

"Maybe we *should* restrain him," O'Loughlin finally conceded.

Five minutes later, Ben located the leather straps and tied down Clarence's arms and legs, and again across his forehead. They turned him so that his neck was exposed, then tightly cinched the strap. O'Loughlin gave him a final boost of ether and then placed the scalpel back on his neck. Both assistant doctors nodded, ready to proceed.

O'Loughlin put one hand on Clarence's forehead and inserted the scalpel. Again, the unconscious man struggled, pulling the bonds tight but they'd secured him well. The bloodshot veins on his neck and face seemed to pulse with his effort. Ben couldn't look away from the fangs—it was all so unnatural.

"Ben, dammit, towel!" said O'Loughlin, shaking him from his thoughts.

"Sorry," he said, and sponged away the dribble of dark blood leaving the cut. It smelled foul—not the coppery scent he was accustomed to, but something else, something like death.

More blood oozed from the wound as O'Loughlin dragged a straight line across the knub. It was a quick trip, only six centimeters.

"My scalpel touched it. That shadow we see through the light. But what is it?"

"Let's find out," said Simpson. "Ben?"

He brought the light closer, noting the blood wasn't shiny at all—it was like some kind of dark ichor. O'Loughlin held the wound open with the scalpel while Ben kept the light steady and continued to mop up blood. Then Doctor Simpson inserted a pair of forceps into the gaping hole.

"I feel it," he said. The sound of the muscles and fat parting around the metal made Ben's stomach knot. Clarence was strained against the belts, hissing and writhing. But then the assistant doctor was pulling something out—something dingy and white and covered in blood. It was hard, like a bone.

Clarence continued to fight, continued to howl in his sleep, but O'Loughlin was keeping his head secure. Simpson was moving slowly, fearful that any sort of jerking motion would cause more harm to the patient.

"What the hell is *that?*" O'Loughlin asked.

The 'bone' kept revealing. It was two inches long, three inches, four, five, six. Judging by the length, Ben guessed it was all the way down into the man's chest cavity. But this wasn't the strangest part.

When the object was halfway out, they discovered it was full of long, hair-like strands. Doctor Simpson nearly let go when they moved, as if they were all worms connected to the thicker piece. A few even tried to wrap around the forceps.

"It's stuck on something," said Simpson.

"No, it's not," said Ben. "It's fighting you. It doesn't want to come out."

The thicker part of the 'bone' was already free—and it was a staggering ten inches long. But all the little strands were folded down now, reaching back into the wound, attempting to pull the mass back inside his neck.

"Hold his head, Ben!" said O'Loughlin. Ben stuffed the soaked rag beneath the wound and overlapped his hands across Clarence's forehead. He could feel the strength in his neck—he was trying hard to sit up.

Once O'Loughlin had a free hand, he wrapped his fingers around the dark, writhing strands and pulled them free. The whole stalk separated from Clarence and O'Loughlin didn't know what to do with it now that he held it. He quickly tossed it into the sink, where it continued to slither like a hundred tiny worms.

Clarence's eyes opened.

The three men were momentarily stunned because the whites were gone, replaced by little orbs of red. They darted around the room, finding all three men. In half a heartbeat, he turned to grey smoke that wafted toward the door, but just as quickly turned back into Clarence. He dropped to the floor and smashed his face against the tile. When he recovered, he eyed the three cowering men, his face twitching, his eyes narrowed. He brought a hand up to his head and punched it until blood poured from the temple.

"For crissakes, he's feral," said Simpson. Ben knew this wasn't Clarence anymore. This was a thing, a creature. An *it*.

And it focused on O'Loughlin and lunged. With speed far quicker than any human, it leapt onto the gurney and launched itself at the doctor, but Ben was still holding the light and he smashed it against the creature's face, the glass exploding. The shock made it roll over onto its back, but it quickly stood and turned into vapor again.

This time when it became corporeal, it was latched onto the ceiling. Seeing the three men rise and huddle together made it realize it couldn't fight them all. Right now, it was confused and perhaps dying without the strange object in its neck.

It flashed a look to the opened doorway and Ben screamed, "no!" and tried to get in front of it but it was too late. It dropped to the ground and ran out.

The trio of doctors gave chase. In the narrow hallway of C deck, Ben saw a few passengers far to the forward end, confused looks upon their faces. It didn't run off that way—a small blessing. But that meant it had to run toward the aft end.

Ben raced to the second-class promenade where the creature was discovering it had taken a bad turn. Its left shoulder was smoking because it had come too close to the promenade windows—they were among the largest on the ship and it spilled lots of the sun's golden light across the deck. So, it pressed itself against the wall and the windows on the other side—

—which was for the very crowded second-class library.

People were turning over chairs, screaming, moving back from the windows or coming closer in curiosity. The creature continued to evade Ben and the other doctors. It was shaking now, its whole body trembling because it had become separated from its lifeline. It made a pitiful wail and ran off. Perhaps it was on purpose or perhaps it knew of nowhere else to go where it could be alone and die in peace.

It ran past the enclosed promenade and right into the open well deck, where the full brunt of the sun's light fell upon its skin.

Ben thought it was trying to sink to its knees, but there was no time. The sun limned across its body and brilliant white flames consumed the creature.

He was vaguely aware of the screaming from those coming out of the library, those already on the well deck and those on the third-class promenade who had the best view of all. Also, those of the creature, which managed a half cry before a wet gurgle and an abrupt silence. The thing that once was Clarence burnt up in the sun in only a few seconds, reduced to nothing but pure, white ash.

It blew across the well deck and slammed into a passenger, the ash covering her body from head to toe. And then Ben took a few steps closer and watched her clear the mess from her eyes and appraise the scene with horror. People were still screaming, perhaps this unlucky girl, too, but Ben was feeling numb and nothing made sense.

Fiona coughed, a puff of white ash bursting from her dry lips.

ASSISTANT DOCTORS' CABINS

2:30 P.M.

AT FIRST, SHE DIDN'T realize what had happened. Passengers were screaming and running away. With the way the man was smoking, she thought he'd come from the boiler room after falling into a furnace. His hand touched hers, but there was no strength behind it.

Because there was no *man* behind it.

As quick as the flames bloomed, they were gone and so was any hint of a person. He collapsed in a puff of ash. Some of it fell to the deck but most of it, carried along by his inertia, slammed into her. It was in her eyes and her mouth and her nose. She didn't taste it but she couldn't breathe either. Each time she coughed, a puff of white blew into the wind.

Hands were grabbing her and pulling her along. She fought back, so confused she'd become with the sudden screaming. But Ben was by her ear and it steadied her nerves.

"C'mon, we've got to get you cleaned up." There were two sets of hands on her forearms, leading her toward the surgery—her intended destination.

"Reid," she said, and coughed more ash. "Reid is . . . missing. You have to help."

"Okay, Reid is missing. Sure," said a voice that did not belong to Ben.

She couldn't see but knew when they'd left the deck because the light wasn't so blinding. A door closed behind her and then warm hands were on her cheeks, dusting them off.

"Over the sink, lass," said the same voice.

"I'm going to hold your hair back, Fiona," said Ben. "Is that alright?"

"Yes, yes, of course."

Cold water dumped across her face as they tried to clear the ash away. When her eyes were clear someone wiped her down with a towel. She stood and turned around to see the older doctor—O'Loughlin, as well as Doctor Simpson. Ben looked as if he'd seen a ghost.

"Are you alright?" he asked.

"No," she said, and broke down. She could feel her tears running clean lines down her dirty cheeks.

The sudden shift in emotion made the men uneasy, so Doctor O'Loughlin said, "I'd better find Ismay. Attempt to get ahead of this recent development."

Simpson said, "And I'm going to make sure no one else was hurt by the . . . conflagration of Mr. Clarke."

And just like that, both men were gone.

Fiona gave her face one last scrub, then turned to throw the towel in the sink. In the basin on the other side, she spied something that she first thought was a spider, then realized it was so much worse. She nearly climbed atop the basin to get away from it.

"It's fine. It can't hurt you . . . at least I don't think so."

Ben grabbed a pair of long forceps and pinched the weird, writhing creature between them. He held it up by its thick, central stalk. The long thin legs seemed to dance chaotically, as if irritated to be touched.

"What is that?"

"I think . . . it's a tooth. A fang, rather. See that middle part there? How it curves at the bottom?"

She nodded.

He took it over to the opposite side of the room and held it up in front of the porthole. When the sun's light fell across it, all the little legs protested, flexing away from the tooth as if they could pull free and escape the harmful light. She heard a tiny hiss, like a steaming teakettle.

And after only a few seconds, the legs relaxed and the whole thing caught on fire. Ben dropped it into the sink as it became ash. He doused it with water and covered it with a towel.

"I just cannot know what's happenin' on this ship!" she said, and she rubbed a hand across her mat of red hair, now dusty with ash.

"C'mon. Follow me and tell me what's happening."

He led her through the door and down the hall while she explained Colin and Reid's absence. The doctor listened with great interest, and she knew it bothered him almost as much as it bothered her.

Down from the surgery was the steward's bathroom. The White Star Line didn't give the surgeons their own bath tub but thought the stewards needed two of them on C deck. Still, Ben had a key and was able to use it.

On the way, they passed Matron Wallis and Ben asked if she'd be so kind as to take Mrs. Lynch's clothes to be washed as soon as she was in the bathroom. Matron Wallis smiled delicately and waited in the surgery.

"You can clean up in here. Matron Wallis will see that you're taken care of." And then he walked off.

"Wait, what are you going to do?"

He said, "I'll go look for the boys. I can access places you can't."

"Thank you. I really appreciate what you've done. You've made us comfortable ever since we arrived." She remembered the gangway and added, "*Before* we arrived."

He smiled and stuffed his hands into his pockets and said, "Listen, after you clean up. I want you to go back to your cabin and lock the door. Wait for me to come see you. Can you do that for me?"

He'd already asked her to do it once. She nodded. "Okay."

"We've had no new victims today. Which tells me one thing: These things hunt at night because they hate the daylight. The sun is downright dangerous to them."

She was inclined to believe him since there was part of a man coating her body.

"Just . . . please bring him back," she said. "I can't lose him too."

Ben nodded, knowing there was a story there but also knowing they rarely had a chance to discuss it.

"Remember: Behind closed doors after dark."

And then he was gone.

F Deck

HIS STOMACH WAS RUMBLING, but he hardly addressed it. Ben stopped long enough in his searches to enter the second-class dining saloon, eat a slab of grilled mayonnaise salmon, potatoes, and puree turnips. He didn't wait for plum pudding to be served.

This was all feeling like his last days at Samaritan Cross. That inability to help suffering children was making its rounds again. This was the biggest, most luxurious ship in the world. They had the same amenities as any first-class hospital. If he couldn't keep children alive here, then where could he? His failings were stacking up, and here on *Titanic* they felt heavier than ever.

His first stop was on the Boat Deck. Ben didn't think the boys would go all the way up there, but perhaps they saw the lifeboats from the well deck and thought they needed a closer look. Or perhaps they'd heard talk of the wondrous machines in the gymnasium. Even Ben thought the rowing machine was majestically hypnotic.

While there, he overheard a pair of officers talking about their combustible victim. He recognized them from the muster—First Officer Murdoch and Second Officer Lightoller. They were smoking—something that Ben knew was prohibited on deck, but they knew the captain was probably occupied.

"What are they feeding those poor saps if they're bursting into flames?" asked Lightoller.

Murdoch shook his head. "Not a passenger, mate. They said he was wearin' a White Star Line apron."

Lightoller shoved the man playfully and said, "Get that cigarette away from me, Will. You'll not be torching me."

"Ah, bugger off," said Murdoch, and he turned just in time to see Ben watching them. He quickly dropped his cigarette on the deck, stomped it out, then picked it up and put it in his pocket. He smiled and said, "doctor," before heading back toward the bridge.

Ben was torn with how the crew was handling the incident. If they made jokes about it, the passengers were less likely to be afraid if they saw something strange. But if they took it too seriously—Ben imagined a great panic. That was unavoidable, he thought, especially with bodies piling up. There were four ladies out there with the same inclination toward blood—four that Ben and the others *knew about.*

After the Boat Deck, he tried the first-class facilities, places the boys may have found interesting, but places from which the stewards would remove them. Ben talked to everyone he came across—passengers, lounge stewards, smokeroom stewards, officers in the corridors. None of them could help Ben because as most said, either eloquently or rudely: "There are children running all over this ship. How could anyone possibly know which two are missing?"

A priest was coming down the staircase, leaning heavily on a cane, when Ben nearly bumped him.

"Apologies, father."

"No problem at all, doctor. How goes the good fight?" Ben thought perhaps he was asking specifics of the infections but realized he was probably speaking of tending to *Titanic's* physical qualms. Ben healed the body, the priest healed the soul.

"It certainly is a fight, that's for sure."

The man laughed. "Tom Byles." He extended his hand.

"Benjamin York. Have you seen anything . . . odd, father?"

Byles shrugged and shifted his weight on his cane. "I saw a man put a message in a bottle and toss it over the railing. Not sure where he expects it to wash up."

Ben smiled and nodded. "Very good, father. Say, you haven't seen a pair of youngsters, have you?" He held his arm up just below his chest. "About this tall?"

"Doctor York, that's probably a third of the ship."

He nodded again. "You're right."

"Are they in some sort of trouble? Medically speaking, I mean."

"I don't really know, father. I just need to find them."

"Then I wish you Godspeed and grace." Byles took a slight bow, favoring his left leg.

"Thank you, father. Have a pleasant evening."

After Byles headed up the steps, Ben moved his search to third-class, hoping the boys had met up with fellow Irishmen, or at least families of similar trappings. Erik and his children were in a daze, but who could blame them? The matriarch was missing, and now one of the children.

The steerage people were far nicer and more receptive than the folks upstairs on the lounge chairs, not a care in the world.

While talking to passengers in the general assembly area, he met a little girl named Sally who tripped down the steps and sliced her knee. He was on his way back for his medical bag when the girl's father handed him a cloth soaked with strong-smelling whiskey.

"I'll let you do it, doctor," said the man. Ben took the rag and cleaned the wound, going slow to minimize the burn, and then bandaged it up with the roll of clean gauze he always carried in his jacket pocket for such a thing.

"Good as new," he said.

Sally held out her dolly—nothing but cloth and straw and sticks, and said, "What about Lizzy? She's hurt too!"

So Ben humored the girl, cut a length of gauze, and bandaged the doll's leg too. When it was over, the father helped Ben to his feet and started to shake his hand, but decided on a hug and a strong Irish pat on the back instead. He offered Ben a drink of the whiskey, which he took, not wanting to seem rude in front of so many. After that, Ben said goodbye and headed back up.

When he was on E deck, he noticed the light was gone from the portholes. He'd squandered three hours below deck. Those emboldened creatures were probably out by now, waiting to lure unsuspecting victims into the dark corners of the ship.

He was about to round the staircase leading from Scotland Road down to F deck when a steward pushing a cart exited the petty officer's lavatory. Ben had been so preoccupied that he almost barreled right over top of it, but at the last moment he corrected his course and simply knocked it on two wheels.

Both Ben and the steward quickly rushed to steady the cart. The man said, "Terribly sorry, sir. Wasn't watching where I was goin'."

"It's fine. Have yourself a good evening." Ben was about to continue by, but on the tabletop of the cart next to a stack of fresh linens was Reid's crucifix.

He picked it up and said, "Where did you get this?"

The steward said, "Down there." He pointed toward the staircase. "Between decks on the landing."

"This belongs to a friend of mine."

"Of course, doctor. I was on my way to deposit it in the purser's office."

Ben nodded his thanks and left for the staircase. He looked around the spot and wondered how it ended up on the landing. Reid wouldn't easily discard such a thing. He did a full circle and finally turned his attention back to E deck. Ben rushed back up the steps and found a quiet corner of the stairwell.

The crew had done a spectacular job of cleaning up the blood, although Ben had no way of knowing how much Clarence Clarke had leaked on his flight to the third-class promenade. But in their cleaning, they failed to search beneath the stairway, in the cubby around the corner.

Ben knelt down and saw a small, child-sized footprint made of blood. He dropped to his hands and looked beneath the stairs—and a pair of eyes looked back at him.

At first, it startled him. Rarely did things watching from the shadows have good intentions. But the more he stared, the more he could see those eyes welling with tears. And when the tears fell it was because the little boy was trembling so hard.

"Are you hurt?" Ben whispered.

Reid shook his head.

"Your mother is sick with worry."

Reid nodded.

Ben glanced down at the blood—he'd tracked it into the cubby and it surrounded his tiny, huddled body.

"Is any of this yours?"

He shook his head.

"Did you see something bad?"

A quick nod.

"Will you come out?"

He shook his head vehemently.

Ben nodded and said, "Okay. Is it alright if I come in there with you?"

Reid hesitated for a moment, as if wondering if Ben was being serious, or if perhaps this was a bad idea. But finally, with a new trail of tears, he nodded.

It was a tight fit, but Ben pulled himself along until he was behind the last step of the staircase. Then it opened wider, and he had room enough to sit up. He put his back against the wall next to Reid. The air was stale there—he smelled the boy's urine. No doubt he'd never left this place. Not even to relieve himself.

For a moment, they sat together in silence. Ben felt the warmth of his tears in the tight space. With their arms touching, he sensed the trembling and the rapid beat of his heart, but it was slowing with each ticking second. Ben tried not to stare as he studied the boy, confirming that he was unharmed—at least physically.

Finally, he said, "You know, I knew a little boy at my last hospital. He didn't talk much. When he was younger, a lot younger than you, I mean, a wagon ran over both his legs and . . ." Ben stopped when Reid's eyes went wide. "Well, it changed him."

What Ben didn't say was the boy suffered from Compartment Syndrome and needed both legs amputated. Although surviving something so terrible, his mind was never the same again.

Ben said, "What I mean is that . . . he didn't talk, but he listened. And he understood. And that was good enough."

Ben dared to reach out and put a hand around the boy's shoulder. Reid flinched but he settled quickly, sniffed back tears and wiped his nose on his sleeve. When his arm dropped, his shirt shifted and Ben could see that his entire chest was healing from an old, horrible burn. It reached from shoulder to shoulder and as far down as the shadow of his shirt would allow. He tried not to stare.

"I'm sorry for . . . whatever made you quiet." Reid nodded slowly and Ben said nothing for a long time. Shadows would pass by the hallway and the boy would tense, but Ben held him close until his shivers nearly departed.

And he finally asked, "Can I take you back to your mum now?"

Reid nodded and shed more tears, but these were of relief, not fear.

Ben put his hands on the floor so he could rotate around on his knees and that's when he came face to face with the wall to Reid's right—and the horrid, bloody drawing that nearly sent him scuttling away.

It was a man, but not quite. There was no bottom jaw, nor eyes. Just two red, angry circles that saw everything. The teeth were the worst part because Ben finally had a missing piece of the puzzle. There were eight long fangs hanging halfway down its face.

What kind of animal has eight teeth like this? he'd asked O'Loughlin.

Apparently this kind of animal, thought Ben. Now he was seeing what killed the man in the cargo hold.

"Did you draw this?"

Reid shook his head and when he got on his knees, he produced a long stick that had been tucked behind him. It was pointed with a bloody tip—the artist's tool for this horrendous image.

"You found that here?"

He nodded.

Ben said, "Okay. Let's get you to your mum." He let Reid go first and before following the boy out, gave a final look at the horrid creature. If that thing was loose on the ship . . .

New York couldn't arrive fast enough.

THE DARK

8:30 P.M.

HE WASN'T SURE HOW far they'd taken him, nor how long it took to get there, but it sure was dark. It wasn't until *Titanic* that Colin saw his first electric bulb. There were hundreds of them on the ship—thousands, probably. Even at night, he'd never been far from light. Until now.

Colin hated this kind of dark, especially when he was alone. He wasn't alone right now, but he sure wished that he was. They were all around him, close enough to touch. But they weren't warm—in fact, they were like blocks of ice, radiating cold that seeped into his spine and made him shiver. None of them breathed because they were dead, and dead people were cold. He remembered touching his granny hours after his mama found her dead—she was stiff and cold, just like these ladies.

Just like his mama.

The only thing worse than the cold was the deafening, rhythmic drone of the engines. Colin knew nothing about this ship, nor any other. But for the noise to be this loud, they had to be right on top of the turbines. None of the scary ladies seemed bothered by the sound.

He couldn't see them that well, but as his eyes adjusted, four shapes came into focus. They were so still, like statues. Colin felt the solid ground beneath his feet. He didn't know where he was sitting, just that it was hard and metal and the ladies were pressed so tightly against him that he couldn't fall off—nor run away.

"Mama, talk to me. Why won't you say nothin'?" he pleaded for what felt like the hundredth time. He pushed on her face but she wouldn't speak. His hands found her eyes and pressed into them—it should've been painful but she said nothing, nor did she move his hands away. He felt the icy stare of the others. They were all women, all better off than his mama. Or at least how his mama had been before .. . this.

They were waiting, although he couldn't figure out why. Anytime he tried to push his way through, one of them would shift to the side and block him in. There was no use in trying because they possessed far more strength than what his little arms could muster.

The only warmth he had was his warm piss running down his right leg. But that sensation passed long ago. He was hungry, thirsty and so, so tired. These ladies were torturing him because he was boxed in so completely that he couldn't lie back. Each time he drifted off to sleep, there was a change in the engine's roar that jarred him back awake. Those jolts made him cry, so he thought it was best to stay awake as long as he could.

"Mama, what are we doing here? Please, please come back to me. I know you're probably dead in there, but if you can hear me, please come back. I wanna go home. I don't wanna go to America. I wanna sleep in my hay bed with the loud kids next door and the old man upstairs who fights with his wife. Please, mama, please. Jack and Micky and Molly and pa—they all gotta miss us by now."

And then the red lights burned in her eyes. It lit in all their eyes, all at once, like an electrician had thrown a switch. She seemed to stare off into space for a moment, then the flames narrowed and flickered low and he knew she was staring at him.

"You don't need to be afraid." It sounded like his mama, but in a way, it didn't. He couldn't explain it—it was like someone was inside her, moving her lips and talking for her.

"I'm very afraid, mama." And he squeezed out warm tears onto his chilled face. The sound barely whispered out—he was losing his voice, the words having trouble fitting past his neck. Was this what happened to Reid? Did Reid see something so horrific that it stole his voice completely?

"There's no need to be afraid, Colin. There's a new world waiting for us. One without pain and fear and anger. One that promises we won't have to beg for scraps anymore. He'll make a way for us."

"Who, mama?"

And then another pair of red eyes joined the fray. They were directly behind Matilda. Colin, in his sleep-deprived brain, thought this new arrival was floating in the air, but it wasn't that at all. This creature was just so tall that it dwarfed the surrounding ladies. Matilda and the others stepped back and took a knee in humble reverence to this cloaked creature. Colin couldn't pull his eyes from its face.

Its long, bony fingers came up and gripped his cheeks. They were so cold that he thought part of his skin would rip away when it let go. Colin was trembling.

The creature leaned in, bearing seven long fangs—and a half one growing back in. Colin fought, but the creature had such a tight hold on his head that he couldn't escape. And slowly, it pushed his head down and exposed his neck. . .

Matilda said, "It'll only hurt for a moment. Just close your eyes and think of home."

The creature came closer, its breath like a puff of death, its teeth dripping saliva, the points bearing down toward his flesh. Colin tried to scream but the noise died in his throat. He thrashed his arms to no effect.

". . . think of the green fields. The fairy circles, the black water, the big . . ."

And the moment the fang broke off and the King tasted the first drop of blood, he knew all there was to know about Colin Olsson and his short, sad life. He didn't care about any of these details—he wanted to grow his coterie since they'd lost one hopeful earlier that day.

But the King cycled through Colin's memories because they both came from the same land, so he privately enjoyed the flashes of a time he'd almost forgotten. He watched Colin's memories from the first time he saw ducks in the pond out from his house, to the time he fell off the ladder and broke his wrist, to the moments when he watched the little girl that he fancied, the one who wore the pretty white dress to church. But most importantly, he observed his time aboard *Titanic,* such as the moment Matilda tracked him down and tried to pull him from a tight crawlspace . . .

The King saw through Colin's eyes as clearly as if he'd been there himself. And he saw another boy trying to save him, and between them, they held the yew stake. The King's cold blood churned. The stake was still on the ship—and he couldn't allow that. He felt its pierce once—he wouldn't feel it again.

"Who is this boy?" he asked his coterie.

"His name is Reid. The little boy in the cabin next door to mine," said Matilda.

"A Bitterblood?"

She nodded.

"Then drain him. And throw the stake overboard."

"I'll take care of it."

The King eased Colin back down against the wall. This time tomorrow he'd be part of the coterie—hopefully along with many others.

"Make sure. I'll not share a ship with that horrid weapon. And remember—if I die, you all die with me."

The coterie bowed as he turned to vapor and floated out of their dark hive.

It had been days since he'd fed. The blood of Ernest did little to wet his palette. He was a unique creature, one that was often better off asleep because his appetite was so insatiable. But with age came experience, and he'd learned to control most of his primal instincts.

But one Bitterblood wasn't enough to stop the rumble in his shriveled belly. He needed more. He demanded more. These humans had already killed a member of his coterie—he had great aspirations for Clarence in the new world. Some deserved the promise of his coterie, but most deserved nothing but death. He wanted to level judgement upon the mortals for taking Clarence . . .

He also needed his bloodlust resolved. The King floated up to the third-class promenade and mixed with the steam exhaust so he could linger unseen by the steerage passengers. He licked the air around several burly men who'd been in a scrape and had clotted blood on their knuckles. Then he watched a little girl sitting alone on a bench, holding her dolly, rubbing a bandage across her knee. He smelled the fresh blood and he wanted to bury his face in it. But even if he slaughtered the entire deck of Bitterbloods, it still wouldn't slake his thirst. Not tonight. He was going to break his own rule. Who would stop him?

He was the King.

BOAT DECK

THE FIRST-CLASS DINING ROOM had been dreadfully busy. Normally, that was the environment where Rebecca and Jonas Williams thrived, but not tonight. The talk of the ship was the poor man who'd burst into flames, making it quite difficult for Rebecca to enjoy her Lobster a la Newburg.

The wind was cool, the air a slap of salt. Each night seemed colder than the last. She rather enjoyed being this high up with only the officers' quarters and the funnels above. There weren't many people here, but it was still early. *Titanic* was one big, voracious party that never stopped, not even for a burning man.

She heard the string quartet somewhere below, probably on the first-class promenade that saw most of the after-dinner passengers. Rebecca only counted six others on the Boat Deck—those who were equally disgusted by the vulgar talk at dinner and needed an early departure.

On her legs sat her Fox Terrier, Lilly. She yawned and looked up, then settled back against the smooth, pricy silk of the dress.

Rebecca looked over at her husband who'd just struck up a cigarette. He fanned the air and dropped the match on the deck beneath his lounge chair. Jonas was several years older—that seemed to be the theme aboard *Titanic*—and the overhead light made for deep shadows around his eyes. But he was a boxer in his early days—a damn fine one, and he was in peak physical shape even after all these years. Right now, he was nearly asleep. The old codger was going to set his dress coat afire.

The last three months had been a continuous party and unlike the other passengers, Jonas wanted *Titanic* to be his winding down. They'd spent their time with Maggie and the Astors, dining in restaurants like the Café de la Paix. She wasn't much for French cuisine but like all other aspects of high-society, one had to live in equal parts make-believe and sincerity. John and Madeleine and Maggie liked that sort of thing. So did Cosmo and Lucy. Rebecca was an American through and through, and she found it difficult to acclimate to European delicacies—even in the presence of other Americans.

As much as Jonas disagreed, she hated the trip and wished they'd never left Boston. But Jonas saw a wonderful business opportunity, made possible by John Astor's influence. Jonas was to open not one but *two* department stores in France. This time next year, their foothold on European shopping would be all but guaranteed.

Jonas stirred and said, "You know, Dorothy said she was standing on deck when that poor lad caught fire. She said he lost all his skin. Then again, Dorothy has been drunk the whole voyage so who the hell knows what she *really* saw?" Jonas lost his words for a moment, then as an afterthought, said, "I bet there's a hospital somewhere on the ship."

"Do we have to talk about such things?" she said, and hid a burp in her hand. The food wasn't settling well on her stomach. Even Lilly yapped at her sudden disgust.

Jonas said, "I just feel sorry for the lad, that's all. I wish there was a way to help. I'm sure he won't ever be well again."

"What would you have us do? Pay for the chap's trip?"

"Now there's an idea. I'll talk to the purser in the morning. He's a fine fellow. Asked me for the address where he might buy my cufflinks."

"Did you tell him they were custom-made?"

"I didn't have the heart," said Jonas. "But it's settled. I'll find out the boy's name and we'll leave him with a little present for when ... and *if* he wakes up."

"You're so charitable, love."

Just then, Lilly hopped off Rebecca's legs and stared up into the sky. Fur bristled on her back, ears pointed down, and she started making a horrid growl, a noise neither Rebecca nor Jonas had ever heard.

"What's wrong with you?" he asked, then gave her a slight jab in the ribs with his shoe. She barely flinched. Instead, she moved backwards and hunkered down, still keeping her eyes on the sky.

Rebecca followed the dog's gaze to the top of the funnel where copious amounts of black smoke were forming a blanket against the stars. The night sky may not have been pretty directly above the ship, but at least they were making good time.

"Where's your valet?" she asked Jonas who was almost back to sleep.

"That way," he said, pointing toward the forward end of the ship. The only thing she saw was a trio of younger ladies playing cards and laughing maniacally.

"Robert! Robert? Are you near, darling?" she said.

"Here, ma'am," he said, appearing on the other side. It startled her, but at least Lilly calmed for the moment.

"Take her for a walk, will you?" she said, handing off the terrier's leash.

"Right away, miss," he said, and headed back toward the staircase that would lead him to the aft well deck.

"Make sure she does her business before you bring her back!"

"Yes, ma'am," he said, his back to the lady.

"It's just . . . she soiled the carpets in our state-room and the entire hallway was foul!"

"Understood, Mrs. Williams. I'll make sure she stretches her legs good and plenty."

"Thank you, darling." Rebecca settled back into her chair and said, "I'm so glad we found him. He's much better than Dunc—"

Jonas wasn't in his lounge chair.

She stood, so shaken by his sudden disappearance. *Titanic* was large, but the space they'd been occupying—it was rather difficult to leave without one noticing.

"Have you seen my husband?" she called to the ladies down the deck. They each shook their heads then returned to their cards. Rebecca did a full circle—Jonas vanished into thin air.

To the left—the girls he would've certainly passed to go back inside. To the right—the direction Robert had taken Lilly. In front was the railing and the promenade beneath them. And behind her was the funnel, large and imposing and nearly black against the starless night.

"Jonas?" she called, and she stepped back against the railing. "Jonas, love, where did you go?"

But then her eyes drifted up to the smoke and saw that something was inside it. Little red lights rotated and focused, but that wasn't what drew her attention—it was the way the smoke parted around the shape of a very tall figure. Rebecca couldn't make sense of it, but maybe she shouldn't have taken Maggie's suggestion of a second glass of wine.

Just then, the post lamps on deck caught something shiny along the side of the funnel. She watched, confused, as water trickled down the edge, first only a thin line but then thicker globs until she realized it wasn't water at all, but blood. And in that blood were chunks of meat.

Rebecca wanted to scream but a sudden surprise silenced it before she made a sound. A large shape fell from the funnel, landing on the railing above and then flopping down onto the lounge chairs in front of her. Warm blood smacked her in the face. The trio of ladies started screaming and sliding out their chairs so they could rush down the deck, away from this awful, awful sight.

Jonas lay right in front of her, his neck torn out, his head lolling to the side so far that she saw the jagged points of his snapped, yellowed spine.

She dropped to her knees and screamed until her throat hurt and when her eyes searched the sky, sought the God who would let this happen to her dear husband, she didn't find Him at all. Instead, she found the vengeful eyes of a creature that was just as much a beast as it was a man. Those red circles in its face flared with hunger as it dropped on top of her, sinking all of its fangs so deep that she was dead before it even lifted her back to the smoke to feed.

F Deck

SHE WAITED BUT BEN never showed. Her mind was playing all sorts of scenarios to explain away Reid's absence, but she didn't like any of the theories to arrive in her sleep-deprived mind. Somehow, she fell asleep just after dark. It wasn't her choice—she'd been running on pure adrenaline after the man exploded into ash.

For a little while, her thoughts returned to her happy place—Kinsale near the water. Back when she was just a girl, and later when she met Emmet. So many wonderful memories permeated one place. It made her sad she had to leave it, and even sadder that she probably would never go back. Life moved forward, even over the bumps and pockmarks.

She'd just started to smell the turf fires and the honeysuckles when there was a heavy knock at the door. She rose so sharply she bumped her head on the top bunk, but she hardly acknowledged the pain. Fiona ripped the door open and there stood her boy and the good doctor behind him.

Reid rushed forward and wrapped his arms around her.

"Reid! You're okay! My boy is okay!" she said, and wrapped him back, burying her face atop his head. His hair smelled odd, something she couldn't place. Who knows what adventures he'd had?

"Are you hurt?" she asked him, kneeling and lifting his chin. He shook his head. "Where were you? We searched this ship over for you!"

But she stopped the berating instantly when she glanced up and saw Ben giving her a sidelong glance. There were no words there, but the implication was clear: Stop yelling at the boy. He'd been through something.

"Where's Colin?" she asked Reid, then looked up at Ben. "Did you find him?"

When Ben didn't answer, she held Reid at arm's length and saw the tears welling in his eyes. And then, perhaps embarrassed, or perhaps overcome with sadness, he embraced her again. He was shaking and she felt the warmth of his tears against her cheek. He'd also wet himself.

Ben stepped out into the hall as Fiona retrieved another pair of Reid's clothes—a grey button-up shirt and black threadbare pants.

Fiona pulled him close after he dressed, her chin resting atop his head. When Reid realized the doctor was back in the cabin, he separated and wiped his nose, then went to the fold-out chair. She was just now noticing the odd stick he'd brought with him—like a natural tree branch but shaped at the end by design.

He laid it aside and opened their bag and started going through his books, looking for something in particular. Finally, he found the one he wanted and took it to the bottom bunk, disappearing into the shadows. Fiona bent low and saw him reading with his back to the world. This was Reid's way of dealing with trauma—shut out everyone and get lost between pages.

She stepped out into the hall with the doctor. At this hour, most everyone was up on deck or in the general area. Dinner had been served a couple of hours ago but she missed it. Now, her stomach rumbled with the smell traveling through the vents.

"Tell me everything," she said.

Ben didn't know much. How could he? Reid didn't talk to anyone, and most people weren't equipped to have a conversation with a mute boy. But she learned several troubling things, not just with Reid but with going-ons across *Titanic*. Reid had seen something bad. He'd been around blood. At least two fell victim to those crazed women. She knew that wasn't the right word, but beast or creature or monster sounded silly in her brain.

Ben stepped back into the room and then turned to Fiona. "Can we . . . can you . . . get him to explain?" He pulled out his notebook and his pen.

"Reid?" said Fiona. "Close the book'n come out, sweetie."

He slid to the front, his eyes far redder than when he entered the bunk. He wiped the wetness away with his sleeve and then Ben placed the notepad on his leg.

"Can you answer a few questions for me? We want to help Colin, okay?"

Reid nodded.

"Will you write what you saw?"

Reluctantly, he picked up the pen. He scribbled a few words across the dingy white paper and then sat back. Ben rotated the words around so he and Fiona could read.

Tillda took Collan

Ben and Fiona shared a confused look.

"She took Colin?" he asked.

Reid nodded.

"Took him where?"

The boy shrugged.

Fiona asked, "Did she say anything to him or you before that?"

He nodded.

"Tell us," said Ben, returning the notepad.

Im fine. Dont be fraid.

Again, Ben and Fiona shared questioning stares. This just kept getting weirder.

Ben asked, "Why would she tell him not to be afraid? Afraid of what?"

Reid tapped his teeth—two fingers on each side. And now it was confirmed. Fiona knew Ben was piecing together what was happening on *Titanic*. Still, he wanted to be sure.

"Show me."

He took the pen and drew a crude face but the fangs were unmistakable. They were sharp, hanging at the edges of the lip in the same spot that aligned with their victims.

"Who is that?" Fiona asked, although she already knew.

Reid slid his finger up to '*Tillda*.'

"Fangs," said Ben. "Just like the ones Clarence had. They're the ones killing passengers."

"You can't be serious. Matilda was a sweet lady. She wouldn't hurt a soul."

Reid shook his head vehemently, disagreeing with his mother's assessment. Perhaps that was true once before, but certainly not now. He gave Ben the notepad and crawled back into the shadows beneath the bunk, book in tow.

This was all so awful. For Matilda, for Colin, for all the others who'd met their end at the behest of these monsters. If Matilda and those other women truly were responsible for the murders of the passengers, it seemed unlikely that Colin was still alive. So what horrors then, did Reid actually see?

After all he'd been through. He would never speak again.

Ben, as if sharing the same thought, asked, "May I ask what happened to him? I noticed his . . ." His voice trailed off and he tapped his own chest.

Fiona hadn't spoken of it in a long time. It had been equally long since she felt as comfortable around another human as she did around Ben. She gave a quick glance to her boy to be sure he wasn't hanging on her every word. Not satisfied, she took Ben by the arm and led him out into the hallway.

At last, she said, "There was a fire. At our house in Killarney. My husband, Emmet, got drunk and almost burned himself up. He got himself out of the house and left me and the little ones to fend for ourselves."

"Oh . . . oh my, Fiona. That's . . . terrible."

"It gets worse."

"He sobers up long enough to go beat on the neighbors' doors, hoping someone could come help him put it out. Then he remembers he has a family. I wake up just as I'm smellin' the smoke. Emmet's got his hands on me, draggin' me through the bedroom door.

"I'm fightin' him, screamin' as we pass my little ones' closed door because I know they're still in there and this smoke and flame is gonna kill 'em."

"Little ones?"

She nodded. "By the time I'm on the street sputterin' and coughin' up black gunk, the house starts to blaze. I know they're gone. Reid's window bursts wide open and flames belch out. That's when I give up hope."

"But he made it."

She nodded again. "He did. A few minutes later as we're sittin' there watching our whole world go up in flames, he comes runnin' out. He had a . . . I mean, I had a daughter. Her name was Erin. Reid tried to save her. He cradled her right against his chest, but she was so . . . so . . . hot. She was burnin'."

Fiona broke down, this story not any easier two years after it happened. She tried to keep her raw emotion low so that Reid couldn't hear. Ben didn't want to seem forward, but he also couldn't bear to see her so upset. He brought her close and let her bury her face against his chest. He smelled nice—a mixture of tonic and his personal scent.

"You don't have to finish this."

"It's fine," she said. "Anyway, Reid carried out his sister, despite the awful pain across his chest. He thought she was just sleepin'. He dropped her on the ground and unfolded the blankets and smoke rose up from her little black face.

"I screamed out and hugged my boy. He cried so hard because the pain in his chest was so unbearable. The fire bit him good. I asked if he could tell me where all he hurt and he didn't say a word. He never spoke again. I can't even remember what his last words were."

"I'm . . . I'm so sorry," said Ben. There wasn't anything else to say after hearing such a story. But she wasn't finished.

"That was two years ago. I never forgave Emmet. We never told Reid how the fire started. Reid thought his father was a hero. And I allowed it. He *needed* a hero. But a year later, everything changed again because Emmet thought he'd found the answer to our money problems—his brother, Cillian, had immigrated to America to open a pub and brewery. He told Emmet to move there and together they'd run it."

"So he did?"

"That's right. Up and left in the middle of the night without tellin' either of us. Used our last penny to get to Philadelphia. I lied to Reid and said his da had to leave unexpectedly and that he'd be home as soon as he could. Only I didn't know when that would be. I didn't know *if* that would be. Emmet had a lot of wild ideas that never came to fruition."

Ben cast a look back inside the cabin and found Reid in the same spot, still turning pages.

"So that's where you're going? To meet Emmet in Philadelphia?"

"Not quite," she said, and breathed a sigh. She hated telling her story, for it seemed like one tragedy after another. But it was important if anyone were to understand the nature of Reid's mutism. "I'm taking Reid to see . . . Emmet's resting place."

"What?" he said, eyes wide. "You poor things."

She nodded. "It wasn't bad . . . for a little while, at least. Emmet and his brother made great money and he sent half of it to us. All of our needs were met. We were able to move to Southampton near his ailing parents and look after them, all while staying in this nice, big house."

"So what happened to him?"

"The bastard was lucky for most of his life but his luck ran out. He was crossin' the street and was hit by a carriage. His brother wrote to me after it happened. It was an awful accident. Was in all the papers."

"When did this happen?"

"Three months ago. We used what little money we had left to buy the first available passage to America."

"Which was Titanic."

She nodded. "I suppose we'll start a new life there. Emmet's brother has promised a little money but not much. Cillian paid for the grave rites and the hole and the headstone. But he found his own financial troubles and had to close the pub and brewery."

"I'm so sorry, Fiona. You've both been through so much. And now all of this is happening."

She nodded and looked back into the cabin. A cool, salty wind blew through the open porthole.

"After the fire, he started to make sounds. Little grunts and laughs. I thought he would one day talk. But when I told him what had happened to his father . . ." She kept her voice level because she was about to break down again. "After that, I knew he'd never say another word."

"Do you have a place to live?" Ben asked. "In Philadelphia?"

She shrugged. "Cillian told us we can have the second room in his flat until we get settled in America. Says it's big enough to squeeze in a bed."

"That sounds awful," Ben said, trying to sound light.

She grinned. "Quite."

"I pray your life in America is better than it was in Ireland, in England, and aboard Titanic."

"Thank you," she said, and looked up at him in a way she never had until now. Something in his eyes caught her off-guard. It was an affection but something else—probably pity. She was torn between wanting to run away—for how could anyone want to pursue a woman with so much emotional ropes pulling her back—and wanting to kiss him. It was unheard of and frowned upon and would probably cause him to avoid her the rest of the voyage, but either way, despite what she wanted in that moment, she didn't get the chance.

R.M.S. TITANIC
⚓
R.M.S. TITANIC

The lights flickered inside the cabin.

Ben caught movement from the corner of his eye which directed Fiona's attention, as well. She turned just in time to see a pillar of grey smoke pouring in from the porthole. Reid also noticed—it was impossible not to choke on it. No sooner did it fill the cabin did it disperse. In its place stood Matilda, only she looked much different from the last time Fiona saw her.

Dried blood caked her entire chin and throat. Through the patches of red, she saw the throbbing veins and the large, dark knub beneath her chin. There was a fang in there, growing, twitching, sending little tendrils throughout her body like a nest of parasites. The worst part was her eyes, dead, yet full of life at the same time. They burned red and angry.

She didn't attack them—her attention turned to the stake sitting against the fold-out chair. Fiona was too perplexed to move as she picked it up and turned around, ready to pitch it out the porthole. Lucky for them, Ben sprang into action.

Without a weapon in hand, he lunged forward and shoved Matilda as hard as he could against the wall. She dropped the stake and went down, not because she was hurt, but because the doctor caught her unawares.

Reid was in the process of racing off the bunk and into Fiona's arms but when the stake clattered to the floor, he took the opportunity and snatched it. Matilda hissed and spun, then launched herself toward the boy, but Ben was ready. He snatched her by the neck and said, "Run!" The creature was strong—far stronger than his slipping fingers.

They turned toward the door but it was filling with more grey smoke. Another woman—a lady neither Fiona nor Reid would've known was Elizabeth Campbell, who'd just killed three passengers in the last hour, blocked their escape. She threw her hand up and shoved Fiona back against the wall.

Seeing an exposed Reid, she lashed out for the stake but he took a swipe at her. Although she didn't seem to fear a boy, she kept her distance from the weapon. Ben thought this was a remarkable discovery that was quickly overshadowed when the woman whose neck he held suddenly vanished. She became vapor to escape his grasp, then quickly materialized on the other side of him.

She grabbed his hair—he screamed out when she ripped some of it from the roots. His blood trickled down his face and dripped from his chin. Both creatures whipped into a frenzy. Matilda came close and sniffed him, then licked the line of blood from his chin to the wound. She made a little aroused shiver and opened her eyes, now burning with twice the intensity. She hissed, bore her fangs and came in for a bite, but by now Reid had spotted the crucifix in Ben's back pocket.

Matilda had driven the doctor to a knee, but the moment the boy held the effigy up, both creatures recoiled. Ben stood, shook the daze from his head, and then snatched the crucifix from Reid's hand and slammed it against Elizabeth's face. She screamed as her flesh sizzled. Her eyes, although closed, ran down her face in white streams.

He felt something touch his other hand. Without even looking down, he knew what had been placed there, and who had placed it. Ben pulled the crucifix away, now with singed flesh attached. When Elizabeth stood straight, body twitching in pure agony, Ben rammed the stake through her chest.

Her eyes flew open, the fires burned bright and hot and quick, and then died out completely. The girl burst into flames and immediately turned to ash. He whirled around in time to see Matilda, who'd been cowering against the wall, turn to vapor and float out the porthole.

Fiona was dazed from her hit against the wall. Reid shook her face with his little ash-covered hands until she woke and looked around. Without questioning, without knowing the outcome of their fight, she screamed, for this was all too familiar again.

"Hey, hey, it's okay," said Ben, trying to sound calm.

"You alright?" asked someone from the door. A huddle of people stood in the hallway. When Elizabeth cried out, the inhuman sound must have projected beyond the cabin.

"We're fine. I'm a doctor," said Ben, and he closed the door. "Up you go." He grabbed Fiona and helped her to her feet.

"What happened?" she asked. He was too busy looking into her eyes for signs of dilation.

"Thank your boy." Although shaken, Reid was smiling. Ben held the stake and realized this was the most priceless thing on the ship. He said, "Did you learn that from your books?"

Reid nodded.

"I think I'm going to be sick," said Fiona, the stirred dust in her nose and mouth.

"We have to go," said Ben. "She'll be back. And there's two others . . . at least two that we know of."

"Where?" she asked. "Where will we go?"

He shrugged. "I don't know. But you can't stay here anymore."

Part III

On a Bed of
Polished Glass

CAPTAIN'S SITTING ROOM

APRIL 13TH, 1912, 11:30 A.M.

FOR THE TIME BEING, Fiona and Reid would stay in Benjamin's cabin. It didn't matter, for it didn't seem the doctors would get much sleep. Last night, as they battled a pair of the infected creatures, the other monsters hunted unsuspecting passengers. There was now too much turmoil on the ship for Ismay to pretend otherwise. At the request of the captain, a meeting had been called between the officers and the doctors.

"That brings this morning's total to seven," said Chief Officer Wilde after a deckhand passed him a slip of paper and then hastily left. Wilde read the names of all the unfortunates the passengers and crew stumbled upon in the early morning hours. Ismay didn't care about most of them. The only two who mattered were Rebecca and Jonas Williams, a pair of first-class passengers who fell victim to their original monster. Ben had already seen the bodies—mangled beyond recognition. This was the work of the creature he'd seen in the drawing.

Ben took a sip of his tea as he looked around the room at the other fine gentlemen. The captain sat at the head of the group, obviously never assuming his sitting room would ever be so full.

Ben said, "At this point, the surgery is overflowing. Perhaps we should look into keeping them in cold storage."

Ismay sat up straight, a look of pure venom in his eyes. "Are you mad? Put them next to the beef and chicken?"

Ben was about to ask what Ismay would suggest but they'd already covered that. The White Star Line chairman wanted to put the first victim in the ash injectors and send him out to sea. If Ismay thought he could dump all the bodies overboard with no one's knowledge, he'd do it.

Instead, Doctor O'Loughlin tried to be more diplomatic. "Bruce, please. If tomorrow we wake up and there are ten more bodies, what then? I'm sure the victualling crew has space."

First Officer Murdock cleared his throat and said, "Rather than figure out what to do with bodies that have yet to pile up, why don't we figure out how to stop these killings?" He turned to Ben and said, "You say this is the work of your four patients. Women, no less?"

"That's right. They have some sort of affliction that makes them need blood. They drink it right out of the victim and leave them dead."

This admission made a few of the older gentlemen twist and turn in their seats. Second Officer Lightoller shook his head and fumbled with the buttons on his jacket.

But it was Third Officer Pitman who turned to Wilde and said, "Sir, don't we have guns? Perhaps the men would ease passenger distress by carrying firearms."

"That's the most ridiculous thing I've ever heard," said Ismay. "This isn't the old world. We aren't barbarians."

Captain Smith gave a long sigh and said, "That's not a bad idea." Without even acknowledging Ismay, he reached into his pocket and pulled a set of keys. He tossed them to Wilde and said, "Henry, will you retrieve them? Two at a time, please and thank you."

Wilde stood and exited the captain's quarters while Ismay shot daggers at Smith. He shook his head and smoothed his jacket. Ben tried to hide a smile that was made even more difficult when he caught O'Loughlin's eye and the old man was grinning into his hand. *Titanic* may have been White Star Line's property, but Smith was the captain and the captain's orders were law.

"So what else can you tell us of these . . . crea-tures?" asked Murdoch.

Doctor Simpson, who'd been quiet thus far, said, "We have a theory. We believe they are the spawn of some . . . unique creature. One we haven't seen."

"Why's that?" Ismay asked.

Ben, Simpson, and O'Loughlin took turns ex-plaining all they'd learned over the last couple of days. They outlined the differences in the bite marks and how those matched up to the fangs seen on creatures such as Clarence Clarke and Matilda Olsson. But then there were ravaged bodies—those of the man they found in the cargo hold, and those of Rebecca and Jonas Williams. It was an entirely unique creature, with different fangs, possessed of inhuman strength, aggression, and bloodlust. This creature didn't simply leave puncture wounds. This one turned people into clumps of meat.

Ismay lit his second cigarette and turned just as Wilde entered the room and said, "We have a problem. The guns . . . they're gone."

"What do you mean they're gone?" asked Officer Pitman.

"Just what I said. The gun cabinet is bloody emp-ty."

"Who else has a key?" asked Ismay.

"No one on this ship," said the captain. "Maybe Captain Haddock?"

That had been *Titanic's* captain during the sea trials, and the man who was going to cross the Atlantic on her maiden voyage. But Smith was popular with first-class passengers, whereas Haddock wasn't a people person. White Star Line chose Smith because the newspapers would love him.

"Find those guns," said Smith. "Check every officer's belongings. And then start checking the deck crew."

"Yes, captain," said Wilde, and then he left.

"I have *my* gun, sir," said Murdoch. "I always like to keep it near."

Lightoller raised his hand. "I have mine, as well."

Ismay turned back to Simpson and said, "You were explaining your theory?" He seemed almost bored with this conversation.

Simpson turned to Ben and said, "You tell him."

Ben nodded. "I believe that if we kill this master creature, the others may die. When we pulled the fang from Clarence's neck, he turned feral. It's as if they're all linked."

Ismay said, "Wonderful. So we have a plan to kill the 'master.'" He rolled his eyes. "And what of these infected women? What do we do about them?"

"Kill them, too," said O'Loughlin.

The tension in the room thickened like jam. Ben knew the doctors were about to lose all credibility, but he was powerless to stop what everyone had already learned was the truth.

Ismay was about to voice his incredulity when O'Loughlin continued. "Those aren't people now. You weren't there, Bruce. None of you were there but the doctor here. Whatever soul Clarence Clarke had was gone before we even attempted to operate on him. If you see any others, do like Doctor York here did with Elizabeth Campbell last night and put something through its heart."

Ismay spoke, his words punctuated carefully for full effect. "Are you really suggesting that we kill passengers?"

O'Loughlin snickered. "I'm suggesting and recommending. If you find one of them with a lump on their neck, kill them. If you don't kill them now, they will escape and kill more than their share later. As you've seen."

The stares would've troubled a lesser man but O'Loughlin held his ground. Ismay said, "If we weren't in the middle of a crisis, I would have you arrested."

Doctor O'Loughlin chuckled and placed a cigarette in the corner of his mouth. "You haven't seen a crisis yet, Mr. Ismay." He struck a match and sucked on the cigarette until the embers flared. "We started this trip with one monster who beget four more. We've no idea how many of 'em are on the loose now. By the time we reach New York, half this ship may be dead . . . or worse."

Ismay breathed a sigh and ran a hand across his head. A bit of his hair dye came away on his palm, but no one said anything. He turned to Smith and said, "We need full speed, captain. Get us to New York quickly. We should light the first boiler right away."

He gently stirred his tea. "No," said the captain firmly.

"No?"

"No, we won't be lighting the first boiler."

Ismay looked around the room to gauge if everyone else shared the same disbelief. When no one else would even look at him, the full brunt of his anger leveled at Captain Smith.

"You *will* light the first boiler."

Smith said, "It's a new ship and we're making excellent time. I'll not have us throw a propellor and add two days to our trip."

"That's unlikely," Ismay said. "The sea trials were a succ—"

"I don't give a damn about the sea trials. This is my ship and we'll be going with my rules. And put whatever the hell you want in your report about me. I'm retiring, Bruce. You can have this bloody ship once I dock her."

Again, the tension returned but this time Ismay ground his cigarette into an ashtray and stood. He smoothed his nice jacket and said, "You're all in service of the passengers. We are a luxury ship. We are on the cusp of outpacing Cunard. Do you not want to see our rival perish?"

Ben said, "This isn't about the damned ship! People are dead. More people are going to die. Don't you care about *that?*"

The fight left Ismay's face and the color fled his cheeks. Clearly, he wasn't accustomed to people standing up to him. He said, "What would you have me do, doctor?"

"There's a printing press on the ship, correct? Have them print a new message that instructs passengers to stay in their cabins. At least at night."

Ismay chuckled.

"I will not do that. And even if I did, it's clear you know nothing about the wealthy. You tell them not to do something, they'll do it for spite. Keep the passengers in good health as best you can, Doctor York. But do not tell them what they bloody well can and cannot do on this ship!"

And then Ismay left, slamming the door behind him. Ben would've been far angrier if he didn't agree the wealthy passengers were like petulant children. *Titanic's* staff would never convince people of the danger, no matter how many bodies piled up. It was doubly hard because the creatures knew what passengers to take and what passengers to leave alone.

The room quieted for a moment, but then Captain Smith stood and turned to his officers. "Time for our rounds, gentlemen. I would like to make one addition. We should change our rotation to six hours on, rather than four." A few of the officers grumbled in annoyance but everyone respected their captain and nodded.

Ben and the doctors excused themselves after the officers left. As they were walking along the Boat Deck, the endless sea stretching all around them, Simpson came up next to him and said, "We're saved. They're adding two hours to each shift."

As they hit the grand staircase with the sun's brilliance pouring through the dome, Ben remarked it was just as full as any other leg of the trip. O'Loughlin asked, "Are you okay? After what you told us happened last night . . ."

"Fine," said Ben. "It was . . . beneficial. We've established the creatures fear the stake. And why that one in particular? We could sharpen just about anything and stab them."

Simpson had already figured it out. "Because their leader fears it. This master."

"Which makes that twig quite important," said O'Loughlin, pausing on the steps to catch his breath.

"He's right. Where is it?" asked Simpson.

Ben said, "Somewhere safe."

"And the girl and her boy?"

"Also somewhere safe," he said. "Where are you two off to?"

Simpson looked to O'Loughlin and said, "We thought we might go talk with the victualling staff to see if we can rearrange their cold stock."

"Oh," said Ben. "I'll meet you down there. I need to wash up." The refrigeration storage spanned both G and Orlop Decks.

They nodded and O'Loughlin, puffing and panting, threw his hand up and then headed around the staircase. "I'm taking the lift."

Ben got off on C deck, intent on going back to his cabin where his stowaways were living until he came up with a better idea.

But as he approached the purser's office, a bald man walking with a cane approached. Ben didn't recognize him at first but that was because he'd been wearing a hat when they first met up on deck.

"Doctor York! Doctor York!" said Mr. Astor. "Just the man I need to see. Could you kindly come to my cabin, sir?"

"Sure. Is everything alright?" Ben followed behind as the man on the cane turned and set off toward the forward end of C deck's lavish, tiled hallway.

"I suppose Nurse Endres and my valet are still enjoying lunch. They've left me all alone with Madeleine and her . . . her," he glanced all around before adding, "*condition*."

"Is it an emergency, sir?"

"I should think so! I've not seen her like this . . . ever!"

Ben expected the worst. He thought for sure he would come upon the young, pregnant French-woman only to find her unable to wake, with vicious veins and a hard nub on her throat. Astor certainly seemed panicked enough.

The man stopped at the door, knocked his cane twice and waited for a lady to say, "C-c-come . . in." She was breathless, but it made Ben's heart rise to hear that she was conscious.

Astor led him into a large stateroom—fancy with a fireplace and plenty of seating, but nothing compared to the captain's quarters, and certainly not Ismay's parlour suite. There on the bed lay young Mrs. Astor, her hair down, the hint of a night-gown hidden beneath the high blanket. She kept her hands on the outside of the covers, balled into fists. She was pale and breathing rapidly but seemed otherwise alright.

"Hello, dear," said Ben.

"Madeleine," Astor said. He came in and shut the door behind him.

"Madeleine. Having trouble catching your breath?"

"Y-y-yes," she said, and her word turned into a hiccup. She was scared, but that was normal when one had never experienced such a thing.

"You're overbreathing. It happens. Did you see something . . . scary?"

She nodded vehemently, but it was Mr. Astor who said, "She was leaning over the railing on the Boat Deck when that poor man . . . the conflagration . . . the . . ."

"Yes, I know," Ben said. He turned back to Madeleine. "I need you to hold your breath and count to ten in your head. Can you do that?"

She nodded and did as he asked, nearly breaking down because she didn't think she could go so long without inhaling. Ben said, "After you count to ten. I want you to breathe into your hands like this." He simulated covering his face with his palms and breathing.

Again, Madeleine did as he asked. Ben had her repeat it two more times and on the third attempt, he pulled her hands down and waited to see if her breathing had returned to normal. It hadn't, but it was slowing. He asked her to repeat the process until she was feeling like herself again.

"Simply amazing," said Astor. He dropped his hand in his pocket but Ben waved him off.

"Unnecessary, sir. She had a fright, is all. She'll be back to normal soon enough. I'll have Mrs. Marsden bring her something to help with sleep."

"Thank you, sir," said Mr. Astor. "Can I offer you something? A drink, a smoke?"

"No, thank you, but I will make a request of you, Mr. Astor."

"Sure," he said, eager to pay up.

"Keep your wife in her cabin after dark."

He seemed vexed by this but said that he would, even though his young wife would insist they rub elbows with the rest of *Titanic's* elite. Ben knew for sure they wouldn't heed any warnings.

As he was standing, he looked over and saw a crucifix sitting on the mantle by the clock. Astor saw Ben examining it and said, "It's Madeleine's mother's cross. She is a superstitious lady. She said the cross would protect us on our voyage. I see no harm in letting it rest on the mantle. It spruces up this ungodly trim work."

"It's lovely. Keep it close. It may just save your life."

Ben was about to leave but Astor ushered him out of Madeleine's room and into the adjoining cabin where all of their baggage was kept.

Astor said, "Are we safe, doctor? Is there a murderer about the ship? Mr. Guggenheim's manservant said he heard a man was bleeding out somewhere downstairs. Had been bitten in the throat."

"We don't fully understand what's happening," Ben said, happy that it wasn't an outright lie. "But I will say this: you're a lot safer in your cabin after dark than prowling the halls and the decks."

"I see."

"If it makes you feel better . . . most of the attacks have been below deck."

Astor nodded. "Except for poor Jonas and Becca. Lovely people. We dined together at the Café de la Paix just a week ago. I'm sure Maggie is distraught over it all. I'll have to talk to her and comfort her over dinner tonight."

"Well, I'll leave you, sir," said Ben.

He was almost through the door when Astor said, "It's curious, isn't it?"

"What's that, sir?" Ben waited at the door without even turning around.

"That the attacks are mostly down on the lower decks. All of us fancy people don't even know about it unless we go looking and asking questions."

"I suppose that's just how life is, sir."

Astor breathed a sigh. "As the way it's always been. Those poor people. Invisible for most of their life. And now look. It's us—the regal elite—who are invisible."

"Goodnight, Mr. Astor." Ben left the room but he didn't go to his cabin as he planned. That rich fool gave him a splendid idea.

Assistant Doctors' Cabins

4:00 P.M.

For the second time in as many days, Fiona was cleaning ash from her body and hair. When the woman—who she later found out was named Elizabeth Campbell—exploded in a shower of white ash, the inertia carried it to the door. Fiona had been laid low early in the scuffle and had fallen between the fold-out chair and the bottom bunk. Most of the ash missed her.

She didn't know the plan, other than wait for Ben to return and put them somewhere safe. Although he didn't say it, Fiona made an eerie realization: The creatures had known where to look for the stake. They sniffed it out as sure as a bloodhound. Even now with it wrapped in a heavy cloth, she didn't like having it so close. The only saving grace was that Ben's quarters were in the middle of the ship, so there weren't any portholes for the monsters to enter.

Fiona and Reid took hot baths, never once leaving the lavatory until they were done. Afterward, they dressed in clean clothes and returned, wet, to Ben's cabin. A stewardess and a pair of passengers going for a spell in the library all stared at them. It was a small fortune that Reid was too young to understand their disgusted looks.

It wasn't the best thing for Doctor York to harbor a pair of third-class passengers. And even worse, one of them was a woman. Men of Ben's stature required good standing, and a poor Irish girl and her son sitting on his bunk surely sent the wrong message.

He didn't tell her when he'd be back, only that the ship's top people were meeting to discuss current events. The voyage was becoming twice as long, at least that's how it felt. This was supposed to be an enjoyable trip, now one that Reid would remember against the backdrop of all the horrible things he'd endured.

His books kept him company. This morning, after breakfast had been delivered thanks to Ben, Reid picked up his current read and engrossed himself between its pages. She hadn't seen him this enamored in a long time, but that was simply a testament to how traumatic his time on the ship had been.

People were in the hallway, loud footsteps that woke her from her dozing. She sat in the chair while Reid spread across the bed and each time her chin touched her chest, something jarred her. Finally, she stood and joined him on the bed, patting his legs so that he would sit up.

"Are you okay?"

He nodded.

"I'm not," she said. "That was . . . awful to see. Are you sure you're alright?"

He shrugged, softening a little, but finally nodded again.

"I saw you put the stake in Ben's hand."

Reid seemed embarrassed by this and he looked down, then nodded reverently. He tried to go back to his book but Fiona stopped him.

"Did you know? The stake, I mean. Did you know what would happen to her?"

Again, the curt nod.

"How?"

He tapped Fiona's chest with his palm.

"My heart?"

He shook his head and used two hooked fingers—their universal symbol for fangs.

"The lady's heart. Elizabeth."

He nodded.

"So they have to be stabbed through the heart to die?"

Reid cracked a smile this time, his chapped lips split from the cold, dry air.

"How do you know this?"

He shoved the yellow book into her chest. Fiona read the title—big, slashing red letters unlike anything she'd ever seen before.

"Dracula?"

He nodded.

She wasn't much of a reader, but knew how to find all the information she needed. It was written by a fellow named Bram Stoker and published fifteen years ago. Fiona had a vague familiarity with the book but couldn't place it. When she failed to draw the parallel that Reid was trying to express, he thumbed through the book to one of the many dogeared pages and pointed.

"I shall cut off her head and fill her mouth with garlic, and I shall drive a stake through her body . . ." Fiona quickly shut the book and said, "Reid! Why would you read such awful things?"

He raised an eyebrow, but then she understood. She was too busy gasping over the horror on the surface to see why Reid found this book important.

"You've read this before?"

He nodded and when she tried to hand the book back, he pushed it toward her.

"You want *me* to read it?"

He nodded again, then grabbed another book from his pile, *The Secret Garden*, and settled in the chair so that she could have the bed.

Later, Mr. Dunford brought their lunch, an agitated look on his face.

"Will you be here much longer?" he asked, trying to sound polite but failing. He was at an end with Ben's impromptu guests.

"Hopefully not, sir," she said. He grumbled and left. Fiona leaned back on the pillow and read.

And she pieced it all together. A book. A fifteen-year-old book. This Stoker fellow knew all about these bloodthirsty creatures.

These *vampires* . . .

B DECK

AFTER LEAVING JOHN ASTOR and his wife, Ben had every intention of going to the purser's office to inquire about their four infected ladies. But he was a doctor, after all, and was required to fulfil his normal duties for several hours after. With the rumors of the 'conflagration man' swirling across the ship, he no doubt entered cabins simply to appease rumors.

Most everyone in first-class thought it was more of a circus sideshow than a tragedy. Ben could've saved a lot of time by being honest, by saying there *was no* burned man recovering below. He blew away on the wind and the same thing may happen to you if you don't stay in your cabin after dark.

Rebecca and Jonas Williams had been reduced to an interesting tale. Half didn't believe it—Jonas was a notorious prankster, after all—so it stood to reason the old codger was hiding in his stateroom so he could spring the surprise on the last day of the voyage. First-class certainly didn't care about the steerage folk who'd either gone missing or lay dead on the tile.

It was almost dinner when Ben tracked down Hugh McElroy, *Titanic's* chief purser. Hugh was a good man, a loud, opinionated Brit who was hand-selected by the White Star Line along with Doctor O'Loughlin and Captain Smith for their larger-than-life personalities and ability to assimilate with the upper-class passengers.

Ben approached the purser's office and waited his turn, listening to the uninteresting conversations of the first-class passengers making their way to dinner. He watched Benjamin Guggenheim and his valet. Captain Smith and Thomas Andrews. Father Byles and a pair of officers. The mood was calm and it often took Ben by surprise how easily men forgot the evil that lurked right beneath their noses.

"Doctor," said McElroy. "You alright? You're too young to forget where you are."

Ben smiled and blinked away the reverie. "Good to see you, Hugh."

"Seems you aren't doing your job so well these days. I've never been on a ship before that needed to move the vegetables and meats to accommodate dead bodies."

McElroy handled a lot of the paperwork aboard the ship. As purser, nearly all operations went through his office. If it happened aboard the ship, Hugh was one of the first to learn about it.

Ben shrugged, seeing the joke for what it was. "I'm good, but I'm not good enough to bring 'em back from the dead."

"It's awful, innit?" he said, turning serious. "I hear captain went to hand out pistols and they were all gone!"

Ben nodded. "That's true. Strange, indeed."

"Bah, there's more guns below deck than any of us up here have."

"Do you really think that?"

McElroy chuckled and leaned in. "You check 'em for lice, not guns. Those people down there are starting their new lives. Tryin' to, anyway. If they owned guns, they brung 'em aboard Titanic."

Ben's attention was drawn to a chirping sound at the rear of the office. McElroy looked irritated and rolled his eyes. "I'm coming, I'm coming. You're hungry."

He approached a cage sitting on the rear counter where a bright yellow canary bounced along the bedding. McElroy pulled a tin of crackers from his breast pocket, crumbled one in his hand, then sprinkled it into the bowl."

"Damned thing hates people. Everyone but me. Whenever the dinner bell rings and all these fancy blokes and lasses fill the stairway, he starts to backtalk. Might just let the cat have 'em." McElroy laughed and shook his head. "Now, Ben, what is it you need?"

The doctor slipped him a piece of paper with four names—the ladies who were the first infected. Ben already knew about Matilda and where to find her cabin. But the Campbell sisters held second-class tickets and Minnie Pembroke a first-class. Beyond that, he was clueless.

"I could get in trouble for this, you know."

"I know. But who is going to find out? Those rooms won't be touched until we arrive in New York."

"I suppose that's true." He knelt in front of the counter and pulled out a lockbox. Ben heard the shift of metal. The canary continued to bounce, perhaps in disapproval of the doctor. McElroy returned and said, "Listen: If anyone asks where you got these, they were on the bodies. Got it?"

"Got it."

The purser slid him five keys.

The only two he cared about were the ones marked A deck. Those belonged to Minnie Pembroke. One was for sleeping and the other for her massive pile of luggage that she insisted stay nearby. Neither cabin had been touched since Evelyn Marsden and Mary Sloan found her unconscious.

As Ben stared at the unoccupied room full of suitcases and wire racks and bags and fancy trunks, he thought it would be a tight fit—but it would work. Before leaving, he looked out onto the promenade and then pulled the window shut.

After closing the door, he rummaged through Minnie's belongings. He felt bad about it, a little odd, but he needed to find a few things for Fiona and Reid. The hotel heiress did not disappoint. She'd been on a shopping trip in Paris—and she'd brought back nice things for her entire family, including a couple of her younger nephews. Or at least that was the talk at dinner.

He stuffed all that interested him into a canvas bag and then went back to the surgery. By now it was getting late, the bugler announced dinner almost an hour ago. Ben's belly rumbled with the promise of food but he wouldn't be eating yet. He banged on his door twice, careful to make sure Fiona was decent before entering.

She met him in the doorway and thrust a book into his chest. It nearly knocked him back in surprise and he gave her an odd, quizzical stare that quickly melted when he took the time to appreciate how nice she looked. She was still wearing the clothes from earlier, but after washing her hair, it dried chaotically like a crown of fire.

"What's this?" he said. "Dracula? That sounds familiar."

"Read it," she said.

"We've more important things to worry about."

"Trust me, you're gonna want to read it. It all makes sense now. I should've known after that tooth . . ."

"What are you getting at?" he asked, entering his cabin and placing the bag on the floor. Reid sat up straight in the chair, as if embarrassed that he'd been nodding off in a room that didn't belong to him.

"The crucifix, the stake . . . I know what we're dealing with—vampires."

"Vampires? What on Earth is that?"

"Something this bloke wrote about. A big, bad monster who drinks the blood of his victims and makes others do the same."

"And you learned that from a book?" He didn't think any of this sounded right.

"I did. And I'm bettin' this Stoker fella is an Irishman. This legend, it sounds an awful lot like the Abhartach."

"What's that?" he asked, leaning against the wall and folding his arms across his chest.

"We had vampires in Ireland long before we knew what to call 'em."

He turned to Reid. "Did she tell you all this?" He nodded. Ben said, "Okay, I'm listening."

"As the legend goes, a long time ago a powerful magician named Abhartach walked into a village near Londonderry and demanded that ten men were to slit their throats over buckets so he might drink it all. Some of 'em laughed at him but others were vexed, so they drove him out of the village and slit *his* throat. Then they buried him in a shallow grave."

Ben looked at Reid who seemed unfazed by such a vivid story. Fiona continued.

"The next night, he strolls into the village again, completely unharmed. Only this time he demands *twenty* men to slit their throats. They put him to death right then and there, then threw the body into the river.

"On the next night, he doesn't ask. He comes and takes his offerin' while they sleep. The village bows to him and he becomes known as the Ulster King."

"So what happened to him?" Ben asked.

"He got famous throughout the kingdom. Several chieftains showed up, this time with a mystic who claimed she knew how to kill him. They stabbed him and buried him standing up, but this is where the legend gets . . . tricky."

Fiona moved Reid aside so she could sit in the chair, then pulled the boy down on her lap. He didn't seem to mind—nor notice.

"My da always said that he went straight to hell and the devil didn't want him. He was too mean. So they made a deal—he could go back to the world of the living and would never die, but he had to abide by the Lord's rules. And that's what happened.

"The next time he showed up, he was horribly disfigured. Tall as a tree. Eight long fangs for breedin'. He snaps 'em off and the tooth burrows and wraps around the body's organs and takes over. Then his fangs grow back and he can keep on fatherin' more . . . children. I guess that's what you call 'em."

"What do you mean by the Lord's rules?" asked Ben, still unsure of this legend but finding it interesting.

"We've seen it. Just as Stoker wrote it in that book of his. The crucifix and sunlight. It's all bad for him, and for his children."

"So how do we kill him?"

She shook her head, smiling until she had dimples. "No, you don't kill the Abhartach. You merely put it to sleep. And you do that with a yew stake. Fortunately, we got one." She nodded to the corner where it lay in its nondescript blanket covering.

"So they didn't come for you. They came for *it*. They knew it was in your cabin."

"That's my thoughts, too. Still doesn't make me feel any safer. Here, read it," she said, and handed him the book again. "It may help you."

"Later. Right now, I have an idea." He picked up the bag and placed it on the bed, then unzipped it to reveal the nice clothes stuffed inside.

"What's all that?" Even Reid came to have a look.

"You two are getting a better boarding pass."

"What do you mean, Ben?"

"You're moving up to first-class."

And despite her insistence they would do no such thing, Ben excused himself long enough for them to dress in his cabin. He took a moment to assess the surgery, now empty of most of the bodies since O'Loughlin arranged for them to clear an entire room of refrigerated goods to store the overflow.

When Ben returned and knocked on the door, Fiona told him to enter. He didn't realize the dress was so extravagant. With her hair pulled back and tamed beneath a wide-brimmed hat, he thought she fit the part naturally. The long, button-down dress trailed the floor, revealing the shapely body he didn't even know was there.

Reid looked equally put-together with his crimped white shirt and black trousers. Even his hair was parted down the middle and oiled to stay in place—something Fiona must have found in Ben's shaving kit.

"You two slip into the role quite well."

"I feel ridiculous," she said.

"You look amazing." And that simple compliment was enough to make her stop tugging at her sleeves. She smiled and accepted it.

"So now what?"

"Now we go to your new room, up on A deck."

"*A deck?*" she said, turning pale. "I don't . . . I don't think we'd fool first-class passengers."

"Sure you can. The trick is to act like you don't care about any of those people."

"I *don't* care about any of them," she said.

Ben chuckled and started putting their old things in the bag. "Good, then you should have no problems. Say little or say nothing." He looked at Reid. "You'll show her how, right?"

He nodded.

"You look really nice, lad." Reid beamed over the compliment.

"And what are we to do up there?"

Ben shrugged. "Enjoy the days. Take him to the library, sit on the Boat Deck or dine in the Café Parisien. But by all means, lock the door and windows at night."

"What will you do?"

"I don't know. But I feel like . . .we have to find them. The vampires. The Abhartach."

Fiona shook her head. "We do not. I've lost too much and I'm near the last leg of my journey. For Reid. We have to survive until we reach New York and then the proper people will look into this."

Ben led them out into the hallway. He said, "Who are the proper people?"

"I don't know, but it's not us."

He nodded reverently. "I have to go. You're in cabin A-16." And then he handed her the key.

"Where are you going?" she asked.

He turned before entering the second-class library.

"To read."

BOAT DECK

9:03 P.M.

AFTER DINNER, BEN WALKED the upper decks. He was afraid of what he'd seen thus far, but he found a reserve of courage because of all the others. It seemed like a typical night aboard the world's finest ocean liner. Men and women were enjoying the cool air, listening to the band play jaunty tunes, and staring out into the unending void of the Atlantic.

Ben leaned over the railing and looked at the black, frothing water. The only lights were those perfect lines of circles, the reflection from the portholes.

He was about to go back inside, for he'd come out without his coat and was chilled, when he spied Thomas Andrews coming up the forward end of the Boat Deck with Captain Smith and Bruce Ismay in tow. The captain and the designer both entered through the first-class entrance, but Ismay lingered, the cigarette ashes blowing back in his face. For a moment, Ben thought he was going to follow the captain but then their eyes locked and Ismay's entire countenance changed.

Ben acknowledged with a curt nod, but Ismay had the smug look of a man who had something to say. He flicked his cigarette over the railing and approached, tugging at his dinner jacket to keep the flaps from blowing wild.

"Mr. Ismay," said Ben politely.

"Aren't you afraid, doctor? It's well after dark."

Ben chuckled and leaned against the railing. To the left and below, the crowded third-class promenade. To the right, the long expanse of the Boat Deck.

"It's early yet," said the doctor. "But I'm sure the people below deck are having a far different experience."

"You know, this is all your fault."

"How so?"

"Those women were under *your* care. And under your care, they escaped. In an asylum, you treat the patients. But you bloody well tie them down first."

"There is nothing to tie down when they can become vapor, sir."

Ismay stared as if he didn't know what to say. But finally, he smirked and shook his head. Ben wasn't sure what the man believed anymore. He had seen none of the supernatural events the doctors had witnessed, but one couldn't argue with the aftermath.

"Doctor York, I spoke with our most prominent passenger tonight at dinner. Mr. John Astor."

"Yes, I treated his wife for overbreathing. Nice girl."

"Uh huh. You also told Mr. Astor to keep his wife's crucifix close by. That it wasn't safe on the ship."

"It isn't."

Ismay looked around, a frantic grimace on his face. But then he focused on the doctor, narrowing his eyes to slits. He came close—Ben smelled the after-dinner scotch on his breath.

"You listen to me, doctor," he said, speaking slowly and deliberate. "My father left me this company. This ship is my legacy. It is the prize that I've waited on for so long. A lot of bad things have happened, but it's nothing the White Star Line and its lawyers and purse can't handle."

"Sir?"

"I'm ordering you to stop stoking panic. We only have a few days left of this voyage and then it'll all be fine. But if you continue down this path, I'll see to it you never set foot on a White Star Line steamer ever again."

Ben chuckled and met the man's chastising stare. "This is my last voyage. So don't worry." He walked off but Ismay grabbed his arm and pulled him back.

"Weigh your actions, Benjamin. I can be an awful man under the right circumstances." He let go of Ben's arm in time for a pair of ladies—Dorothy Gibson and her mother—to walk by. Ismay's face changed as surely as a street performer changed acts.

"Evening, ladies! I hope you're ready for Mr. Hartley's encore. I hear they're setting up in the lounge!"

And then the three of them were gone.

Ben smoothed his jacket and thought about what the man had said. It chilled him to the bone, but it was hardly surprising. Ismay was a powerful man and he would do whatever it took to stay that way. It would be wise to give him a wide berth on the ship.

But the moment Ben entered through the first-class entrance with the frosted dome blotting out the stars above, he found the man talking to Quartermaster Hichens just by the purser's office. Ismay gave him an icy stare, then stuffed a cigarette into his mouth. Ben dropped his head and continued on down the steps.

He ended up in the second-class library on C deck, a stone's throw from the surgery. As he stared at the darkness through the black windows, he thought of how awful it had been for the readers to see Clarence lumber by, smoking and sizzling.

At this hour, the library steward had gone to bed, but the doors remained unlocked and a few passengers, those wanting an escape from the constant noise and music, found themselves there. By electric light, they wrote letters or shorthand telegraphs to be sent via the Marconi radio in the morning. Ben sat by the windows at a small table, reading through the book that should've never found its way into the hands of a boy young as Reid.

It was all falling into place—the creatures mentioned in the tale were real. Ben read all about Dracula, not as a work of fiction but as a cautionary story for how they should proceed with their own problems. The master vampire was powerful indeed, but as they'd seen with their own resident creature, vampires had weaknesses.

Ben needed to act during the day. If this Abhartach slept while the sun was up to recharge his power, then he'd be easy to kill, or at least more vulnerable. There were a few differences in the vampire lore of Dracula, but enough cross-referencing to feel confident in fighting the beast.

So far, they only had two weapons—a crucifix, which could not kill them, but only weaken and distract them—and the yew stake. Any piercings of the heart were good enough for the infected vampires, but according to Fiona, a yew stake was needed to kill Abhartach.

No, not kill. Put to sleep. Ben wasn't entirely sure, but he thought the creature had been on the ship since the beginning and that someone had woken it. The yew stake was bloody when Reid found it, meaning it was already in the creature. And then, either intentionally or by accident, it was removed. After that, the master vampire was awake.

Ben was reading the passage of Van Helsing's order of destroying the boxes of dirt from Dracula's homeland when someone touched his shoulder. The book skated across the table and Doctor Simpson quickly rushed ahead of Ben to grab it. He said, "Sorry, doctor. I should've announced myself. Dracula, huh? Sounds odd." He handed Ben the book and placed his medical bag on the table.

"Yeah," he said. He returned the book to his pocket, forgotten—and forgotten with it, the last passage that would later become the most important one of all.

"It's quiet," said Simpson. "I suppose we'll wake to more death."

"Probably so."

"There's been no more infected, so that's a good thing."

"I've been thinking about that," said Ben. "We killed one of them, two if we count Clarence, because they were lying in beds all over the ship. They're smarter than we think. Now . . . I think they're hiding them until they turn."

"But where?"

"Somewhere dark. Somewhere without many people."

"That can't be too difficult to find," said Simpson.

Ben shrugged. "Maybe not. But there are no portholes below G deck. This ship isn't even half full. They could be in a number of places."

Simpson shook his head and wiped his hand across his sweaty brow. "We're going to have our hands full. And we can't keep storing bodies in the freezers."

"New York is just a few days away, John. And then we'll have help." He hated to repeat Fiona's words, but after his altercation with Ismay, perhaps the best course of action *was* simply to survive until they reached America.

"That's what I keep telling my—"

A person ran past the window, full-gait toward the aft-end well deck. Both doctors stood and looked out just in time to see another zip by. Then another and finally a fourth person. Now they could hear screaming and shouting.

Ben was the first through the door with Simpson on his tail. They raced down the promenade, past several curious onlookers until they reached the entrance to the third-class assembly area. People were crowding around a man who was seated with his back to the wall.

He was gasping for breath, his hand clamped across his throat and blood gushing between his fingers. Simpson said, "Christ Almighty, I left my bag on the table! Keep pressure on it, gents!" And then he was gone, racing back to the library.

"It was a child! A damned little boy bit my throat clean out! Is it bad?" The man's wide, fearful eyes searched the crowd. "Where is Ennis? Ennis, is it bad?" He was screaming, a look of pure shock in his eyes.

"We're all going to die on this bloody boat!" someone from the crowd shouted. "We're all stuck here, waiting to meet the Lord!"

More cries of agreement. Ben knelt in front of him, feeling the warmth of the man's blood soak through his pants. He put a hand against his throat and held tight until Simpson returned with supplies and took over.

Ben backed out onto the well deck again and spun around, noticing all the eyes upon the scene. People were hanging above them from the third-class promenade. A few fancy ladies and gents up on the Boat Deck. Father Byles stood by the door of the library, leaning heavily on his cane. Horrified looks all around, and then Ben's gaze fell to the shadows on the promenade at the portside of the library.

A trio of red eyes watched the panic.

He wasn't sure what made his courage rise, but Ben chased after them, hopping a bench and ducking an exhaust vent on the well deck. By the time he reached the shadows, the eyes had dispersed, but he saw all the way down the promenade and figured they didn't go that way.

Ben rushed up the second-class steps until he reached B deck. It was empty, the pretty tile shiny under the flickering electrical lights. He raced down the hallway, spotting a trail of grey smoke near the far end.

Halfway down, the smoke stopped—and darkened until it resembled a cloud of coal dust. He stood still, watching as it reversed direction and slowly crept his way. Ben retreated a few steps toward the aft end of the ship just as the smoke settled only ten feet in front of him.

It billowed out, twisted and turned with a low groan that sounded like warping wood. In the middle, a tall, gaunt figure emerged, wearing a black robe with a high collar that surrounded most of its hideous bald head. Its mouth was turned in a grimace—only one fang remained in its jaw but the likeness to the drawing under the stairwell was unmistakable. Ben backed away, for that was the natural order of things when confronted with a nine-foot-tall monster. It spread its arms wide, and beneath it stood several others—three women, two men, and a little boy, all bearing fangs. Ben had to wonder if the child was Colin, turned after going to find his mother. They choked the hallway with their lingering smoke. Each time the lights flickered, Ben was left in the dark with their creeping red eyes.

He reached to his pocket but realized with dread that he'd left the crucifix with Fiona. Even worse, the yew stake was sitting in his cabin. All he had was the book and that wouldn't do him much good in an actual fight with a vampire.

Ben knew this was the end. These creatures and their darkness would cover the whole ship and by the time *Titanic* pulled into Pier 59 in New York City, the boat would run aground because there'd be no one left at the helm. As the creatures started forward, moving slowly to build the tension, to get Ben's blood pumping so their feeding wouldn't be so much work, he stumbled against something that didn't feel like the wall.

Quickly, he whirled around, sure that he'd been surrounded by more of them, but it was just Father Byles, standing in the middle of the hallway. Ben felt awful for this—the kind priest had followed him from the well deck, curious and concerned that Ben took flight so suddenly. He would go to the grave knowing he'd killed a man of the cloth.

"Father ... I ... I ..."

"Move aside, doctor."

Byles stepped past him. Ben whirled around, awestruck by this brave man who hobbled forward on his cane. But up came the walking stick, a move that curiously made the entourage of vampires stop. Even the tall master creature hesitated, arms dropping to the sides, the red dots flaring with malice.

The priest gave the cane a full turn until the bottom was at the top—it was a cleverly hidden long cross. Golden electric light gleamed from the crossbar. The bevy of vampires recoiled, a collective hiss that made Ben cover his ears.

"In the name of the Father, and of the Son, and of the Holy Spirit, I order you off this ship!" He took a step forward, the vampires retreating still. *Titanic* seemed to groan.

"In the name of the Father, and of the Son, and of the Holy Spirit, I order you off this ship!" His voice was louder, booming in the tight hallway.

The master vampire dared to advance, bounding past its minions. It raised a hand and brought its nails down on Byles's arm but the priest merely staggered back while keeping the cross high. The creature lumbered back, vexed by the pain in its eyes.

The priest repeated his blessing, louder each time, driving the creatures back down the hall. Ben watched as he fumbled for something in his pocket. He pulled out a small glass vial filled with a clear solution, and on the next reiteration of his blessing, he tossed it onto the floor at their feet.

The vial burst, the liquid sprayed, and any that landed upon the creatures turned to fire. Two of the women hit the ground, unable to turn to vapor with the flames leaping at their bodies. They rolled around, screaming and hissing and speaking words that Ben had never heard.

Byles retrieved another as the master vampire hunkered low, the shadows gathering around him. He was about to charge but the priest was ready.

"In the name of the Father, and of the Son, and of the Holy Spirit, I command you off this ship!"

The beast roared, blood and spittle flying from its lone tooth in little tendrils. It lunged, ready to barrel over Byles and his cross, but the priest tossed the vial at the last moment, striking the creature's face. It exploded in a shower of glass and water, but turned into smoke and fire. A sickly, rotten stench filled the air. The master vampire roared in pain and anger, but then it was twirling around, gathering shadows, gathering smoke until finally it was no longer there. Ben watched the infected vampires join it, diluting the dark smoke into a massive dingy grey cloud, and it all blew out the window and disappeared on the deck above them.

Boat Deck

THE KING WAS ANGRIER than he'd ever been. In his escape from B deck, he snatched an unsuspecting woman from a shadowed corner on the Boat Deck who'd been trying to smoke a cigarette away from her husband's watchful eye. The King tasted the exhale of smoke as he bit into her throat and sucked her blood. With only one remaining fang, feeding was difficult. But lucky for him, he was an evolved creature, so he turned the dying woman to the side and chomped her flesh with the hundreds of tiny teeth that hid behind his monstrous ones. When he was finished, he dropped her off the funnel.

He stood on the edge with his coterie. They were many, but not nearly many enough. By the time they reached New York, some four days later, he would have enough to maintain control of the ship.

"The situation has changed," said the King, listening to the delicious screams below as the humans discovered the body.

"His cross, my King," said his coterie of six women, two men, and a child. "It burns so hot."

275

"He is a hunter. Skilled in bringing us pain. If we're not careful, this could become dangerous."

"What would you have us do?"

"We'll be arriving in our new land in a few days. Titanic cannot communicate with other ships. Destroy the means."

"I will do it," said the woman who was once Pearl Sinclair. And then she joined the smoke coming from the funnel and disappeared inside it.

The King said, "Do not feed on anyone who is paramount to operating the ship. The cattle are yours. But be wary. You are being hunted."

"We understand the risk, my King. All for the glory of our new world."

"Yes," he said, growing weary. Maybe he started his coterie too soon. Maybe he should've eaten Ernest Burr and then retired for the rest of the trip. Either way, it was too late to change things now.

Just as Matilda was about to jump from the edge of the funnel, the King put a large hand to her shoulder and stopped her. She looked at him quizzically, her dead eyes vengeful and eager to serve.

"Yes, my King?"

"I have an important task for you. And this time, you'd better not fail."

F DECK

APRIL 14TH, 1912, 3:02 A.M.

IT HAD OCCURRED TO Erik Olsson, on at least three occasions in the last two days, that he should jump right off the ship. From the third-class promenade, the smack of the water would probably kill him instantly, saving any further pain. Matilda's disappearance would've been strange two days ago, but now she was one of the many unaccounted-for steerage passengers. He had no hope left. His wife may have been sick in the beginning, but now he believed she was dead.

And what of Colin? The boy was headstrong and defiant but he was a good child. Of all Erik's children, Colin was the one who related to him the most. He was certainly the only one who tried to communicate. And even though Matilda didn't know it, Erik had been learning how to speak English for the past two years. He couldn't understand most of it—the words were tricky and felt odd in his mouth, but he was making progress. One day, he hoped to join in a conversation. Life would be grand.

He gave up the search earlier that day. It was useless to ask for information. The most knowledgeable people certainly didn't come from Sweden. Sure, Erik made a few friends over drinks, but the only ones who spoke his language knew very little. Despite third-class having a perpetual party, no one had seen Colin or Matilda.

The only saving grace was the ease with which he found beer and ale. He drank his fill, night after night until the pain in his heart moved up to his head. Micky hated to see him wallow, and the boy was dealing with the grief in his own way. If not for him, Molly and Jack would've been much worse off. They'd lost their ma, and their da wasn't in any shape to parent.

But Erik couldn't end it all. The children needed him. Once they arrived in New York with hardly a penny, he'd pull himself together. He didn't want to think of that. He couldn't possibly shoulder that responsibility right now. So, he did what came naturally and jumped headfirst into a bottle of ale.

He staggered his way back from a card game up on deck. When he rounded the corner, there stood Matilda and Colin, hand-in-hand, eerie smiles upon their faces.

"My . . . my babies!" he said, and lunged forward. He wrapped Matilda in a tight hug and knew something was wrong almost instantly. She didn't feel like herself, nor did she smell the same. Her skin was so cold, as if she'd swam in the ocean. Colin was the same when Erik pulled him close. The boy was light as a feather, nearly floating.

"I'm sorry we've been away," she said, voice purring like a kitten. Erik separated and appraised his wife, horrified by her changed appearance.

"What's . . . what's wrong with you?" he asked.

"What do you mean? I'm fine!" she said.

He didn't notice that she was speaking his language.

"You're bleeding," he said, and rubbed her chin. She allowed him to touch her, and she even remained still when he noticed the fangs. "What . . . what's happened, my love?"

"We're free, Erik. We can be whatever we want now."

"Papa, it feels good," said Colin, his eyes like little flickering dots of light.

Erik was trembling but he refused to look away. He put his hand on Matilda's cheek and ran it down to her neck. When it reached the nub on her throat, she snatched his fingers and pushed them away.

"I want you to be a part of our new world. Do you want that, Erik?"

"I do. Yes, I do," he said.

"I need you to do something for me. It isn't hard. But it's so very important. Will you do it for me, love?"

"Please, da?" chimed Colin.

"Of course."

He wasn't sure how it happened, but the next moment he looked around, they were standing outside their cabin. The door was open and Micky and the little ones were sleeping soundly.

Matilda said, "I need you to go into your lockbox and get your gun."

"My gun?" he said, horrified. "It's my family's last possession. We said we'd keep it hidden until we got to America so I could sell it."

Matilda crept close and put a chilly hand to his cheek. "You don't need to do that now, *älskling*. He will make everything right for us. No more hunger, no more pain. And no more need for money."

Erik wasn't sure what she was talking about but he nodded. How could he ever say no to a request from his wife and son?

Gingerly, he stepped across a sleeping Jack and fumbled through his things until he found the lockbox—which, incidentally, wasn't locked at all. He grabbed the pistol and stuffed it into his waistband, and then padded his way back out. Erik never knew how important it had been that his family remained asleep.

Back in the hall, Colin said, "Is it loaded?"

He checked to make sure, then nodded.

Matilda wrapped him in a hug and he felt his son's tiny fingers along his waist. She whispered into his ear, "We'll be together soon. You'll see. But for now, you have to do your task and you have to do it well."

"I will. But . . . I don't understand. What is it?"

He blinked a few times and that's when he noticed the gun was in his hand. Erik did a full-circle, now finding himself in a different part of the ship—somewhere he'd never been before. Just in front of him was the fancy grill of an automobile.

Movement from the side startled him so badly that he raised the gun, only to have it peeled out of his hand. He felt pressure on his finger and he worried it would break. But then the gun was back in front of him, offered by the grip.

A giant creature stood over him, its face a mask of pure rage. It was so old and decrepit that the burn wounds across the temple and forehead were unnoticed.

So were the eight missing fangs.

"Guard me with your life," it said, and then pushed the lid off a large wooden box. The creature's bottom half turned to black smoke until it was wafting inside it. Seated, it added, "Kill anyone who comes near. Do you understand me?" Erik slowly nodded.

The creature stared at him for a moment, perhaps gauging the Swede's resolve. But Erik would do whatever it took to make his family whole again.

Finally, the beast lay back and pulled the lid on top.

R.M.S. Titanic

Sunrise

ALTHOUGH IT WOULD NOT be *Titanic's* worst night, the hours before its last sunrise were among the bloodiest. A cool, almost unbearable wind kept most of the passengers indoors, but it didn't matter. The monsters running unopposed still found easy prey.

Eugene Daly sat on the steps between F deck and G deck playing his uilleann pipes. The sound belted all the way down the hallway but he didn't care. He loved the song—it was a childhood favorite, after all. His music was so loud, in fact, that when Lillian Goodwin, a third-class passenger traveling with six other family members, came down the steps behind him to ask him to stop, he never heard her scream. She jerked toward the ceiling, struggling and squealing and thrusting her bare feet until they gently stopped, blood dripping off her toes and splattering on the steps.

On the forward end of the deck, beyond gates that kept the classes separate, pool steward Isaac Widgery was wishing he could get off to bed but first-class passenger Howard Case wanted to take another lap across the water. Isaac excused himself to the drying room to collect the man a heated towel. When he returned, Howard was lying face-down in dark, bloody water, dead as a dormouse.

Just above their heads on E deck, six-year-old Robert Spedden was kicking a ball down Scotland Road after sneaking out once his parents fell asleep. There weren't many people so he ran at a full gait. But then the ball disappeared through a darkened doorway that stank of coal fire and blood. Rather than retrieve it, he returned to his parents' cabin and shut the door.

On D deck, Father Byles and Ben barricaded themselves in the priest's cabin. Byles used a thick wedge of charcoal to draw crosses on all the walls, the door, and the porthole window. Ben fell asleep while the man was still mumbling blessings over the whole cabin.

On the aft end of C deck, Matilda Olsson and Catherine Campbell drained the last dregs of blood from lift operator William Carney and then dumped his body over the railing. If any of the humans possessed the same keen vision as the creatures, they would've seen around twenty other shapes, bobbing around in the wake of the steamer's prow.

Higher still, the carnage was more understated but still felt. Edith Rosenbaum had just spilled her third cognac across her breast because she was too drunk and too sleepy to hold the glass steady. When a pair of passengers raced by her door, screaming and yelling for help, she simply dabbed the mess and rolled back over.

In a cabin across the deck, Reid sat in a chair, unable to sleep even though his mother seemed to have no trouble at all. The linens smelled odd here, and it took a moment to realize it was the unfamiliar scent of absolute cleanliness. He was thinking about Colin and how the boy was either dead or one of them now and hadn't asked for either awful thing. And that made him sad and he dropped his head and cried silently into his knees.

Margaret 'Maggie' Brown, who'd earlier passed a pale-faced and frightened Robert Spedden on E deck, made her way up the first-class staircase to see a thin line of blood running across the outside of the frosted dome. For a moment she thought there was a body lying with it, but it was too dark and the glass too thick. And then, the shape that may or may not have been a person, lifted away.

On the Boat Deck, Harold Bride and Jack Phillips were wide awake, attempting to fix the broken Marconi radio. Neither could explain how the wires had come disconnected, nor how the terminals were all bent and broken. Harold suggested sabotage but Jack wouldn't hear it. Who on this ship would want to do such a thing?

And perhaps the safest place of all, further down the Boat Deck toward the bridge and the cluster of officer cabins. None of the decorated men heard the noise, nor did they see the floating bodies washing past the hull. Visibility at night was low, after all.

By the time the sun was rising in the east, just beyond *Titanic's* bow, the creatures were back safe in their hiding spots, tucked away from common people and the watchful eyes of the crewmen. It was a cold morning, would be an even colder night. The sun ticked higher in the sky, casting long shadows across the waking deck.

It would be *Titanic's* last sunrise. The last touch of heat. The last time the etchings on the wood and metal would be read. The last day for music, for hot presses in the kitchens, for printed menus and iceberg warnings, for laughter, for amazement of man's greatest design. And for most, life.

It was the silent, creeping death that would grip the ship and everyone on it in a mere seventeen hours.

D Deck

THE LAST THING BEN remembered was Father Byles ushering him downstairs and into a cabin. He didn't even know what deck they were on—his survival instinct had flooded him with adrenaline. He and Byles talked for a little while but none of it made sense. Ben had seen enough patients in shock to recognize it in himself. Once they were safe, the adrenaline evaporated and his body succumbed to the weariness. After that, a ship's worth of vampires could have stormed in without waking him.

When he finally did open his eyes, it was morning, although he didn't know what time. For all he knew, he'd been asleep for days. Byles was nowhere to be found—only his bags and a steamer trunk.

The cabin was nice—not quite first-class but certainly not steerage. Second-class, for sure. Only now the walls were all marred by thick charcoal crosses. Ben wasn't sure if these would work to keep out the monsters but so far, they were safe.

The door opened and in walked Byles with his tie loose around his neck. He was leaning against the cane again, only now Ben would never see it as an old man's walking stick—it was a weapon against the monsters.

Byles had been trying to sneak back inside, but once he saw Ben awake, he dropped the ease in which he was entering and opened the door wide. Judging by the sounds behind him, no one was letting the most certainly horrible night ruin their day.

"Are you alright, doctor?" asked Byles as he pulled up the only chair to the bed. Ben was still in his uniform, wrinkled and smelling of sweat.

"Ben, please. And I suppose so. How did you know? The creatures . . . you faced them with no fear."

Byles knotted his tie. "I'm plenty afraid. But I've faced them before. Not these particular creatures but ones like them. The world is full of 'em." His eyes darkened and he added, "But never a master. That's the first time I've seen one of those. I can't fight him. I'm certainly not equipped for that."

Ben wanted to argue the point but let it drop for now. Instead, he said, "Thank you. I'd surely be dead had you not come along."

"Dead. Or worse."

"Yeah."

This discomfort hung in the air for a moment while Ben dwelled upon his words. Finally, Byles finished his tie and slapped the doctor on the leg and said,

"You need to have breakfast. Gather your strength. You're in for a busy day. Lots of . . . unpleasantness turned up on Titanic this morning."

"I figured as much," said Ben. The priest was a kind man and he didn't want to say outright that lots of bodies had piled up.

When Byles stood, Ben saw the top of a flask in his jacket pocket. Normally, he would've assumed the man had a love-hate relationship between God and alcohol, but he'd already seen this magic elixir in battle.

"What is that?" Ben asked, pointing.

Byles pulled the flap of his coat aside and said, "Blessed water. The power of God is pure anguish for them."

"Do you have more?"

Byles kicked open the steamer trunk, revealing at least a dozen bottles of the water, all in neat little rows. Next to them was a bundle of short, stout stakes, probably of oak or birch. Ben smiled, feeling a tiny breath of confidence.

"Why do you travel with these things?" he asked, waving his hand over the holy water and the high cross in Byles's hand.

The priest shrugged. "You never know when you'll stumble upon evil." He leaned down with a groan and pulled back his pant leg, revealing a healed, but horribly disfigured scar, like the bite of a wild animal—but Ben knew better. Byles said, "I was un-prepared once. Never again." He let the pant leg drop.

"So you're here to hunt these creatures, then?"

Byles chuckled and leaned back in the chair. "I'm doing no such thing. I'm officiating my broth-er's wedding in New York one week from today."

"It's good fortune you're here then."

"Yes. Good fortune, indeed." Ben didn't think the man saw it the same way. "You've been trying to help them, I see."

"We've a duty to protect all these people. You, with your knowledge and your weapons. You also have this duty."

"Wrong," said Byles flatly. "I've a duty to bring them to God. I'll try my best to quell the beasts while I'm here but I fear it may be too late. We don't know how many are on the ship now."

"At least seven," said Ben, making his best edu-cated guess based on the ones he'd seen so far.

Byles narrowed his eyes and shook his head. "Seven is a lot. Enough to take over the ship if they're smart. By the time we reach New York there'll be no hope for us."

"Unless we can find these things while they're sleeping."

"True. But this is a big ship and they're crafty. Or at least they're led by a creature that is. They were able to kill all night long and disappear without a trace. We cannot hope to put a stake through all of them."

"I've put a stake through one already," said Ben proudly.

Byles raised an eyebrow and said, "Did you? Tell me about it."

Ben explained how the creatures stormed Fiona's cabin and tried to make off with the stake, but he almost died by one of them before getting lucky and finding her heart with it.

"Where is this stake now?"

"In my cabin."

"Yew?"

"I think so."

Byles nodded. "Keep it close. Protect it. It's the only thing that can hurt the master."

"It's just a sharpened stick."

"It's more than that. It's the same one he's felt before. This particular stake has power over him. He knows you have it and his minions will do all they can to take it."

That put Fiona on his mind and it occurred to Ben that he'd left her to the wolves—not the creatures running rampant at night, but perhaps something more sinister—first-class passengers.

He stood and gave himself a stretch. "I have to go. I need to talk to someone."

Byles nodded and leaned against the desk by the bed.

"We could meet later for lunch if you'd like. Perhaps we can discuss how best to survive until we reach New York?"

He slipped past Ben and opened the door and gazed out into the hallway. Ben said, "Where are you going?"

Byles acted as if he'd been slapped. He straightened his tie and said, "It's Sunday, doctor. Just because there's monsters onboard doesn't mean we shouldn't have church service. You're welcome to come."

First-Class Dining Room

9:30 A.M.

IT WAS DIFFICULT TO tell how bad the passengers fared during the night, at least from first-class. Fiona had gone down to the dining room on D deck but the crew had already cleaned up whatever messes had been made. The air had a distinct acrid scent from the chemicals used to scrub the blood from the tiles. The White Star Line employees knew the route first-class passengers would take to reach their dining saloon and had planned promptly and accordingly.

She wondered why first-class passengers would have their dining hall so far below deck where they risked mingling with second-class passengers but Fiona worked it out. D deck was close to the center of the ship and would offer a less turbulent dinner should the waves become choppy. Just imagining the ship teetering side to side was difficult, for it may as well have been a floating city.

Having been a member of the upper class for less than twenty-four hours, Fiona realized it wasn't meant for her. Just watching these prim and proper people ready themselves for breakfast was an endeavor to itself. They had to find the best seating, the proper arrangement at the table, then there was cutlery to navigate. Fiona had never seen so many utensils for eating fruit. A lady across from her donned a pair of white gloves, as if the thought of handling peach fuzz was too much. The more she settled into this temporary role, the more she wanted to run from it.

"They say the Marconi machine is broken," said an elegant lady at the next table to a group of equally elegant passengers.

"Where on Earth did you hear that, Ida?" said the man to her left.

She looked wounded by his question. "My love, I asked the operator himself. I went up on deck and knocked on the door and told him I wished to send a message to Jesse."

"Don't trouble him with our happenings," said the man.

"He would love to hear all about it! The boy loves a good mystery! But alas, it won't happen. Those gentlemen upstairs say they'll be lucky if they can get it fixed before we arrive in New York."

Fiona turned away from the conversation when she saw Reid and another woman across the room staring at one another. The lady looked perturbed but that was to be expected. Fiona took Reid's arm and pulled him close.

"She doesn't like you staring."

He nodded.

"You can go back to your eating now. He's fine," said Fiona to the woman, probably louder than she needed. A few forks hit the table to the right, but otherwise people were silent. The lady's face darkened and she glowered, but only for a moment. Her eyes quickly averted to her food.

Almost immediately, Fiona felt embarrassed. Would she always fight Reid's battles for him? Surely the boy was capable, even without a voice. As she watched him eat, she wondered if shielding him from the world was the best option.

They were seated at a half-sized table in the corner, an island to themselves. No one tried to talk to them, especially after the outburst. They didn't know Fiona was a complete lie. They simply assumed she came from money and hadn't figured out how to be wealthy yet.

But Reid was a dead giveaway. The woman across the room continued to stare, although her glimpses were quick. Fiona gently knocked Reid's elbows off the table and showed him which fork to use to spear his peaches. Fiona could have blended in but the old money knew that Reid was dining above his station.

"What's the first thing you want to do when we get to America?"

He thought about it for a moment, then tapped the hard spot in his pocket—a book.

"You want to read? Of course you do."

He shook his head, and since this was the extent of their communication for the past couple of years, more was imparted in that simple shake than what most people would realize. He wanted to read, yes, but that wasn't his only meaning.

Reid held up his hands and traced a large box.

"A building. A building with books?"

He nodded.

"A library?"

His face lit up. She knew where he wanted to go.

A few years ago, her sister visited them in Killarney and brought a picture book from all the places she'd traveled. Reid was interested in many of the locations but nothing quite like New York's grand library. There were no pictures of the inside but he didn't need them. He saw the size of the building and could dream. Fiona had nearly forgotten about that—and now she would do whatever she could to make sure he saw it.

"Do you want to go for some air?"

He nodded, grabbed an apple from the plate in the center of the table and put it in his pocket. Then they slid out and made their way back up on deck.

It was a cold, dry morning but lucky for them, Ben had secured fancy coats to go with their fancy clothes. Not many people were deterred by the weather—at least the skies were clear. It was a fine day for sailing.

Reid stood on the railing of the Boat Deck, watching the water far below them. Something about the sun that morning cast it in a shade of blue that was the most beautiful color Fiona had ever seen. It was so pure. And it joined beautifully with the icefloes far to the north of the ship.

If they squinted, they could see them—jagged white icebergs rising out of the water like dragon teeth. They were probably massive—some taller than the ship. But they were far away and the captain—a man with thirty years of experience at the sea—knew how to navigate these cold waters.

Titanic had several ice warnings that morning, the information published on clipboards around the ship. Fiona didn't care to read them—weather was always a dreadfully boring subject.

After only a few minutes of relaxing on the lounge chairs, Reid grew bored and Fiona grew cold. They went back inside and she wondered how well her clothes would be received back on her original deck with the steerage class.

They didn't see many passengers in the hallways, not because they were afraid but because a man by the name of Father Byles had orchestrated two church services. While Captain Smith was presiding over an Anglican ceremony in the first-class lounge (foregoing the planned lifeboat drill), Father Byles split his time between mass in the second- and third-class lounges.

Fiona and Reid only caught the latter one and once it was over, the people dispersed and she found Ben seated at the front. When he saw her, he stood straight as an arrow and smoothed his hair back.

"Fiona. You really shouldn't be down here."

"It's where we belong," she said. "I didn't take you for a religious man, doctor."

He flashed a look to Father Byles, who smiled and raised an eyebrow. Then he said, "There's a lot we need to discuss."

"The doctors are no longer the specialists," he told her later as they sat in the second-class library with Father Byles. It was busy—lots of people were penning letters or checking out books.

"How many did you see?" Fiona asked.

"There's at least six of 'em. And . . . one of them is a child. A little boy. I never met the lad, but I assume it's Colin."

Reid looked up, eyes welling with tears. The heat rushed to his cheeks, but he couldn't express why he was so upset.

"So you're like Doctor Van Helsing," Fiona said to the priest and realized how odd it must have sounded.

Father Byles nodded and smiled. "You're referencing Abraham's book. Dracula."

The mention of it made Reid look up from his newest tale, something far less violent than vampires and those who hunted them. He smiled, happy that someone else had read it.

"You know the book?" asked Ben.

"I certainly do. Abraham was one of us. A hunter. He did the world a service by writing it, although the information doesn't apply to all vampires."

"How many of them are out there?"

"Plenty, but the master aboard this ship is the worst I've ever seen. He is no Dracula. He is far more powerful."

Ben told her, "You were right. This is the Abhartach."

Byles nodded. "A vampire we all thought was lost forever. But there's no mistaking it now. The fangs . . . you see, this is how he spreads his filth. According to legend, he can make eight vampires every night. The fangs continue to grow back."

Ben explained Clarence Clarke and how the man became feral once the fang was removed from his throat, as if his connection to the master vampire had been severed.

Fiona asked, "Is there no way to save the people who've been infected?"

Byles shook his head somberly. "No, my dear. Those people may walk and talk as before but I assure you, they're dead. Their soul no longer lives in their body. This is a horrible burden for them because they only know suffering. It is a mercy to kill them."

Reid looked up from his book, nearly blinking back tears, and returned to reading. No one seemed to notice, so lost were they to Byles's knowledge.

"So what can we do?" Ben asked. "To help as many people survive the voyage as we can."

Byles considered for a moment and then said, "We need to convince the captain to speed up and to send word ahead to New York. I have contacts there who can come aboard the ship and cleanse it. I'm just one man. You're all . . . you have the right heart, but this goes far beyond us."

Fiona said, "Won't be getting word out anytime soon. The Marconi machine is broken, or so I've heard."

Byles nodded solemnly. "That's not surprising. We're dealing with a smart master."

Fiona smirked. "He's a king. A dead ole Irish king has taken over."

Ben conceded the point. "I fear we're an island to ourselves."

Byles said, "That we are, doctor. You all should hide. In the daytime, stay outside. Travel the ship in groups. And above all else, go nowhere that harbors shadows. Pray we do not have a worse attack."

Fiona chuckled, a change of tone that was enough to garner even Reid's attention. She said, "Worse? How can it get any worse?"

"Right now, they're feeding from the steerage class because they don't want to jeopardize the ship. If we stop or if another vessel were to catch wind of what's happening, the vampires would die because we'd all abandon the glorious Titanic to a rescue ship." Byles waved his hand around the room, to the patrons reading and talking about the ship's happenings. "Without them, without *blood*, they'll starve."

That made Fiona realize a horrible truth. "If the vampires think their food supply is ending . . ."

"They won't care to even hide anymore," said Byles. "Or be selective. It'll be a feeding frenzy."

Ben said, "That's why we need to warn everyone. We can go around knocking on doors if we have to.

You have all those stakes and bottles of water. Let's hand them out to the passengers."

"We can do that, but the passengers won't listen to me," Byles said. "I'm just a crazy old preacher who doesn't align with half of 'em."

"But us. The doctors." Ben turned to Fiona. "And you."

"Me?" she said. "Those rich bastards can smell the low-class on me."

Ben said, "Maybe so. But not third-class. Dressed like that, those folk may listen to you."

She nodded, although it would likely have the opposite effect that Ben wanted.

He chuckled and shook his head. "Ismay will be furious."

Byles said, "He'll be grateful to save at least some passengers."

"Let's hope so," said the doctor.

MOST OF THE FIRST-CLASS passengers were polite to Ben but he didn't think any of them would heed his words. He ran into John Astor and his wife before dinner and it was almost as if they'd never met. A doctor's uniform garnered respect, but in the throng of society's high-class who were off to eat, he may as well have been steerage.

He found no better luck in talking to the Strauses, Benjamin Guggenheim, nor Dorothy Gibson. As he was about to approach Margaret Brown on the grand staircase, someone put an arm on him and pulled him aside.

Doctor O'Loughlin was in his finest attire, no doubt eating in first-class with someone quite important. Since it was Sunday, Ben assumed the captain but he was wrong.

"I'm off to have supper with Ismay," said the old doctor. "He's been askin' the officers where you might be."

"Why?" But Ben already knew.

"Maybe he's heard rumor of a desperate doctor tellin' all the high-class t'stay indoors. I told you these rich blokes won't listen. Might as well let 'em be fodder."

"I can't do that."

"Benjamin, this is above us. We cannot help anyone. I know you had your share of . . . tragedies, at your old hospital. That wasn't your fault and neither is this."

Ben nodded. "But we've a duty to help all that we can, doctor. Keep Ismay busy for me. Once I finish up on A deck, I'm going to lock myself in a room for the rest of the trip."

"Alone?"

"What?"

O'Loughlin smiled, his eyes beaming with happiness. "I see the way you look at her. And the way she looks at you."

Ben felt his face going red. "Yeah, well this isn't exactly the best environment to explore that, now is it, doctor?"

The old man chuckled and leaned against the railing for support before going down toward B deck. He said, "If we wait for the best environment, Benjamin, then we'll never make tough decisions. Whatever happens on this ship, remember that."

Then he placed a cigar in his mouth and limped down the steps.

R.M.S. TITANIC

Just like any normal night, passengers chose not to go straight to their cabins after eating. Some of them remained long after the final course of dinner (lamb in mint sauce) to talk politics or fashion. Some ventured off to the smoking lounges and several more out to the decks, despite the cold air.

Despite the murders.

Ben knew it was a losing battle with each person he warned. Up on the Boat Deck, he spoke with a pair of ladies—a Clara Bonnell and her niece Abbigail. Both listened for only a moment before deciding he'd lost his mind.

"We heard the awfulness of what happened to the Williamses," said Clara from beneath a feathery, wide-brimmed hat that she couldn't keep in place because of the wind.

"Don't forget Mr. Sinclair and Mrs. Mauve," said Abbigail. Both were first-class passengers who found their end just last night.

"Oh, right. Dreadful business. Just terrible."

"Indeed," said Ben. "So you'll go straight away to your staterooms then?"

The ladies laughed. Abbigail said, "We're supposed to play bridge with Dorothy later tonight. It would be rude for us to say no on such short notice."

"Your lives are at stake," Ben said, pushing the frustration out of his voice. "Surely you can play in the morning?"

At this, Mrs. Bonnell laughed and said, "Darling, I plan to drink enough tonight so that I skip over the morning entirely! Now if you'll excuse us." The girls headed down the promenade with locked arms, laughing at the doctor's gall the entire way.

And such was the case of all the passengers who couldn't see over their piles of money to the dangers just in front of them.

As he was passing the gymnasium, the door opened and the stagnant smell of sweat wafted out. He looked inside and found a pair of men on the stationary bikes but that wasn't what caught his attention. Ben entered, the steward approaching, probably to tell him to buy a ticket from the purser. He saw the doctor's uniform and took a step back, nodding politely.

Along the back, set against a wall of polished mahogany, hung a map of the world and a side view of the White Star Line flagships. Ben approached the latter, seeing the decks of *Titanic* laid out for the first time.

Something stirred in the back of his brain. He'd been all over this ship in the last few days—most of it, anyway. There was something Ben was missing. Something he wasn't seeing. Maybe it was the places where the creatures hid or the routes they were taking to snatch passengers and then disappear as if they'd never been there. This diagram was good, but he wanted better. He wanted blueprints.

And only one man onboard would have them. Thomas Andrews, *Titanic's* designer.

C DECK

A FEW OF THE passengers listened to Fiona's warning but not many. Whereas first-class didn't think this calamity could befall them, the steerage folk simply didn't care. Sure, the parents pulled their children closer, but for a lot of these people, life had been a constant race for survival. Sickness and disease took them all the time, so the atrocities happening aboard *Titanic* weren't enough to force them out of the assembly areas. After all, drink made everything better.

She wanted to go with the doctor but felt it was impolite to ask. Ben seemed to be one of the few who was taking things seriously, and the only one she trusted. There was something else there, too, but she wouldn't allow herself to think of that. The last thing Reid needed was for Fiona to muddy the waters of their life even further.

"Come on, with ya," said a voice behind her as she entered F deck from the stairs. Matron Wallis had a group of children, ushering them down the hallway. They looked somber, some of them so little they could barely keep up on their short, stout legs. A few clutched dolls and wooden toys. "We're going to have a great big party in the lounge. How does that sound?" A few of them mumbled something but none seemed pleased. Reid tugged Fiona's shirt and pointed to the group, curious of where they were going—and why.

Fiona took a knee and whispered, "I think . . . their parents are missing. So they're all going to sleep together where the matron can watch them. Very nice lady."

Reid nodded and swallowed a lump in his throat, then took her by the hand so she could lead him on.

The sun would soon set and she knew she needed to be inside her cabin with the door locked. While on C deck, she passed the surgery, wondering if Ben was there, then continued on to the library. He wasn't in there either, and when she came back out, a voice was calling out to her.

"Miss, miss!" it said. She turned toward the end of the promenade, and just where the well deck started was a sliding lattice gate that hadn't been there an hour ago. This was a thoroughfare from steerage class to first- and second-class. They were being segregated even worse now and Fiona thought it was ridiculous considering the monsters could turn to vapor.

The voice belonged to Micky, Matilda's oldest son. He was holding little Jack in his arms, the boy staring blankly with red-rimmed eyes. Fiona approached the gate and gave it a shake but it was locked. Micky looked disturbed.

"What's wrong?" she asked him, but knew it was a silly question. What *wasn't* wrong?

"It's me da," he said. "Gone missin', too. I'm thinkin' the worst! Little Jack here won't stop cryin' for him." Poor Erik was probably part of last night's slaughter if Fiona had to guess.

"When did you last see him?"

"Yesterday morning. He don't stay with us much. He . . . grieves to hisself. But he's been bummin' cigarettes from a fella downstairs. One of them engineers."

Scotland Road, she thought. That's the only place Erik could've come in contact with an engineer, unless he went much further down in the ship. She nodded and said, "But you can't reach that part now."

He shook his head. If there was a gate here, there were probably ones down below, too. At least for the night. And while it was possible for steerage to reach Scotland Road, it was no doubt difficult for most to manage it, especially with a hysterical child in tow.

"I'll look for you," she said. "I'll find him."

"Oh, thank you, miss. Thank you!" At his excitement, Jack stirred and started crying. "You hear that, Jackie? Da is gonna be back in a jiffy!"

And then he turned and disappeared through the doorway on the far side of the well deck. Fiona took the steps leading upstairs, not realizing that Ben was on the same deck, about to knock on Thomas Andrews's door.

Inside the cabin, Reid pulled on her hand and directed her attention to the window where the sky was starting to purple.

"I know, it'll be dark in an hour, but I won't be gone that long."

He shook his head, fearful.

"Listen, I have to do this." And she said no more in hopes of protecting the boy. But the truth was she didn't want to speak of how awful it had been for Reid when Emmet died, and she didn't want the same fate for Micky and his younger siblings. The Olssons had already lost their mother, after all.

Reid glanced at the clock on the mantle and Fiona said, "One hour, okay?" She handed him the crucifix and pushed it into his chest. He hugged it like a straw-stuffed toy. "You don't need protecting anyway. My brave little boy." Reluctantly, he nodded. She glanced over his shoulder to the window and the last rays of sunlight. It would be nightfall in *less* than an hour, but she didn't want to tell that to Reid. Fiona was trying to be brave, too.

Back below deck, she found most of the doors of the steerage class closed and locked. That was a good thing but, she wasn't so sure they were all in bed. Somewhere below she heard uilleann pipes and if she stayed completely still, the music from the general assembly area on the other side of the ship.

Fiona and Reid's old cabin was standing open, but the ash was gone. Someone had cleaned it. She gave a little shudder when she thought of how close they'd died in there. If not for Ben. If not for Reid . . .

The cabin next door—the Olssons'—was also empty. Micky had probably taken his siblings to be around people. For that, Fiona didn't blame him. Not everyone was like her—some found comfort in fellowship.

From F deck up to E deck, she encountered only one steward.

"Are you lost, love?" he asked, inspecting her fancy dress. "There's a better way to reach the Turkish Baths than this ole dirty hall."

"I'm not lost, thank you." She carried on but could tell the steward didn't believe her. Either way, he was content to let a fancy lady keep her pride.

On Scotland Road, she found it completely deserted—something that didn't feel quite right. A few of the doors were standing open, heat wafting out. She walked the length of it, listening to the sounds of the engines grow stronger the closer she got to the aft end of the ship. And when she paused at the dark doorway she'd ventured toward only a few days ago, a sense of dread overcame her.

Fiona had no way of knowing that Robert Spedden had paused here after kicking his ball into the void and promptly turned around without retrieving it. Nor could she know about engineers Hodge and Coy, who found the first boiler room so off-putting they kept their heads down whenever they walked through on their way to the engine room.

She took a step toward the darkness, knowing with every fiber in her body that this was a mistake, that this was where all the bad things on the ship were lying in wait for sacks of blood like herself to wander by. And as her foot crossed the lighted hall of Scotland Road and touched the darkened metal of the catwalk leading to the boilers, she knew something was watching.

The lights behind her flickered, enough to make her cast a quick glance over her shoulder. When she turned back, four sets of flames were staring at her, so close that she felt the cold wafting off the dead creatures' skin. She managed a scream, but it didn't matter. Strong hands grabbed her forearms and pulled her in until the darkness swallowed her.

A DECK

BEN HAD JUST RAISED his fist to knock on Thomas Andrews's door when it opened and a man appeared in front of him. It wasn't Andrews, but one of the Guarantee Group. Ben looked past him to a throng of others, all holding nearly empty glasses of scotch. Thomas Andrews recognized his dress at once and muscled his way through his men.

"Doctor? Is everything alright?"

"As right as can be, sir," said Ben. "I have an odd request. May I see your blueprints of the ship?" The others in the group looked at Andrews as if he'd asked for a large sum of money. *Titanic's* blueprints were a heavily lauded trade secret of the White Star Line. Rivals such as Cunard would love to get their hands on them.

But Andrews, polite and helpful as always, said, "Of course, doctor. Just a passing interest, might I ask?"

The men parted and let Ben into the room—Andrews's quarters were unlike any he'd seen on the

317

ship thus far, but he knew too little of architecture and design to pinpoint the reason. Still, it was fancy.

"I want to see if there's a pattern to the initial infections," he said. "It may help to see if they have anything in common."

"Of course," said Andrews. "You're referring to the vampires?" Ben cast him a curious look, to which the entire Guarantee Group began laughing. Andrews elaborated. "I'm a fellow Irishman, just like Bram Stoker. I read his book many years ago. You don't really think that's what's happening aboard the ship, do you?"

"I do. If you saw the things I did, you'd believe it too."

"No need to argue, doctor. I *do* believe you." He turned to his men and said "You best be leaving, boys. It's suppertime!"

As they filed out, Andrews crept close to whisper. "But the vampires aren't what you need to be worryin' about. It's Ismay. He's been effin' and blindin' about ye."

"I'm sorry to make trouble, sir. I just don't want more death."

"Neither do I. And if my documents help with that, then by all means." He waved his hand over the desk. "I'll be having my supper now. Lock the door when you leave, eh?"

He stepped out into the hall and pulled the door shut.

Ben forgot about the ship's calamities long enough to appreciate the artistry for creating blueprints. He'd seen the ones drawn up for his hospital but those were straightforward. This was like layering pieces of a puzzle, and the end result had to float.

For the first twenty minutes he examined the upper decks, noting that while the staterooms were large, the amount of open space meant there were few places the creatures could hide. Witnesses said that both Jonas and Rebecca Williams fell from one of the funnels, but Ben supposed they'd been dropped.

That led him to follow the exhaust route down into the boiler rooms and Ben wasn't sure why he didn't think of this before. Those places were dark and spacious enough to hold the creatures, but as Byles said, they wouldn't do anything to affect the ship's passage. They wouldn't feed on the stokers and firemen.

He then remembered the first boiler room wasn't lit and if he'd been smart, he'd have left the stateroom immediately and took as many able-bodied sailors to check it.

But another thought struck him as he bumped the desk and he heard a metallic ding from his pocket. He reached in and pulled out all the keys McElroy had given him. Checking the room numbers, he laid them on the blueprints, right above the corresponding rooms. These had been the first victims of the King. He cursed himself for not figuring this out sooner.

Minnie Pembroke, A deck, cabin fourteen. Sisters Catherine and Elizabeth Campbell, C deck, cabin sixteen. And then Matilda Olsson, F deck, cabin sixty-eight. The keys were almost in a perfect line. Ben inspected the side-view diagram and followed the line straight down the forward end of the ship until he reached—

Christ in heaven

—the cargo hold. The first corpse. The box. The damned monster moved straight up the ship, infecting as he went. Ben remembered the last passage he'd read in *Dracula*, how the creature had to make the trip to London sleeping on earth from his homeland.

In a box.

Ben had been standing right over the creature's bed and didn't even know it. He had to find Byles. They had to get to the cargo hold and destroy the box and whatever was inside it. Maybe it would weaken it, maybe not. Right now, it was the only chance they had to be more than just survivors.

He tidied Andrews's stateroom, then let himself out the door. As he turned the corner to head down the grand staircase, a powerful hand grabbed his arm and pulled him away. He almost lost his balance as he hit the wall. A beefy hand covered his mouth and something pressed into his stomach.

Quartermaster Hichens was staring at him with a grimace, his eyes narrowed to angry slits. Slowly, he pulled his hand away but the object at Ben's stomach remained. He looked down and Hichens pushed the gun harder into his belly.

"C'mon, friend," said Hichens. "We're going to go for a little walk."

R.M.S. TITANIC

The quartermaster kept behind him as they weaved through the crowd of men and women returning from *Titanic's* last dinner. He didn't know Hichens well, but assumed the man was crazy enough—and paid enough—to put a bullet in him if he made any sudden movements. For now, he was content to walk with the man, all the way down to E deck.

On the way, he found Father Byles on the staircase but the look on Ben's face kept him away. He turned his head to the side so that Hichens wouldn't realize the exchange. Ben hoped the man didn't get involved. Vampires were one thing. Politics and money were another.

Hichens pushed him into a room off the forward end of Scotland Road, just as the black and white cat who'd been sleeping in the cubby beside it, hissed angrily and ran off. Ben assumed this was the man's own cabin—it was messy and stank of cheese. There wasn't much room, so Ben sat on the bed while the beefy man hovered over him.

In just a few moments they were joined by Ismay who looked rather pleased to see the doctor with a frantic look on his face. He stepped into the room and moved to the corner, as if afraid of getting his fancy clothes dirty.

"Get him up," he told Hitchens, who then grabbed a handful of Ben's shirt and hoisted him to his feet.

"I can stand on my own," he said, but Ismay detected the sarcasm and gave Hitchens a nod.

The beefy man slammed the pistol into the corner of Ben's temple. His body crumpled but luckily the bed was there to catch him. After that, the world was swimming. He felt blood running down his cheek. Sweat fell from his brow and stung his eyes. And when he was making sense of the world again, he was sitting on the bed with his arms tied behind his back.

"So you've been stealing, have you?" said Ismay, holding up one of the keys McElroy had given him earlier.

"You don't understand," said Ben.

"I understand you've been a thorn in my side since this voyage started. No more. I relieve you of your duties, doctor."

Ben smiled. "You can't do that. Only Captain Smith or Doctor O'Loughlin has that authority."

As if bored, he plucked the gun from Hichens's hand and held it against Ben's temple—in the same spot where he'd been struck earlier. He tried not to wince.

"And what if I just dump you overboard, hmm? One more body isn't going to matter at this point."

Ben said nothing, for the man was so far gone into his fantasies that no words would've mattered. He closed his eyes, wondering if this high-class millionaire had the guts to pull the trigger.

Luckily, no. He handed the gun back to Hichens and said, "Watch him. Don't let him leave, at least for the night. Then we'll decide what to do with him."

"I have to relieve Oliver at ten, sir."

"Yes, of course," said Ismay, sliding back into his prim and proper façade. "Lock him in."

Both men left and Hichens pulled the door shut. He heard a shuffle outside. They'd propped something against the other side, obviously forgetting the doctor's hands were tied behind his back. Ben didn't know what to do—but Byles needed warned. Byles needed to know where the creature slept. He glanced over at the clock—it was just past eight.

A DECK

NIGHTTIME CAME AND HIS mother still wasn't back. He didn't think she would be—both knew when she left it was less than an hour before the sun would sink beyond the horizon. Reid had only hoped she'd been quicker. But now, nearly two hours since she'd left, he was starting to think something was wrong.

They're out there now, he thought. *Out there killing and infecting.*

He figured at a quarter to nine that most people would still be out—if they were emboldened by drink and good company. If he waited until the late hours, the ship would feel deserted, just like on the night Colin was taken.

After closing his book and setting it aside, he slid off the bed and approached the door. He looked out the window, as if staring long enough would will the sun back into the sky. Then he gingerly turned the lock and opened the door.

Out in the hallway, he heard voices. On the forward end, he saw a pair of people, or at least that's what he hoped he was seeing. The way the walls and lights converged on the vanishing point made it all blend together. Reid was feeling brave, so he stuffed the crucifix into his back pocket and left the room, heading toward the aft end just in case those people weren't people at all.

There was only one other place on this ship where his mother could be, and that was with the doctor down in his cabin. Reid had a methodical mind, much better than what teachers thought of him back when he could talk. So it wasn't difficult to see the layout of *Titanic* in his head and chart a path right down to C deck.

But on the stairwell, he heard beautiful music coming from further below. For a moment, he stood there listening, drawn in by the calming hymn. It was like being back in church again, a treasured memory of him and Erin and their parents. There had to be a dozen people down there singing, so he figured his mother just might be in the crowd.

Reid descended to D deck and ventured down the darkened hall. He saw the light and shadows and of course, heard the singing. There was even a piano, the melody crisp and beautiful.

He didn't know this place was the second-class saloon, nor that the Reverend William Carter was leading not a dozen, but one-hundred and six people, in song. A lounge steward at the back was pouring coffee into many rows of cups to stave off the chilly night.

Reid stood by the opened doors listening, calmed and captivated by the hymn. He'd never heard it before, but was moved by the words:

Eternal Father, strong to save,
Whose arm hath bound the restless wave,
Who biddest the mighty ocean deep
Its own appointed limits keep;
Oh, hear us when we cry to Thee,
For those in peril on the sea!

He listened to the refrain, leaned back against the doorway and counted heads, looking for his mother or even Ben. He'd have settled for Father Byles but none were to be found. Reid had spent the voyage either in steerage or first-class. None of these second-class people were familiar. The brave boy had a job to do. He couldn't listen to the pretty music all night.

Back on the staircase, he climbed to C deck and turned toward the surgery, paying no attention to the gate strung across at the edge of the prom-enade. He was about to push through the doors but saw the old man walking down the hall—Mr. Dunford. He was a crabby fellow and made no secret that he didn't approve of Reid and Fiona staying in the doctor's cabin.

Once Mr. Dunford disappeared down the hallway, Reid stepped to the door and tried the knob. He didn't expect it to turn, so when the door swung in, he stood there for a moment, looking perplexed yet satisfied. Quickly, he hurried in and closed the door.

He switched on the light and found no one. Ben's bed was made up and the chairs were straight. The notepaper and pen set were placed perfectly in the middle of the desk. The doctor had not been here tonight.

Reid was about to leave, perhaps to check the third-class promenade where he'd seen bodies a couple nights ago when he spied a bundle sitting against the wall.

The stake.

Now, he was feeling *really* brave. Reid placed it on the bed and unrolled it. There was still a smear of blood on the tip but it was dry now. He gave the stake a swing, then a stab, feeling as if he could take on a vampire, despite being a mere eight-year-old boy.

But this was awful business, he thought. His mind raced back to Father Byles's words, about how those infected were living in anguish and how it was a mercy to put an end to them. Could he do that for Colin? Reid wasn't sure, but he would try. Colin was a sweet boy who didn't deserve anguish.

He opened the door and looked toward the forward end but saw no one. Then he turned to the aft end just in time to see hands reaching for him. Reid tried to squeeze back into the room and shut the door but he wasn't quick enough. The stake clattered to the ground as he was hoisted into the air.

"What's this? Snooping around?" said Mr. Dunford. "You're that boy from steerage. Whose clothes you got on?"

Reid tried to fight him, but Mr. Dunford grew weary of his 'unwillingness' to give an answer. He threw Reid over his shoulder and stooped down to pick up the stake. Then, he started walking toward the forward end of the ship.

The boy beat his fists against Dunford's back. Stopping only once, he adjusted Reid on his shoulder and said, "If you don't stop that I'm gonna throw you down the steps and this twig over the railing! And you'd better hope I don't get the two of ye mixed up!"

He continued on, moving further away from the doctor's cabin and the last familiarity Reid had aboard the ship.

The lights flickered.

Down the hall in the direction Reid faced, a tendril of smoke bled through the gate and materialized on the closest side. A tall, gaunt man with an enormous bulge on his neck dropped to all-fours and slowly stalked Mr. Dunford.

Reid screamed only air.

He beat his fists on the old man's back but it only hastened his footsteps. The monster grinned, its fangs gleaming in the flickering lights. They were already bloody—this thing had fed tonight.

Reid continued to pummel Mr. Dunford but the old man just stopped to put him on the other shoulder, closing the gap between them and their predator.

Changing tactics, Reid reached behind his back, over Mr. Dunford's arm and tried to get in his pocket. The old man was still fighting him. Each time his fingers touched metal, the old man readjusted and thwarted his progress.

By now, the vampire was upon them. It stood up and wiped its chin, then licked the blood away from the top of its hand. The creepy smile never left, nor did the flames diminish in its eyes.

It reached up, ready to pull Reid off the old man's back when he finally wrestled the crucifix from his pocket. He held it up for the creature to see—and the hallway was filled with an inhuman screech as it fell back and shielded its face from the holy trinket.

At such a noise, Mr. Dunford dropped Reid and he stumbled forward. The stake clattered to the floor. Reid banged his head on the tile but kept his hold on the crucifix, which was the most important thing of all.

Flipping around, he faced the vampire who was crawling toward him. It snatched him by the shoe and dragged him a few feet when the cross came up and sent it reeling away. Reid gave chase, feeling braver than ever to see the beast turn to vapor and disappear through the gate at the far end, just the way it had come.

And without even checking on Mr. Dunford, he snatched the stake and ran off to find his mother. He kept the crucifix close to his heart, just like she showed him.

THE DARK
9:20 P.M.

EVERYTHING ABOUT THIS PLACE was an assault on the senses. The stench of blood hung in the air. Coppery and thick. It mingled with the smell of metal and coal and smoke. A deafening, repetitive crash sounded below her, and the air on her skin was cold and tinged with fine dust.

She remembered what happened—the powerful hands pulling her into the darkness, the tight, icy grip on her throat so she didn't scream, her head banging against the metal catwalk as they dragged her through the bowels of the ship.

At first she thought she was blind, but then noticed an orange glow beneath her, toward the left side of her body. It was so dark and so loud. This place was maddening. Just in front of her, a pair of red eyes blinked and stared. Her first instinct was to run off, but she felt them next to her.

Fiona's hand slapped at her throat, fearful that she would find one of the angry-looking knubs. Much to her relief there was only warm, sweaty skin.

"You aren't one of us yet," said Matilda in the darkness. She was close enough that Fiona could smell the coppery sludge on her breath.

"Where are we?" she asked. Her vision was adjusting to the dark.

"Somewhere safe. Somewhere the humans won't check."

And then she pieced it all together—they were in the first boiler room, standing atop the unlit furnaces. If anyone walked to the engine room, they wouldn't see a group of creatures above them. As Fiona's eyes took in more of her surroundings, she counted four shapes next to Matilda—they were hanging from the underside of the catwalk, as if attached by glue. There were more, she knew. These were the ones who stayed behind to guard her.

On the next catwalk over were two people lying on their sides, breathing deep as if it were difficult. Their eyes were clamped shut, throats bulging. These were vampires still undergoing the change.

"You oughta be thankin' me," Matilda said, her voice somewhere between sweet and raspy. "They all wanted to eat you but I told 'em you'd make a fine addition to our coterie. You . . . and that boy of yours."

Fiona hoped Reid was still safe in the room. Maybe he was asleep by now, crashed against the bed with a heavy book across his face.

"We'll find him. The King wants the stake back. Do you still have it?"

Fiona thought it serendipitous that Matilda used the same lofty title for the master vampire. After all, it made sense because it was currently ruling *Titanic*.

Matilda grew irritated by Fiona's lack of acknowledgement. "No matter. Once he tastes you, we'll know everything."

"And where is this King of yours now?"

"He'll be here soon, I'm sure of it." Matilda put a hand against her cheek—it was like a block of ice. "We aren't your enemy, sweetheart. Don't fight us. He'll make you whole, Fiona."

"I'm already whole."

She laughed, and was joined in by the others as if it were an involuntary response—three women and one male, who quickly giggled and then returned to quiet stoicism.

"He will take away your pain, your fears, your silly dreams that go nowhere."

"You know nothin' about my pain."

"But I will soon. We're all together. And when this boat pulls into New York on Wednesday, we'll proclaim from the tallest buildings that our time has come. We will rule the nights. Don't it sound wonderful? Don't you wanna join us?"

Fiona chuckled and crossed her arms over her chest. "I think I'd rather die than become like you."

Matilda let the insult hang in the air for a moment. The way her eyes flickered, Fiona was certain she was going to lash out, perhaps take a chunk from her neck. But no, the tension bated and the vampire took a step back, as if wounded.

She said, "Our King will arrive shortly. And when he does, he'll decide that for you."

QUARTERMASTER HITCHENS'S CABIN

11:10 P.M.

IT TOOK LONGER TO untie his hands than he thought it would. That hit on the temple gave him an awful headache and his vision was blurry for the first hour after waking up. But as he lay on the bed, he rubbed his wrists together until the knots gave, and he could finally slip his hands out. But this still didn't help him get out of the room.

Not only was the door locked, it was also barricaded from the other side. The handle wouldn't even turn. *Titanic* was a stout ship and her doors wouldn't easily break. Ben threw his shoulder into it several times until the rattling made his head hurt even worse. Even under more typical circumstances, he didn't think he could muscle his way out.

So, he sat on the bed and waited. Eventually, Hitchens would need to come back to sleep. The ship on the other side of the door was quiet, but if he listened close enough, he was sure that he heard screams. A frigid wind rushed through the porthole—so frigid that he quickly closed it, shutting out the salty air for good.

He was nodding off to sleep when he heard a noise in the hallway. So happy he'd been to be rescued that he rushed to the door and banged without thinking first. This was probably someone Hitchens sent to check up on the doctor. Behind the door, the chair lifted away with a metallic scrape and then the handle turned. Ben expected to be punished for untying his hands, so he sat on the bed and waited for it.

But it was Father Byles, a frantic look upon his face.

"Doctor? Christ Almighty, what have they done to you?" He rushed forward and took Ben's face in his hand and turned it to the side to inspect the purpling knot above his eye.

"I'm fine, but we have to get out of here." Ben didn't wait for him to agree. He stuck his head into the hallway and looked around, saw no one, and then walked through until he reached Scotland Road. Byles was chasing behind him.

"I never would've imagined Ismay would go to such lengths! How awful! If I were you, I'd lodge a formal complaint with the White St—"

"I know where the King is sleeping," said Ben. "In the cargo hold. I've seen his bed."

This stopped Byles from uttering another word. He said, "It won't be there now. It's out hunting."

"But what if we destroy its bed? What then?"

"All master vampires must sleep on consecrated earth from the place they were born. If we get rid of that, he won't be able to rest and he'll grow weaker by the day."

"Then I say we go make the damned thing uncomfortable." Ben turned to the stairs and raced down them two at a time.

SCOTLAND ROAD

11:30 P.M.

IF REID WOULD HAVE been twenty seconds earlier, he would have seen Ben and the priest rounding the corner to F deck. He probably wouldn't have paid attention, so intent was he on the black boiler room entrance. It was all making sense now—the night Colin disappeared, the night the vampires chased him into a cubby beneath the stairwell. All the bad things were right there, beyond that darkened doorway. Reid squeezed the crucifix in his right hand, the stake in his left.

Nervously, he stepped onto the catwalk and waited for his eyes to adjust. The smell of coal and fire was strong in the air, as was the coppery stench of blood. It was nearby, and he hoped it didn't belong to his mother.

He heard agitated voices down below—angry enough to project over the roar of the engine room, but still too far away to understand their words. Reid was quiet as a church mouse as he gingerly descended the catwalk until he was in the boiler room. The ground was slick with coal dirt, but he hardly paid attention. As his eyes continued to adjust and he attuned his ears to what was happening in front of him, the world fell away.

"The King isn't coming," a man said in a raspy, angry voice.

"He's out hunting," cried another, a dainty sounding woman. "As we should be!"

"We will wait for him!" said a voice that Reid knew belonged to Matilda.

The man, growing more agitated, said, "*You* can wait for him. We know you're afraid of failing him, but we are hungry!"

And then Reid saw four pillars of smoke rise and disappear through a vent. All that remained now was Matilda. His heart dropped—his mother was there, too, but at least she was still alive.

Fiona, now emboldened because only one vampire remained, tried to dart off the edge of the boiler. Reid figured she couldn't see and thus was about to plummet to her death. But in her rage, Matilda saved her life. She grabbed Fiona by the hair and jerked her back. Fiona struggled and screamed and groped at the hand that caused her pain. Reid joined her scream, but nothing would come out. He was holding the crucifix and stake but felt so paralyzed with fear.

He wasn't very brave, after all.

Matilda put one hand across Fiona's chest and the other continued to pull back her hair, exposing her throat. The vampire sniffed her and laughed.

"Maybe they're right," she said. "Why am I waitin' for my King when I could be out there feastin'?" Her hand moved up Fiona's chest and lay gently across her throat. "And you do smell delicious, after all."

The creature bared her fangs and inched closer to Fiona's neck . . .

Reid watched, helpless. In the span of a second, his mind raced back to when things were better at home, when his father was still alive and still slogging his mom, although he never let her know that he'd seen on a few occasions. He still believed his da was a good man who just let life force his hand sometimes.

Reid thought of his sister and how they would play make-believe and she always wanted to be a dragon, even though girls were supposed to be a princess. He loved her so much and he'd been just as helpless in the fire as he was right now. He couldn't save his sister. He couldn't save his father. And now, he couldn't save his mother.

But then something clicked inside of him, like a light switch turning on. Fiona was all he had left. His mother was his everything, and he would not lose her like this. Not after all they'd been through. Maybe he was a little brave, after all.

He opened his mouth to scream.

The air in his throat thickened.

R.M.S. TITANIC

Fiona's head throbbed. The creature was pulling her hair out from the root, but it didn't matter. In a few minutes, hair would be the least of her worries. She'd stalled the vampires this long, but now Matilda was growing impatient and hungry. Fiona smelled the woman's rotten, icy breath as she descended.

Her fangs had just touched the skin but stopped because an odd, choked noise caught their attention. The hold on her hair relaxed, and she could turn and look through the catwalk.

"M-m-m-mama!" said Reid, voice cracking. "M-m-m-mama!" He said it over and over again, as if his first words in two years were stuck in his throat. Each time he said it, the words were more powerful, less punctured by his waggling tongue. "Mama! Stop hurting my mama!"

"Reid!" she screamed. "Run, little one, *run*!"

CARGO HOLD

"THIS IS A BAD idea," Byles whispered as they entered the Orlop Deck and proceeded toward the automobile. It was too quiet, but Ben told himself this was the last place the vampires would be—there were no people here, no blood.

"Why's that?"

"Because we should wait until daylight. You have the yew stake. We could put it through his heart while he sleeps."

"I'm not so sure that would work," Ben said. "Because the fellow who became the King's first victim must have pried off the lid, and it would've been during the daytime. Let's just burn the box now and gain what advantage we can."

"Okay," Byles said, although he didn't sound convinced.

Ben wondered what they would do if the King was already there, sleeping. He reminded himself that there were still several hours of nighttime left. Plenty of time to feed and infect more people. He never thought such a thing would be a consolation.

The cargo hold looked the same as it did on the day Ben found the dead man. Boxes neatly stacked except where there'd been a scuffle. He wondered if the poor man attempted to fight the vampire, or if his death had come swiftly without pain. Ben didn't think so. These creatures drank the pain as much as they did the blood.

"Nice auto," said Byles, running his palm along the sideboard as they squeezed past it. Ben was in the front and he looked back to see the priest staring at his own grizzled reflection in the window.

"A little too extravagant for me. Since when did horses become obsolete?"

Byles chuckled. It was a silly conversation to have under such circumstances. As soon as they were clear of the fender, Byles had his hands on Ben's shoulders, shoving him down toward the car.

"What the h—" was all he could say before noticing the glint from the shadows. A loud bang made Ben's heart skip a beat. The flash from the gun's muzzle was close enough to his face that he felt the heat on it. Byles cried out in pain as Ben rushed the assailant.

The man got off another shot but it went wide, exploding the car's headlamp. Ben grabbed his arm and held it high while the man squeezed off two more shots. And with them locked in battle, Ben saw it was Erik, Matilda's husband. He had a crazed, sleep-deprived look in his eyes.

Ben wrestled with him, holding the gun high and switching positions until he was facing the car. Byles lay slumped against it, holding a hand over his shoulder. He was trying to get to his feet, to join the fight and hopefully overpower Erik, but it was over in just a few seconds.

The Swede brought the metal down against Ben's temple—and for the second time of the night, his body crumpled from the hit of a gun. He staggered back and collapsed against the box.

"Stop it! Stop it this instant," Byles cried, getting to his feet.

Erik cocked the gun—his eyes were emotionless. His arm was shaking as he took a few steps up to Ben and leveled the weapon at his head. Byles continued to scream and shout and Ben thought to himself: *Stop wasting your breath, Father. He doesn't speak a word of English.*

BOILER ROOM ONE

11:36 P.M.

REID WAS AS SURPRISED as Fiona that he spoke. Something felt odd in his throat—and in his brain. It was as if there'd been a deck of cards in his mind, scrambled and strewn about. And now, they'd been laid straight and put back in order.

"Mama!" he shouted again, but in his excitement and fear, he failed to realize his newfound voice would also draw the vampires.

It wasn't just Matilda who remained, but a large, bulky man with a thick neck. He'd been hanging upside down beneath the catwalk as if he were about to build a cocoon. Once Reid started shouting, his eyes lit and he dropped to the ground, not even twenty feet from the boy.

"Run, Reid, run!" Fiona shouted.

"Don't run, boy," said Matilda. "Let's talk, shall we?"

She put her hand around Fiona's waist but kept a hold on her hair, then together they gently glided down to the boiler room floor. Fiona's eyes were so full of fear so Reid, without even a thought, raised the crucifix.

Matilda and the male vampire cowered behind Fiona, holding her out as if her only purpose was to absorb the awful, holy power. They were hissing behind her back, growing angrier the longer Reid held the cross. His little arm was shaking—they knew he wouldn't be able to hold them off forever.

"How about a trade?" said Matilda. "You toss me the stake and I'll toss you your mama. How's that sound?"

The male vampire turned to smoke and drifted up, probably hoping Reid would miss it in the darkness. But the creature materialized on the ceiling, perching like a spider. It was trying to flank Reid, and the boy didn't know how to stave off two vampires from two different directions.

"No one else has to die," said Matilda.

Reid hesitated for a moment, and then he put his back to the boiler. Another tendril of smoke dropped from the catwalk above and materialized as Colin. The little boy's eyes were so dead and vacant. Reid felt a tear running down his cheek. He deserved so much better than a life of living in the shadows and drinking blood.

"Hey, pal," said Colin, his voice hardly changed in undeath. "Can you put that thing away?"

He was pointing to the cross, but he had his eyes closed. Even though he wasn't looking at it, he was still agitated enough that his nose drew up as if he were smelling something awful.

Reid almost did as he asked. He was smart enough to know all of them were the same, and that this was a monster wearing his friend's face. Colin took a step closer, then another. When he was within striking distance, he stopped.

"Join us, Reid. When we get off this ship, we can all be together. Our parties will be way better than those of the folks upstairs! Your mama won't have to worry about feedin' ya. She won't have to worry about where you live."

"Reid, don't listen to him!" Fiona said. Matilda jerked her hair harder.

"No more movin' from place to place. No more eyes lookin' down on you for being poor. We can be all we wanna be, Reid. I just need ya to put down that awful cross and give me the stake."

The fight was slowly leaving him, but that's when they all heard a loud hiss from the engine room. Metal scraped metal, voices screamed and shouted. And then, the steady pulse that had been present for the entire trip, slowed and then disappeared.

The engines had stopped.

CROW'S NEST

11:37 P.M.

"I'M TELLIN' YA, THAT'S screams!" said Reginald Lee, hanging off the edge of the crow's nest so he could look onto the Boat Deck behind them. "No one is out, Fred. Not a damned soul that I can see."

Frederick Fleet shook his head. "Because it's bloody freezing. What d'ya expect?"

"I don't like it one bit, Fred. It's too calm tonight. Sky is all clear. That probably means we're due for a storm."

"Then we'll worry about it tomorrow night," he said, then produced a metal flask from his inner jacket pocket. "Here. You need this more than I do tonight."

"I can always count on you for a drink."

"Well, I nicked it from the officers' mess, so don't tell no one."

Lee laughed and said, "Who am I gonna tell? You're my only friend."

Fleet was about to say that he had lots of friends, namely Evans who was another lookout aboard *Titanic* who grew up a street over from Lee, but that's when a drop of blood landed on Fleet's wrist. He wouldn't have even noticed it had it landed on his glove or sleeve—but the little droplet of warmth hit the thin sliver of flesh between them.

As he watched, another drop hit his thumb, then the back of his hand. Lee, who'd just lowered the flask and was handing it back, noticed it as well. Together, the men looked up the pole and into the darkness.

A pair of flames watched them. There were enough stars in the sky to illuminate the half-naked woman clinging to the pole. Blood dripped from her fangs and landed on Lee's forehead, but he hardly flinched.

The woman had been stalking them, but upon being discovered, she hissed and let go of the pole, dropping on Fleet, ready to feast. He screamed out and perhaps the luckiest thing of all had been his hat falling down, just long enough to block the vampire from going in for the kill. Frustrated, she ripped the hat away and tried again, but by now Lee was pulling her back by the shoulders.

"Off him, you bloody harlot!"

She changed targets, whirling around and grabbing Lee by the face. He screamed as she squeezed. He dropped to his knees and once Fleet was sure she would not turn back, he pulled the stake from his pocket and jammed it into her back, hoping he found the heart like the priest had told him at Mass that morning.

In a move of pure anguish, she turned back and tried to fight, but she lacked the strength. Both Lee and Fleet shielded their eyes as the crow's nest suddenly became like daytime. The vampire turned to holy white fire in an instant, and when they looked back, she was gone. Their bodies were covered in ash.

"Hell, Fred, you saved my life!"

"Thank that priest at breakfast."

"Yeah, he gave me one of them pointy sticks too, but I threw it right in the bin. That was right stupid, huh?"

But Fleet was no longer listening.

He'd just cleared his eyes in time to return them to the horizon and that's when he saw it . . .

The sky was black, as was the water—like satin sheets joining together. The water was so calm, a sheet of polished glass under an explosion of stars. And because there were no turbulent waves, they didn't see the iceberg looming in the distance, growing larger with each passing second. They'd seen it too late—Fleet knew this at once.

He rang the bell three times, ash unsettling into the air. After that, he lifted the telephone and listened through the crackling static until a sleepy, yet perturbed voice answered. It was Sixth Officer Moody.

"What is it? What did you see?"
"Iceberg! Right ahead!"

PART IV

WATER LIKE A THOUSAND STINGING KNIVES

Cargo Hold

ERIK WAS TALKING FAST, but it was all Swedish so Ben didn't understand it, so he certainly wouldn't be able to reason with the man. Tears streamed down from his vacant eyes. The gun was pressed to Ben's forehead, but the barrel was rubbing his skin raw because Erik couldn't keep his hands steady.

Byles was shuffling to his feet, creeping up behind the man, but Ben knew it would be too late. He also knew that any kind of intervention would probably just anger the man further.

"I'm sorry about Matilda," said Ben, as some sort of soul consolation he wished to impart, here at the end.

The barrel of the gun relaxed for a moment, the fight suddenly leaving the man at the mention of his wife's name. Ben figured now would be the time to strong-arm Erik into submission, but he didn't have to do it.

A great piercing wail sounded from outside the ship, like a dragon taking a bite out of the hull. Cold air whipped in just before icy water blasted the cargo

359

hold, tossing crates and sacks aside as if they were pebbles. Ben was struck in the back by the torrent and pushed forward, his body knocking over both Erik and Byles. It was cold, the freezing water unkind to his achy bones and muscles. The salt burned the wound at his forehead.

The car, turning on its side, was enough to save the doctor and the priest. Both slammed against the fender hard enough to dent the metal. Erik screamed as he was pulled under the water, and it was the last they saw of him.

"C'mon!" Ben shouted, pulling the priest by the collar. They climbed atop the car and rolled down to the floor on the other side. The water was rushing up around their ankles, growing deeper by the second as they tried to outdistance it. Byles was hurt, but he still tried to keep up.

Together, they raced toward the aft end of the ship, listening to the shouting from below, listening to the pounding, screeching metal, the hiss of extinguished fires. One by one, the watertight doors dropped. Ben's frazzled mind forgot if there were any in the cargo hold, so rather than risk being trapped, he ushered Byles up one of the many crew ladders, hoping the doors above hadn't already cut them off from the rest of the ship.

Boiler Room One

AT THE SAME MOMENT on the other end of the ship and a deck below, Reid was about to hand over the stake to Colin. He was smart enough to know that there was no way out of this. In a minute, the vampires would probably kill him, and then his mother. Fiona still stared at him with wide, fearful eyes that begged him to run.

Matilda still held her by the hair, the vampire's fangs poised to take a bite.

Colin crept closer. His eyes were like a pair of tiny furnaces. "C'mon, Reid. Let's all have a little fun, yeah? Give us that nasty thing. I promise he'll replace it with something' so much better."

The fight left him and he was about to lower the arm that held the crucifix when the lights flickered and went off. If the tension wasn't already so high, they would've felt the shudder beneath their feet. But this far from the forward end awarded them with nothing but a loss of electricity and a strange shift from the engine room.

The vampire stalking him from the ceiling dropped behind Colin just as the lights came back on. He tried to swing at the boy, for a fist would've put him out of the standoff in an instant. But Reid had been expecting it and he stooped just in time to avoid getting a bloody lip.

When he sprang up, he was leading with the crucifix. The hulking vampire hid his eyes and recoiled, as did Colin. Both of them hunkered low to the ground and backed away. But Matilda's frustration had run its course.

Rather than look away, she sank her fangs into Fiona's neck. Both Reid and Fiona screamed—one of fear and one of pain—and then he was racing past the vampires so he could slam the crucifix against Matilda's cheek.

She recoiled, spraying warm blood—his mama's blood—all over his face. In an instant, her skin was sizzling and smoking and filling the space with an awful stench. She pulled back so violently that the cross ripped from his fingers. It was attached to her melting face. She wanted to remove it, but each time she touched it, her fingertips smoked. Reid took advantage of her hysteria.

Without even thinking, he lunged with the stake, not sure exactly where the heart was located. Any hole in her chest was better than no hole. With all his strength behind it, the tip burrowed through her patchwork shirt and kept going. It was like thrusting a stick into mud.

The lights in her eyes snuffed out and then the dim boiler room lit up as she became nothing more than ash. Reid and Fiona both fell over, for the woman they'd been entangled with was suddenly no more. He swiped the crucifix and rolled over just in time for Colin and the man to descend on him. He was quicker and sent them skittering back again.

"M-m-mama!" he said, still feeling the words stick in his throat. She was on her feet, pure adrenaline moving her along. They raced through Boiler Room One and into number Two. If they'd had their wits about them, they would've noticed something was wrong—that the engineers, firemen, and stokers were in a panic, that they'd swung all the dampers shut, and that many of them weren't even on the dirty coal ground but climbing the catwalks to get out.

"He's going to kill you, Reid!" screamed Colin from behind. "He'll come for you and he'll come for your mama!"

Fiona's hand was covered in blood—blood that continued to seep between her fingers as she clutched her throat. She staggered away with his help, but it was awkward—he was still facing behind them to keep the monsters at bay.

But once they'd reached Boiler Room Five, the creatures stopped following. He didn't see them turn to vapor—they were just gone. When he turned to face the forward end of the ship, he knew why.

Water was rushing in from the front. He saw men wading through it just before the watertight doors came down. Behind them, the door leading back into Boiler Room Four also went down. Reid followed the stokers up the steps and to the catwalk. None of them cared about a boy and an injured lady, not after what they'd seen in the next boiler room.

Halfway up the steps, Fiona collapsed. Reid, not nearly strong enough, tried to get her on her feet, but she wouldn't budge.

"Help! Somebody please help my mama!"

But no one would help. They were too busy addressing *Titanic's* latest calamity. He turned back to face her and for a moment thought about pulling her fingers away to assess the damage, but decided not to do it. Right now, she was keeping the blood in, and that was important.

"Reid . . . go get . . . go get help," she said, her voice weak and strained. How awful it would be for him to regain the ability only for her to lose it.

"No! You left me, mama! I'm not gonna do the same to you!"

"I'm sorry. I had to."

"I know. I'm just . . . I'm just sayin.'"

"Listen to you," she said, and reached up and pulled his hair back behind his ears. "My sweet angel. I'm glad I got to hear it again."

"Don't talk like that, mama. C'mon! On your feet, dammit!"

"Reid!"

"Then listen to me, mama! We got to go!"

He heard more yelling down below, and the roar of water somewhere close. Reid knew little about ships, but he did know there were more big doors on the lower decks—those with the golden tracks and the heavy gears that wound them shut forever. If those closed, they'd be trapped.

Fiona got to her feet but almost passed out again. Reid put the cross in his back pocket and threaded the stake through one of his belt loops. Then he took his mother's arm and draped it across his shoulder. With all his strength, he lugged her up the steps, not sure how he was going to get her all the way back to the surgery. Not sure if the doctors would even be there to help.

R.M.S. Titanic

11:40 p.m.

LIFE IN THE MOMENT of *Titanic's* collision—and in the moments to follow—seemed to stop all across the ship. As the ice struck her starboard side, far deeper and with much larger teeth than realized, chunks of it fell onto the well deck, some pieces as large as a man's head. Quartermaster Hitchens, just hours after holding a gun to Doctor York's stomach, now held the trembling wheel, feeling every poke and prod of the berg down below. Throughout the doomed vessel, the impact was felt with spotted reverberations.

Eugene Daly emerged from his cabin on F deck, yawning and rubbing his eyes against the night's heavy drinking. The hallway was empty, save for an approaching bedroom stewardess. Above him, he heard footsteps running across E deck.

"Everything alright, miss?" he asked the passing girl.

"Just fine," she said, and he saw the tip from a stake hiding beneath the stack of towels in her arms. "Right as rain."

Back inside his cabin, he locked the door and crashed against the bed.

Several decks above, First Officer Murdoch had the unpleasant business of tapping on the captain's door and informing him the ship had just struck ice. The captain, who'd already felt the shudder, threw on his coat and trudged toward the bridge.

On the same deck, aft end, Dorothy Gibson was playing cards with her mother and a few friends as they watched the ice sail by, a large, grey sentinel in the otherwise black night. They were too deep in their drinks to care, so they laughed at it and started another round of bridge.

Downstairs, just beyond the encroaching water at the Orlop Deck, Ben pulled Father Byles against the wall and removed the man's jacket. The bullet went clean through—a little muscle damage, but nothing life-threatening. Ben needed to take him to the surgery to clean it up.

Lawrence Beesley, second-class passenger and schoolteacher, stepped out of his cabin after donning his favorite robe, a gift from his sister. On the way up the steps to C deck, he noticed a tiny slant in their direction, almost imperceptible. Once he reached the well deck, he saw a few passengers joyfully kicking the chunks of ice, oblivious to any danger—just the ones they'd ignored for almost a week.

Only minutes after the collision, an angry yet sleepy Bruce Ismay inspected the damage alongside Thomas Andrews and Captain Smith. They could go no further than the mail room on the Orlop Deck, for all the envelopes and parcels were floating in the frigid, churning water.

Doctors O'Loughlin and Simpson, sleeping a mere three rooms apart, both woke at the ship's shudder and promptly dressed. They didn't know what had happened, but each had a soured stomach, and knew their services would be needed before the night was over.

Reid Lynch had every intention of getting his mother to the surgery, but she was too weak to make it. She'd lost so much blood and her words were slurring. She was talking about Erin and the fire and she swore never to do that again. He wasn't strong enough to throw her over his arm the way Mr. Dunford had thrown him earlier. He settled for pulling her onto F deck just before the deckhands wound shut the watertight doors. Their old cabin was empty, the door swung open. Reid put her on the bed and checked her heart—it was beating, but faintly. He didn't want to leave her, but he had no choice. He had to go for help or she would die.

And just three minutes before Ismay and company inspected the damage, the King emerged from the bowels of the ship having taken a much closer look.

He stood in the ankle-high water, cold to everyone else, boiling to him. Salt never felt nice on his skin but he didn't care. At that moment, he was seething because his box and his sacred earth was washed away. He would grow weaker until he died—not the pretend death of a yew stake through the heart, but the terrible, permanent death that was malignant in the mortals. He would go back to the Pit and be punished for all eternity.

There would be no coterie. No new world. No owning the night. *Titanic* would rest at the bottom of the ocean before the night was over.

"What do we do, master?" asked Catherine Campbell behind him. He turned to her—the vampire's face was splotched with blood, her dress drenched in salt water.

"The ocean will keep coming in," he said. "We are too far from land to survive."

"I don't . . . I don't understand. You are powerful. You were to give us a new world! Why, why did you promise us this?"

Quick as a viper he grabbed her by the throat. If she had a need for breath, she would've passed out. But Catherine's eyes only flickered and dimmed.

"I am robbed of that new world, as well." He released her throat and shoved her back against the steps. The lights flickered. Behind her stood three others of his creation. They were just watching. He didn't have answers, so he said, "My children. We are done. Tonight will be our last night on this earth. Man's creation is grand, but it is not infallible. And in a few hours, it will most certainly fail."

"It was all for nothing," said Ronin Dixon, the King's latest servant. "This keeping in the shadows and only drinking the Bitterbloods!"

The King stepped forward, his very presence enough to make his coterie retreat.

"Then tonight we feast," he said. "If we're to go down with the ship, if we're to never see America, then let us have our fill of blood."

"Even . . . the Sweetbloods?" Catherine Campbell said, smacking her lips.

The King's face twisted into a grin. "They'll be assembling on deck soon. That's where they keep the lifeboats. Wait until they're desperate. Wait until their blood is pumping. And then gorge yourselves on it until the sun comes up!"

The vampires smiled, defeated and bitter, but happy to face death through an avalanche of blood. They became grey smoke, twisted together like a nasty cyclone, and disappeared up the steps.

The King sat down and pulled back his robe. He rubbed his long, bony fingers across the wound on his chest. It was hardly visible now with so much rot and ruin, but each time his nails graced the spot where a stake had found his heart not once, but twice—he winced.

When Matilda Olsson bit Fiona Lynch, the woman's memories passed to her. And although the former was dead and the latter would probably be soon, the King still saw through her eyes until Matilda's death. He saw them there in the boiler room the moment the ship hit the ice. He saw the boy and he saw the yew stake.

The King wouldn't let either leave the ship. He would snap it over his knee and kill the boy who wielded it.

WHEN BEN AND BYLES opened the door to his cabin, just nine minutes after the collision, they had no idea that over one-million gallons of water had already invaded the ship. Even if they had, neither would've thought much of it so early into the night. Ben, like all White Star Line employees, had bought into the propaganda that the ship was unsinkable, and a mere iceberg was hardly cause for concern. When passengers thought of maritime problems, it was always a collision with another ship, not ice.

"Sit down," said Ben. "Pull off your shirt. This is going to sting like hell." He grabbed a bottle of spirits from his medical bag. Often there was no need for medicinal cleansing, especially when drinking alcohol was so readily available and cleaned just as well. Father Byles gritted his teeth and waited for Ben to pour.

His eyes clamped shut as the stinging alcohol dug into his wound. Ben patted it gently with a sterile cloth until he was certain the area was clean.

"How bad is it?"

Ben pulled his desk light over as far as the cord would allow. "Not as bad as it could be. Straight through. You're lucky. I'd hate to dig out metal. We'll sew you up and send you on your merry way."

"Thanks, doctor," said Byles, grinning politely.

Ben tried to keep him talking while he threaded the needle. "That fella who shot you . . . he's the husband of one of the infected. Name's Erik."

"In the service of the King, I'd assume."

Ben doused the needle with the alcohol and put a hand on Byles's chest, choosing to fix his front before his back. He took a deep, steadying breath, then pushed back in.

"I suppose so. Is there no limit to this damned creature?"

"Oh, yes," said Byles, gritting his teeth as the thread wound through his flesh. "We've struck a blow . . . well, the ship did the work for us, rather. With the way the water was rushing in, I'd say his box is no more."

"That's good, right?" Ben swiped away the fresh blood.

"Yes and no."

"Explain."

"The creature can no longer rest to regenerate. If we hurt it, it can no longer heal. But I fear now that it's vulnerable, it will act . . . reckless."

"Reckless?" Ben quickly pulled the stitches tight, then cut the excess thread. He nudged Byles forward so that he could treat the rear wound.

The priest nodded. "If the vampire feels hopeless, he will kill everyone on this ship. Vampires move about because the world becomes wise to their patterns. But the world is big and there's lots of shadows to fill it. Right now, the creature is . . ."

"Stuck. With nowhere to go."

"That's right," said Byles, feeling the needle sink into his back.

"But now it's exposed. Now we can kill it."

"Not likely, but if we ever stood a chance, it's now. We need to stab it through the heart and out the back. It'll bother us no more after that."

Ben felt his heart drop. He looked over to the corner where he'd left the stake, only now it wasn't there. The priest winced as Ben pulled him to his feet, thread still hanging down his back. The cloth covering was on the bed, laid out flat. Someone had unrolled the stake and taken it.

"It's gone. Christ, it's gone!" said Ben, looking beneath the bed and the desk. "Perhaps Mr. Dunford or one of the bedroom stewards took it."

"Calm, doctor. Who knew that it was here?"

Without answering, he handed Byles a sterile cloth and said, "Keep this on the stitches until the blood clots. I'll be right back."

And then he excused himself from his cabin and went to the surgery. Before going through the door, he spied Mr. Dunford exiting their shared lavatory, black circles beneath his eyes. When he saw Ben approach, he took a step back. It was probably the frantic look on the man's face, or perhaps the blood on his shirt and hands.

"Doctor? Is everything alright?"

"The boy and his mother . . . the ones who stayed in my cabin? Have you seen them?"

Mr. Dunford dropped his head as if in shame. "I did, sir. The boy, anyway. He may have very well saved my life with that crucifix of his."

"What happened?"

"I didn't mean anything by it, sir. The way I treated him, I mean. I thought he was snooping."

"Did he have a stake?"

"He did, sir."

Ben nodded and turned to walk off. Dunford asked, "Sir, did you feel the bump? What do you think it could've been?"

The doctor turned back and said, "We've hit a berg, is all. But these ships can take on a little water. Get yourself in a cabin and lock the door."

"Yes, doctor."

Back inside his own cabin, Byles was running water from the sink over one of the cloths. He saw Ben enter and said, "The water pressure is low. That's probably not a good sign."

"Reid has the stake," Ben said.

Byles nodded. "Then let's go find him. We have to get it back."

"I'll find him. You need to get to your steamer trunk. I have a feeling we're going to have need of your holy water."

Byles straightened and nodded solemnly. "Alright, doctor. I'll meet you up on deck."

F DECK

A LOT OF THINGS happened at *Titanic's* final midnight. Captain Smith, having assessed the data with the clinometer and learned the ship had started to list to the bow *and* starboard, knew it would sink without Andrews's professional opinion. He was heard saying, "Oh, my God," upon reading the angle.

At midnight, First Officer Murdoch began preparing the lifeboats, but was delayed because he had to find a hammer to first break the ice that had formed on the ropes holding down the tarpaulin. Although he'd never admit it, he thought this whole thing was silly.

Also at midnight, the crew moved through the ship waking passengers. This was difficult for many reasons—some had been drinking, some didn't want to be bothered so late, and others simply had a language barrier that prevented them from understanding the captain's simple instructions: Get dressed, get up to the Boat Deck.

And finally, at midnight, Fiona Lynch thought for sure she would die. The ship was still, the engines no longer purring. The propellers would turn no more. She was so cold but her forehead was hot, at least it was the last time she felt it. Now, she couldn't even raise her arms above her head. One of them was tingling because it had fallen off the bed and laid on top of the crucifix.

It took a moment to realize where Reid had carried her. She was back on F deck, in the original room she'd paid for back when they had aspirations—although under duress—of going to America. Only now that wouldn't happen, at least not for her. She'd never teach Reid to ride a bike, never see him grow up, fall in love, have children of his own. The world had stacked too much against her, and tonight was the final straw. Fiona's story ended here.

Sometime between waking and sleeping, a vampire entered her room. It was a man, thin and mustached with a bloody cheek. He bent down and sniffed her face, then left without even taking a bite. That's when she knew she wouldn't make it—even the creatures thought her blood smelled foul.

Outside the room, she heard raised voices, although she wasn't sure if they were from a single conversation. She drifted in and out, so it could've taken place over two different moments.

"You've got to put your lifebelt on, love," said a man, an authoritative voice. "And get to the Boat

Deck. Why, if you'd have seen the mail room, you'd march right up!"

And then, a mother and child. The little one sounded so frightened, voice breaking. "But I don't wanna go up on deck. It's cold, and Jimmy took my jacket."

"You can have mine, sweetie," said the mother. "It'll go right over your lifebelt. See?"

Fiona's vision was darkening. She hoped Reid was safe. Wherever he was, she prayed he stayed away from the monsters—and now, away from the water.

R.M.S. TITANIC

12:15 A.M.

THE FIRST-CLASS PASSENGERS ASSEMBLED in their lounge up on A deck. It was a frigid night, but that didn't stop half of them from drinking cold whiskey and brandy. They looked a sight—half the women in their furs, marred by the cork vests underneath. None of them took it seriously and before long, many were heading back to bed.

Wallace Hartley led the White Star Orchestra into a soft ragtime tune, something to keep the passengers orderly and their feet tapping against the cold. Their music was bland and forgettable, and the most notable part about them was that none of the eight musicians would survive the night.

Harold Bride and John Phillips, having just repaired the Marconi machine a few hours earlier, were put on standby. They were to use the new distress call tonight, but neither thought it would be needed. This was all just a precaution, after all.

Just inside on the grand staircase, a few passengers grew worried at the sight of Thomas Andrews racing up the stairs, two at a time. When he reached the bridge and found Smith stirring his second cup of tea, he announced what the captain already knew: The ship was certainly sinking. And, what he *didn't* know: It only had one or two hours before it all went under.

If passengers had thought to look up, they would've seen Colin Olsson and Ronin Dixon perched atop the first funnel, watching the flurry of activity below. There was no more smoke coming from the funnels, only a thin line of steam. They were ready to pounce, feeling every beating heart on deck.

While Ben was searching for Reid and he for Ben, they missed each other by a matter of minutes on the second-class staircase. Ben had the right idea to search F deck while Reid thought the doctor must have been up on the Boat Deck with everyone else. The boy still carried the stake, but he felt exposed without the cross. As he made his way up to C deck, he didn't see the dots of red watching him from the shadows, and once Catherine Campbell knew his location, so too did the King. Hungry shadows gathered deep in the ship. There was still time. The boy had nowhere to go.

Doctors O'Loughlin and Simpson were tending to Catherine's latest victim, a man lying across the tile of C deck with no blood left to pump from his wound. He was alive when they reached him, but passed soon after the old doctor tried to stem the flow of blood.

He wasn't the first victim of the night, and he certainly wouldn't be the last.

F Deck

12:31 A.M.

SHE'D HAVE PROBABLY SLEPT forever if not for the cold water rushing by her hand. Out of pure instinct, she pulled it back, the last of her strength spent in flopping it up to her chest. Now that the cold water was seeping through her shirt, she felt a bit energized, so she brought her fingers to her lips and licked. It was nice and cool, but tasted awful. The chill through her body was just what she needed to keep herself awake. Somehow, she was still alive.

Her mind was light and free and her vision was returning. But something wasn't right, for as soon as she tried to sit up, she saw Emmet sitting on the bed. He was looking at her with a mixture of kindness and sadness, for he probably knew she was dying.

"You have to keep still," he said. "We don't have much time." She saw a thin black thread pull away from her throat, and that's when she felt the pain coursing through her body. She tried to fight against it, but he pushed her arm down and said, "Stop it. If I have to start over, we'll never get up on deck in time."

"Reid. Where's . . . Reid?"

"I don't know. He's probably up on deck with everyone else."

"Emmet, I'm . . . I'm sorry. I'm so, so sorry."

"I'm not Emmet, Fiona. Can you sit up? I'm almost finished here."

She was weak, but she did as he asked, and now her eyes were clearing and the pain was becoming too much to bear. Fiona thought she was going to be sick.

"He spoke, Emmet," she said. "Our boy . . . he's not mute. He said mama."

"That's great," said the man who wasn't Emmet. "You're lucky, Fiona. Whichever one of them bit you completely missed your carotid artery. But you've still lost a lot of blood. You're going to have to take it easy. We have to get you to a lifeboat."

"But Reid is . . ."

"I'll find Reid."

Just then, her mind cleared. He tugged the thread and leaned in as if to kiss her, but he was only cutting the excess with his teeth. When he pulled back, she snatched his face and kissed *him*. He didn't fight her—in fact, he relaxed and returned it. She tasted the sweat and salt on his lips, felt the muscles in them twist into a smile.

They sat in silence for a moment. Fiona's eyes continued to clear until she could see the doctor watching her, great concern on his face.

"Do you know who you kissed?" he asked.

She nodded weakly. "I kissed Benjamin York, the only kind soul left on this ship."

He grinned and shook his head. "I'm not so sure about that. C'mon, we have to get out of here. This deck is flooding fast."

She rotated her wobbly legs and stepped down on the floor, and that's when the frigid water permeated her dress and socks and she cried out. It was so, so cold. The water was moving, sloshing lazily back and forth but rising nonetheless.

"I don't know if I can walk," she said, and when she stood, she went right back down on the bed. "Sorry, let me try again."

Ben grabbed her around the waist and draped her arm across his neck. Her wound hurt so bad—it was throbbing with each beat of her heart, but she supposed it could've been much, much worse.

As they began trudged out of the room, Fiona shouted, "Wait! The crucifix."

"Where?"

"There, in the water somewhere."

Ben leaned her against the doorframe and dropped to his knees. Somewhere across the deck they heard a loud, terrible groan. Furniture was sliding toward the sinking end. Ben splashed around until his fingers touched the cross, then he lifted it, shook the water off it, and grabbed Fiona.

The deck was empty and Fiona could already tell the ship was listing to the side. As her vision returned, she saw the water was higher on the left side of the hall's trim work than on the right side. A few of the manual watertight doors were closed, but lucky for them, not all. They could pass through and leave the water behind.

At midship, Ben stopped and waited. Fiona was about to ask why when she saw a pair of red eyes far at the other end. If not for the dimming of the lights, she would've never seen them. The creature looked around, then turned and left around the corner.

"Can you climb?" he asked her.

"Climb?"

He pointed back toward her cabin and said, "That watertight door is closed. The one on the aft end is still open, but I don't feel like fighting a vampire to get to it. This is our only option."

Fiona followed his finger up—there was a ladder directly in front, leading up to E deck. She swallowed the lump in her throat and felt the weakness in her knees. She wasn't sure she could do it.

"I don't . . . I don't know, Ben."

Then the lights flickered and went out. They were standing there, listening to each other's breath, listening to the water creep toward them until she felt it seeping into her socks again. When the light came back on, she quickly grabbed the ladder and went up.

Boat Deck

THERE WERE MORE PEOPLE on the Boat Deck than Reid had ever seen amassed all at once. Most were first-class—it was easy to tell with their nice jackets and furs and large, floppy hats. The women were cold and irritated, many nursing drinks from long-stemmed glasses. Almost all of them wore White Star Line lifebelts over their bedclothes.

"Please, sir!" said Reid, approaching the nearest crewman, who turned out to be First Officer Murdoch. He'd just helped swing a lifeboat out on the davits and was ushering in the hesitant passengers. Reid tugged at his nice jacket. "Please, my mother needs—"

"Well get in, lad," said the officer, taking him by the shoulder and pushing him forward. So far, this boat was filled with young women, two who looked drunk. One of them held a shivering little dog inside a blanket. They stared at him with cold eyes, despite the fancy clothes Ben had given him. When Reid didn't step aboard, Murdoch shoved him out of the way. "Either get in or move!"

And then the boy disappeared into the crowd. The grown-ups were too busy right now. His mother wasn't a priority even on a normal day, much less when the crew were trying to get the first-class passengers to safety.

More people lingered inside the gymnasium and the first-class entrance than out on the deck. Reid couldn't blame them with the frigid wind. It seemed silly to abandon such a sturdy ship for a flimsy boat out in the middle of the Atlantic, vampires notwithstanding. Like most of the adults, he didn't think the ship could sink . . . until he looked at the water next to it.

He followed the circles of light reflected on the waves. They formed a perfect line, the same distance out from the edge of the ship until reaching the front—and that's when the distance tapered. The lights grew closer and closer to the water until the sea consumed them. The forward end was already going down. But the ship wouldn't *really* sink, would it?

"Look at them," said an older gentleman by the door of the first-class entrance. He appraised the small crowds of people around the lifeboat. "They're orderly right now. In a little while, it'll be madness."

His wife, who'd been gripping his arm with the force of a bear, said, "Why do you think that, Isi?"

This time, he crept close to her ear, almost too close for Reid to hear his whisper. "Because there aren't enough lifeboats for everyone."

The old woman looked appalled. "Why in the world not?"

Again, the whisper. "After dinner last night, Mr. Andrews told me that only the bare minimum was brought aboard. That too many would clutter the deck."

"Oh," she said. "Then I suppose it's alright. The ship can't sink if they made a decision like that."

"That's what I think, too, Ida. That's what I think, too."

Either way, Reid was horrified. He was running out of time. The vampires fed every night and if all their food was up on deck . . .

He made his way back toward the aft end, just past the gymnasium. That's when he spotted an important-looking man with slicked back hair and a cigar in his mouth. Reid knew it was a long-shot but the man wasn't talking to anyone, simply observing as if his thoughts hadn't yet caught up to his actions.

"Sir? Sir!" he said. "My mother . . . she's injured and she needs help right now!"

He seemed to shake from a trance, then found Reid standing in front of him. His entire countenance changed and he smoothed his coat and adjusted his lifebelt.

"What did you say?"

"My mother, she's injured and needs help."

"Well I'm not a doctor, boy. I'm the owner of the ship." Realizing this information meant nothing to Reid, he added, "Where's your mother?"

"F deck, cabin sixty-six."

"F deck?" he said, and almost laughed. "And the forward end, too? I'm sorry, boy, but that part of the ship is probably under water by now. I suggest you find a lifeboat. Look there, Mr. Murdoch is about to lower that one right now . . ."

But Reid wasn't hearing it. He ran off, blowing past Lifeboat 7 as it lowered with less than half its maximum occupancy. He didn't even realize he'd passed up the first-class entrance and thus the staircase to take him back down to F deck. As soon as he saw the closed doors of the officers' quarters, he turned back around, only to face the beginning of tonight's mayhem.

A woman was screaming because Colin had jumped onto her back. She tried to fling him off, but only managed to lose her frilly hat. He sank his teeth into her neck, a fountain of blood spurting out. A trio of men rushed to pull him away, but he finished his job, ignoring all the fists that landed against him. Through the mess of limbs, he saw Colin looking back at him, his eyes red and fierce with fresh blood.

And then he snatched the nearest man and dragged him atop the gymnasium roof and out of sight. A few seconds later, Colin climbed up the dead funnel and sat at the top. He wiped his lips and gleefully watched the panic below.

Two more vampires climbed up the railing from the first-class promenade down on A deck. One officer pulled out a pistol and fired, but the shot missed, serving only to further panic the passengers. Two more shots and Reid felt the spray of blood on his face—and he didn't think it came from the vampire.

He stepped back, tripping over someone's heel, and went down. A foot kicked his gut and his bladder released. The warmth felt nice on such a cold night, but he didn't think of that in the moment—in the moment, he was shielding his head from the stampeding passengers startled by both the vampire and the officer with the gun.

He found grace through a stout, fancy woman. As he rolled over, he saw her with her arms out, blocking the rush of passengers trying to barrel over her.

"Settle down now, we have a kid on the ground!" she said, her accent strange and unlike anything he'd ever heard. When she was satisfied no one was going to plow over her, she put her hands beneath his shoulders and lifted him to his feet.

"T-thank you!" he said, then checked his belt loop to make sure the stake was still secure.

"Get in a boat, fella. You might not get a chance before long."

He nodded, then rushed off toward the first-class entrance. More people were pushing past him, caring little that he might go right back down to the deck. Finally, he burst through the door, but someone was coming out—a frantic woman who was being chased by a vampire—the lady who was with Matilda when Colin was taken.

Behind them came a trio of crewmen, all trying to fight the creature, or at least turn her attention away from her intended victim. The door slammed Reid against the wall and he took a moment to catch his breath. The creature bent the lady over the railing, nearly breaking her back. She was screaming a sound so raw he knew he'd never forget it.

The crewmen were trying to pry the creature off her. Two had her arms, peeling them away. One had her hair, but she was stronger than all three. Slowly, she was shortening the distance between her fangs and the woman's neck.

Reid rushed toward them, unsure why he'd grown so brave, and jammed the stake right through her back. The tip passed easily enough, and lucky for him the victim moved to the side and the stake bit into the railing and not her.

The vampire whirled toward him, her flesh breaking down, and Reid kept his hold on the shaft while it tore through her body. Then, a torrent of screams as she turned to fire and ash. The woman against the railing screamed again, then limped away.

"Hey, Walter!" said the burly man to one of the crewmen who'd sat down to rest. "This lad is stronger'n all of us!"

Reid smiled. He turned toward the aft end of the ship and flicked the ashes off his stake. It probably wouldn't be the last time he used it tonight.

E DECK

WATER HAD ALREADY WASHED up the staircase from F deck. Ben and Fiona made it out just in time, and he was certain her cabin was submerged by now. It broke his heart to think of it. There was no way all the passengers reached the top deck. Many were asleep, probably not even waking until they heard the water trickling beneath their doors. The children, who didn't know better to wake an adult . . .

Then there were the ones trapped by gates and other obstacles. While most of the furniture on a ship was bolted to the floor, some of it was not. Ben had already passed one hallway that was blocked by tumbling luggage and chairs.

Some passengers couldn't read—or at the very least, read English. Those were the unfortunates who had to follow others up to dinner and back down. They couldn't navigate such a labyrinthine ship, and they certainly couldn't hope to follow panic-stricken passengers.

On the forward end of Scotland Road, water began to chase them. Ben could've easily outrun it had he not been pulling a severely injured woman along. When he stopped to adjust her against his shoulder, he looked down in the water and saw a drenched, matted wad of straw. It was Lizzy, the doll that belonged to little Sarah with the hurt knee. Ben knew before the night was over, he'd have to return to help the other passengers.

The watertight doors on E deck weren't closed, at least not yet, but he didn't think that would happen. The crew had abandoned the lower decks. While closing the doors may have slowed the flooding, leaving them open meant Fiona didn't have to suffer another ladder. They rushed to the aft end of the deck and climbed up the second-class stairway.

But a gate prevented moving further up than D deck. Ben gave it a shake, but was sure it was locked tight. They were going to have to go back toward the sinking end of the ship—and hope there wasn't a gate blocking them from the grand staircase.

It was eerie seeing the ship so deserted. They passed through the first-class dining saloon, already prepared for tomorrow's breakfast that would never come. Ben took it all in—every silver fork, every linen cloth, every table napkin with the White Star Line embroidery—it would all be at the bottom of the Atlantic before the sun came up. Past the dining saloon, in the reception area, they saw bodies.

Men, women, and children lying across the floor with very little blood, meaning these were vampire victims and not tragedies of the sinking. Ben placed Fiona in a chair and checked every one of them, grimacing at the pale, clammy skin and the two devastating puncture wounds. Again, he thought of how lucky Fiona had been.

"They know Titanic's sinking," said Ben. "They've abandoned all moderation." He turned back to Fiona. "We have to get you to a boat."

"No!" she said, and sat up. She put her foot out to brace herself, for she almost tumbled straight forward. "We have to find Reid."

"You aren't in any shape to go finding anyone."

"I'm sorry," she blurted.

"For what?" he asked, taken aback.

"For everything. We saddled you with so much responsibility, and your only crime was seeing to Reid when he dropped his father's cross from the gangway."

"You and Reid . . . you're good people. And it's you who have been saddled with a lot—a lot of heartache and a lot of responsibility."

"And now this."

"And now this," he said, and stooped by her. "One day you'll look back on all this and remember it as the day your life started. Titanic was supposed to be about starting over, right? Let's make sure it still happens."

She smiled, but before either said anything, a terrible bang sounded in the hallway behind the grand staircase. The lights were dim and he tried to see what was happening. He grabbed the crucifix from his pocket and held it out, listening as something metal crashed against the tile.

The gate leading to the forward end had come down.

But the vampires didn't use the gates . . .

"Christ, Almighty!" said O'Loughlin. He stepped into the reception area, favoring his right leg. Behind him came Doctor Simpson.

"Ben? Christ, are you alright?"

"I'm fine," he said. "She's not."

The doctors surrounded Fiona and it was O'Loughlin who said, "Jesus, Ben. Hell of a stitch job. Were ye underwater when ye did it?"

"Funny."

"Not much more we can do," said Simpson, checking her pulse and pulling back her eyelid. "Lost a bit of blood, did ya, love?"

Fiona nodded.

O'Loughlin turned stern. "Get her to a boat, Benjamin."

Simpson nodded. "Listen to the old man. Titanic? She's going down sure as we're sittin' here."

Ben nodded. "You two haven't seen her boy, have you?"

Both shook their heads, ashen faced and sad. O'Loughlin said, "We're headed down below to help. Heard a pair of stokers say people are trapped in the E deck lavatory."

Simpson said, "It's not looking good. So much death. It's everywhere."

"But no vampires," O'Loughlin said.

"At least not down here. They are waiting upstairs, I'm sure."

The old doctor smiled and nodded. He stood and tapped Simpson on the chest. "We'd better be going if we're to beat the water."

Simpson nodded. Ben stood and pulled Fiona to her feet. She was hot now, burning up, in fact. She needed cool air and to get off this ship. But he had a duty to help her find Reid. He turned to the doctors then shook O'Loughlin's hand.

"Been a pleasure, boy. Best of luck to you."

"Right, Ben," said Simpson, taking his hand. "We'll be right behind you. Get that pretty lass to a boat!"

And then, they ran off through the dining saloon and disappeared into the blackness that was soon to overthrow *Titanic*.

It was the last time Ben saw either of them.

Boat Deck

A LOUD BOOM STARTLED Reid and almost sent him diving onto the deck. He saw the brilliant white light fall over everything and then disappear. They were firing off rockets toward the front of the ship—it must have been dire if they'd resorted to that.

It was obvious how much of the ship had gone under. Only fifteen feet separated the bow from the water. A prominent slope made the rear of the ship higher, and Reid saw the stars through the railing rather than the ocean. The more he ran toward the aft end, the more his calves hurt because it was all uphill.

He wasn't sure where he was going, only that he was panicked and wanted to find help for his mother. Maybe the adults were right. Maybe he needed to find a boat. This sturdy ship wasn't looking so sturdy anymore. But they weren't loading boats on this end, at least not yet. He took a moment to recover his breath, and that's when a trio of grey pillars appeared in front of him.

Colin and two ladies, barring his passage. A few people screamed and rushed off, a few down the second-class staircase and even one man who tumbled over the railing, hopefully landing on A deck.

"He's looking for you, Reid," said Colin. "We gave you a chance, now it's over."

He pulled out the stake and the creatures froze, but they weren't afraid of it in the same way they were afraid of the crucifix. The first lady whose name Reid didn't know was Minnie Pembroke, a creature with fourteen kills behind her, lunged, intending to snap his arm off before he could raise the stake.

But then the door to the second-class staircase burst open and a fast-moving shape shoved her out of the way. She was caught so unawares that she tumbled around and fell against the already tilted railing.

Father Byles grabbed Reid's hand and helped him to his feet. In his hand was the staff—the long-cross that sent Minnie over the rail, her body becoming smoke in the process.

"C'mon, boy. We have to get you in a boat!"

"My mama!"

"So you talk now?"

Reid didn't have time to explain. Colin lowered his head and lunged, but Byles was ready. Gripping a bottle of holy water by the neck, he smashed it over the boy vampire's head. The glass embedded in his flesh, making it hard to stop the flames once his skin began to burn. Colin looked up with bright red eyes and hissed. Byles slammed the cross against his cheek, knocking him back. Like Minnie, he rolled over the side, but he never turned to vapor.

"Let's go!" said the priest, and Reid ran after him.

More people were displaced by the sudden appearance of vampires. Grey smoke heralded death, and it was easy for them to materialize, feed, then disappear again. The forward end of the Boat Deck was nothing short of chaos. Those who'd been trying to get into a lifeboat now found themselves overcrowded and pushed aside because others were desperately trying to avoid becoming a victim.

And then, the passengers saw the creatures' true strength.

When Reid and Byles reached the entrance to the grand staircase, four vampires touched down in front of them. The passengers fled, running toward the aft end. When they reached the edge of the gymnasium, seven more vampires dropped from the roof and the funnels. They were boxed in, the vampires stalking.

"Stay behind me," Byles whispered.

But Reid was doing nothing of the sort. He gripped the stake tight in both hands, ready to wield it as surely as a broadsword. Visions of King Arthur's knights danced in his head.

The vampires on the aft end lunged, two of them snatching victims. A young, fancy woman found her neck opened up, blood pouring down her nice dress—it was a stark contrast to the white lifebelt. Her husband beat the creature with the stock of a rifle, but they snatched him too, then wrestled him to the deck and started feeding.

On the forward end, the group of four vampires advanced, but that's when the doors to the first-class entrance and the gymnasium blew open and out came Byles's reinforcements.

Some passengers had listened, after all.

John Astor, with an opened bottle of holy water, slung it across the deck, lighting them all on fire. While they writhed on their backs, he straddled the nearest one and jammed a stake right through its heart. He toppled over when the creature turned to ash and was no longer there to support him.

Behind him was a young Edith Rosenbaum, her stake held high. She advanced on one of the creatures who'd just put out the flames across his midsection. He grabbed her arm, was ready to bend it back and break it but Victor Giglio, Benjamin Guggenheim's valet, shoved his stake right through the creature's chin until it was lodged in its brain. Edith pulled free and stabbed it through the heart.

Ernest Carter and Frederick Fleet took down one with holy water and a hatchet. Eugene Daly another with a sharpened piece of trim work. Shopkeeper Henry Rudd held down one creature with the crucifix his sister gave him while saloon steward William Moss poured holy water down its throat. The creature's eyes widened as its fangs melted along with everything else between its throat and stomach.

The good people of *Titanic* pushed back the creatures until they'd seen enough of their brethren laid low. The ones that could flee turned to smoke and whipped away to regroup. One crisis averted, at least for the moment.

Reid turned back to Byles and found him leaning against the wall, a piece of his arm hanging down his sleeve. It looked so awful the boy had to turn away. Byles was in great pain, but he tried to cover the wound with his hand. Still, blood was gushing between his fingers.

"Couldn't bite my neck with a cross in its face, so it took my arm instead." He laughed, but Reid could tell it was forced.

"Have you seen the doctor?"

"Ben went looking for the two of you. Where is your mama, anyway?"

"She's hurt. Very badly."

His face darkened and he nodded. "I'm sorry, lad. With any luck the doctor has seen to her wounds and has already placed her in a lifeboat."

Reid hoped that, as well, although he didn't believe it.

There was no use in asking Byles for help. The man couldn't even make a fist with his limp fingers. He certainly was in no shape to help carry his mama up to the Boat Deck.

He handed the priest the stake, but Byles pushed it back with his good hand.

"No, you keep it. My fighting is done. I have to make sure these people find heaven after they find the water."

He lifted himself off the wall, leaving a bloody streak across the stark white paint. Then he hobbled away, holding one hand in the air, as if to talk to God. Others seemed to recognize the gesture, and before long there were people kneeling at his feet, offering their confessions. He prayed over them, his voice gravely and weak.

Reid wanted to stay and listen, comforted by the words, but he knew he had to find someone able-bodied enough to bring his poor mama to the boats.

R.M.S. TITANIC

12:58 A.M.

AS THE ORCHESTRA ABOVE repositioned at the grand staircase, the King stood at the flooding end of Scotland Road. With such a long, wide hallway, water rushed in and weighed down the port side of the ship, creating a heavy list that would remain all the way to the bottom. Everything beneath E deck was nearly gone. His box, his earth, the automobile and the first-class passengers' pricy exports. Nearly two million pieces of mail never to be delivered.

The ship smelled like saltwater more than blood, but he didn't need scent to hunt. Every single human was in a panic, their bodies sweaty, their hearts beating fast. They were easy to see through the walls, even easier to hear floundering below deck.

A group of engineers were trapped by watertight doors down between Boiler Rooms Three and Four. He bent low and lifted it, listening to the joyful cries of the men who assumed the pump teams had come to rescue them. Once the door was a foot from the ground, hands appeared along the bottom rim as they tried to help their 'rescuer' hold it. As their weak human muscles struggled to keep it in place, he turned to vapor and passed beneath, twirling around their legs, only to appear behind them.

"Christ, I'm losin' it!" said one man just as they let go of the door. The way one of them screamed out, he was certain the metal came down on toes or fingers.

He watched them, listened to their hearts, enjoyed the fear. How he wished there was light, but the furnaces had all been doused when the iceberg was sighted. Still, they knew they shared the room with something evil. And as they turned around and found his two, glowing eyes hovering nine feet in the air, they barely managed a scream. He tore through them in an instant, opening wide so he could drink long and deep.

After the boiler room, he floated through the vent and glided down the slanted aft hall of F deck. The water was encroaching behind a group of Bitterbloods—they were stuck at a gate, desperately trying to rattle the bars from the hinges. None of them possessed the strength, nor the organization to get it done. They would drown here, if not for the King. He materialized a few feet behind them and waited for one to see him. Sure, he could've drained them all before they knew what was wrong, but he wanted the thrill of the panic—he wanted their blood pumping fast enough to burst their hearts.

And moments later, he passed through the gate, now bloodied and dripping.

Up on the first-class decks, he found fewer people. Any who saw him either dropped into a ball along the floor, or turned and fled the other way. In a little while, the lower decks would be gone.

His head swam with all the memories and thoughts of the victims he and his minions enjoyed tonight. There'd never been a feeding like this and he was unequipped to deal with the slight madness that came with it. This was what the mortals would call drunk—only his drink was not wine, it was the lifeforce of the cattle.

A few of his vampires had already met their end, but that was to be expected. A death at the hands of a stake was far better than at the radiance of the sun. He'd known vampires in his day to meet such a horrible end and wished that fate on no one. The passengers were emboldened to fight the vampires, but not the King.

On C deck, a woman who'd been hiding in a linen closet sprang out and attempted to stab him, only she failed to realize he was much taller than a common man, so his heart wasn't in the same place. No matter, though, for the King reversed her stab and snapped her arm off at the elbow. Rather than drink her, he left her to flounder while another pair of would-be vampire hunters dropped their stakes and ran off.

The holy water was a bigger concern. A man, cornered at the end of a debris-strewn hallway pulled a bottle from his belt and slung it at the King. The glass burst and a few drops hit his cloak, but it wasn't enough to start a fire—just smolder and hiss. Still, it gave rise to his anger and he split the man apart like some exotic fruit.

As he made his way to A deck, he looked out on the starboard side and found a trio of lifeboats in the water. The mortals probably couldn't even see the furthest one now, but the King could—twenty-eight shivering passengers with nowhere to go.

Once the ship vanished beneath the water, he'd skip from boat to boat until there was nothing left but wood and tack.

R.M.S. TITANIC
1:06 A.M.

IF THE OFFICERS HAD known how little time *Titanic* had to live, they may not have waited until an hour after striking the iceberg to begin setting down lifeboats in the frigid Atlantic. As of one o'clock in the morning, only four boats had left the davits and begun to row slowly away.

Nineteen-year-old Helen Bishop was the first passenger to step foot into a lifeboat. She was pregnant, although she wouldn't know it for quite some time. The baby would be born in late December—and die two days later.

Joining her was Dorothy Gibson and her mother and Margaret Hayes with her shivering Pomeranian. All four ladies would've rather faced the vampires than the icy wind and the prospects of lowering down into the black sea. Like Reid Lynch had thought less than half an hour ago, the flimsy boats couldn't possibly be better than this unsinkable ship.

Although the first lifeboat to be launched did so with little trouble, the same could not be said of the others. The second boat—Lifeboat 5—launched with thirty-five people, including Doctor Henry Frauenthal, a large, beefy man who jumped from the railing and landed upon Mrs. Annie May Stengel. He thought he'd felt something trying to grab his leg—at least that's what he would later say at the official inquiry in New York.

Lifeboat 3 launched next, as First Officer Murdoch was outpacing his counterpart on the port side of the ship (Second Officer Lightoller, who wouldn't launch the first boat until Murdoch had launched *three*), carrying half its capacity.

Among them, Robert Spedden (without his ball), who was carried down to the boat while sleeping. Later, he wouldn't remember much of anything where the sinking was concerned. The fates of the passengers aboard *Titanic* seemed cursed even after the ordeal. Like the fragility of Helen Bishop's baby, Robert Spedden would be struck by an automobile and killed while chasing his ball in the street, just three years after surviving a sinking ship full of vampires.

Next was Lifeboat 1, carrying an obscenely sparse *twelve* people down into the water. Among the passengers, Lady Duff Gordon and her husband Cosmo. Seated at the other end, five stokers who'd been in the right place at the right time. Their greasy faces were shiny with sweat as they stared up at the ship and rowed away.

Up above them, the ship had taken on a notice-able portside list. One had to dig in his heels just to walk across deck. The remaining starboard lifeboats weren't hanging free on the davits now—they were touching the side of *Titanic*.

Having just repelled a vampire attack on the port side, Isidor Straus urged his wife Ida into Lifeboat 8. Headstrong to the end, she refused and offered her maid the spot, then pulled Isidor across the Boat Deck until they were seated on a bench by the officers' cabins.

"Why did you do that?" he asked.

She smiled warmly, listening to the blood-curdling screams all around them. They felt something push against the wall behind their bench.

"Because we have lived together many years. Where you go, I go."

BOAT DECK

FIONA NEEDED A HOSPITAL. It was possible he could've cauterized her wound on the ship, but the surgery, down on C deck, was likely flooding. Even if he could've gotten her past the water, there was no guarantee the surgical equipment was still secure.

"C'mon," he said, pulling her to the Boat Deck. Her feet were dragging and she kept her right hand cradled close to her body, fingers clenched. She'd most likely suffered nerve damage—the vampire missed her carotid artery, but hit something else instead. Ben dragged her past the orchestra, still playing upbeat music despite the blood splatters on the windows.

Out on the Boat Deck, he found evidence of dead vampires—the wind had blown away the ash long ago, but the initial burst of white fire remained, painting the deck with soft, pale spots.

"Reid . . .," she said, voice weak again.

He turned her around and lifted her by the jacket, then propped her against the wall. A young boy passed by, older than Reid and sporting a White Star Line jacket. In his hands were four lifebelts.

"Can I have two of those, boy?" asked the doctor.

He seemed taken aback that someone had noticed him. His face was pale, eyes gaunt. For a moment, he stared at the belts as if he wasn't even aware he was carrying them.

"You can have one, sir. I need the rest for me, my ma, and my sister."

"Okay, one then."

He handed it off to Ben and disappeared into the tight crowd. The crewmen yelled above his head, still seeking women and children for the boats. The starboard side had launched most of them, at least those on the forward end.

Ben used his knee to hold up Fiona so she didn't slide off the wall. He pulled off her coat, revealing the pretty dress beneath. The skin above her breasts was so pale—pale to match her face. And her lips were blue, not only from the cold but also from losing so much blood. Her eyelids fluttered. Now that he had her beneath one of the electric lights, he saw the horrible stitch job on her neck, yet it was holding. Ben needed a new profession.

"Slip this on," he told her, pulling her out enough so the belt could slide over her body. He tied it in the front, then quickly put her jacket back on before the chilled air hit her.

"The ship . . . we're sideways," she said.

"Yeah. Leaning quite a bit now."

"Not enough . . . boats."

"And that's why you need to get on one right now."

"Not without—"

"I'll find him, Fiona. You have to survive this. You have to get away from the ship."

He thought she nodded but he wasn't sure. Either way, he lifted her and dragged her down the ship toward the aft end. All the boats up front were gone—he looked over the railing and gasped by the closeness of the water. Two boats drifted out there, but darkness consumed the others.

Fiona was heavier now, but that was because they were walking uphill. The railing at the far end of the Boat Deck was pointing toward the sky, rather than straight ahead. Between them, a throng of people were following the officers toward the next set of boats when a vampire dropped from the roof of the first-class lounge.

It was a man—one that Ben had never seen before. The doctor dragged Fiona toward the bank of lounge chairs just as the creature pounced. As it wrapped its arms around a freezing girl, its eyes widening as a stake ripped through its chest, exploding its heart. Ben had never seen one die from the front before, and its eyes vanished like puffs of smoke before fissures split its skin open. Then, the quick return of ash.

When it was dead, Reid stood over the mound, the yew stake trembling in his hands.

"Ma-mama!" he said, then pushed the stake through his belt loop. He rushed forward, almost knocking over both Ben and Fiona. With what little strength she had left, she raised her arms and draped them heavily across his shoulders. He leaned into her, kissing across her neck. Ben could feel the warmth of their tears.

"You . . . sound wonderful," said the doctor, rubbing the ash from the boy's hair. He'd heard of this before—extreme trauma could take away a person's voice—and give it back. His hand moved to his cheek. "Is this *your* blood?"

Reid shook his head. "Let's go, mama. Let's get off this boat right now! He's comin' for us!"

Ben thought so too. They'd been after that damned stake since the beginning.

"Let's go, we can probably put you on that one." Ben pointed to the one that was quickly crowding over. With the forward end boats already gone, people were slowly descending into panic.

Lifeboat 9 was dropping toward the water, but people were still swarming it. Murdoch waved a pistol toward the crowd and they backed away. Once he handed over the davits to his crewmen, he moved onto the next boat, already half full.

"C'mon, mama," said Reid, pushing his way through.

Fiona turned back to Ben and kissed him—she was so cold, blue lips shivering. She tried to say something but was too weak.

"I didn't hear it, love."

She pulled herself close to his ear and whispered, "Come with us."

But Ben knew he couldn't. Even though Murdoch had adopted a less stringent boarding procedure than Lightoller on the port side, he had work to do. Now that Fiona was safe, he would see to the other passengers. Despite his desire to move on, he was a doctor to the end.

He pushed his way through the crowd and Murdoch put a firm hand against his chest—it was hard enough to rattle his teeth. When the officer finally recognized him, he said, "Sorry, doctor. Go on, then." His words came out in trembling, cold steam.

"I just want to speak to the boy."

He stepped up on the railing and Reid approached. Ben said, "I want you to look after your mum, okay?"

"Come with us! You can sit right here. There's plenty of room!"

"I know, lad. I know. But I can't in good conscious board while so many are fighting for their lives."

When his eyes teared up, Ben quickly added, "But I'll find one before it's too late."

"Promise?"

Ben hesitated and sighed, but said, "I promise." He hugged the boy and looked over his shoulder at Fiona, who was leaning heavily against another woman. "Take care of her, okay?"

"I will."

Ben separated and waited for Reid to find a spot next to his mom, then disappeared back into the crowd.

R.M.S. TITANIC

Fiona jolted awake when the davits creaked. She groped at the lady next to her, feeling as if she were flying. She looked over the edge of the boat, now hovering thirty feet from the water. The boat to the right of them was already off the davits and rowing away and the one to the left hung just a few feet up. Fiona and Reid's boat had dropped almost to A deck.

Reid held her hand. It was so cold. His eyes were so fearful. He was about to say something, but another rocket went into the air, forcing her to close her eyes against the stark white blaze.

426

"You gotta stay awake, mama!" he said, and he pinched her cheek. Her eyes fluttered open again.

"I'm trying, Reid. Mama's trying." Her thoughts turned to the days leading up to *Titanic's* departure and how things could've been different. She thought of the man selling the sweets on Simnell Street. She said, "When we get home, I'm going to get you all the gingerbread you want."

"Home?"

She understood his confusion. They hadn't called anyplace home in a long, long time. She ran her fingers through his hair. Ash fell into her hand.

"Home can be anyplace we want it to be."

He nodded, satisfied with that answer, then leaned against her. She draped her arm around his little body and made the same discovery Ben had earlier tonight—something was wrong with her hand, but she was happy to be alive—at least she found her boy at the end.

She cast a sleepy look around the boat and already knew too many people were inside. Why did they allow so many to climb aboard? They would be lucky to hit the water without the whole lifeboat capsizing.

A commotion stirred her from another hopeful sleep. This had already happened twice before, vampires touching down on the deck and trying to feed. But this time was different. This time, all those retreating to the aft end of the ship were running toward the sinking end.

Those in the boat to the left started screaming, and then two people flew overboard. They screamed all the way down until they hit the water. Fiona's boat rocked on its davits—everyone rushed to the edge to look over and that almost sent them right in after the unfortunates. But they quickly moved back just in time to watch the rest of the carnage unfold.

Something was grabbing the passengers out of the boat. She heard slurping sounds, and when the bodies flew over the edge, they were missing heads.

A pair of sailors in the boat fought back at the unseen creature. They shoved oars like clubs but it didn't matter. Fiona watched with horror as a giant beast stepped up to the edge of the boat, then sliced its claws across the ropes on one of the davits.

Everyone in the boat tumbled out as it hung vertically. Those around Fiona stifled their screams when the boats slapped together. Then, the creature sliced the other rope and sent the empty boat down on top of dozens of floundering passengers.

She held her breath as the beast stepped up to the davits above her boat. Whatever officers had been lowering the boat must have either run off or were cowering against the deck. The beast was sniffing the passengers beneath it, red eyes passing over everyone. Reid burrowed beneath her coat, face hidden.

The monster gripped the edge of the deck, splintering the wood. It was the calm before the storm and all seventy people inside the boat were avoiding eye-contact, praying, and silently sobbing in hopes the creature would move on.

And as luck would have it, the beast's attention was suddenly averted to the front end of the ship, like a bloodhound locating its prey. In an instant, it changed to black smoke and was gone.

Fiona thought they were going to be stuck—a few men even suggested they climb out of the boat and enter through the windows on A deck, but then Officer Murdoch reappeared with another sailor and the two began to wind the boat down into the water. Reid trembled beneath her arm.

"We're getting out of here, love. We're getting out of here."

BRIDGE

1:35 A.M.

THOSE CORNERED IN THE ill-fated Lifeboat 13 tasted so nice. It had been a mix of all classes, but their fear had been as one. Like cornered rats, their adrenaline surged through their bodies, carried along by bright, oxygenated blood. And he would've moved onto Lifeboat 11 had his coterie not informed him of something hopeful.

Ronin Dixon had just sunk his teeth into Sixth Officer James Moody and learned all about his life growing up in Scarborough but most importantly learned about the telegraph *Titanic* received forty-five minutes ago.

Quickly, the King rushed past terrified crewmen and passengers, finding pure enjoyment over the collection of white vests to hit the deck. When he reached the empty bridge, he perused the line of telegraphs that had been brought there as per White Star Line procedure.

It was an answer to *Titanic's* distress call. A ship called *Carpathia* was on the way but wouldn't arrive for another four hours—now just over three hours.

The ship would beat the sun, he thought with satisfaction.

An officer entered the bridge, saw the hulking monster, then quickly turned and left. The King paid him no mind. He stepped through the door of the bridge and looked out to the well deck, now taking on water.

For once, he was glad that he didn't understand modern technology. His coterie was to destroy the radio, but now in light of the iceberg, the radio had saved him.

The ship, this *Carpathia*, was coming. It didn't matter if any of the humans lived—most would die in the water, anyway. All that mattered was that he secured passage. True, his box and his earth were gone, but he could survive without those. He would use his influence and suggestive powers to get more earth.

But if he could leave the ship, so too could the stake. He had to find it. He had to make sure it was splintered into a thousand pieces. Even if he lived after tonight, even if his coterie blossomed in America, and even if *Titanic* rested at the bottom of the ocean, he would forever be haunted that the stake was still out there.

The King floated up to the top of the funnel and stared down, amazed that so much of the ship was already underwater. The aft end was slowly lifting.

Propellers—something he'd only seen in the minds of others—would be out of the water within the hour. He counted the lifeboats, like little pumpkin seeds floating along a stream.

His stomach grumbled. He threw his head back and grinned, then soared back toward the deck, led by his unbridled bloodlust.

B DECK

1:50 A.M.

THE LIGHTS WOULD FAIL anytime now. Ben was sure of it. The only reason they hadn't gone out already was because some brave engineer was working tirelessly to keep them on. Once the electricity failed, he'd be flailing about in the dark—and no matter how packed the sky was with stars, he wouldn't be able to find his way topside.

Water surged into the ship through the larger, square windows of B deck. On the forward end, the portside lifeboats didn't have to drop more than ten feet to reach the water. Ben pounded on doors, pushing open the ones that were unlocked, kicking in the ones that were. Most everyone in the places he could reach was already topside, and those he couldn't reach could not be helped now.

Titanic listed heavily to the portside, and he feared that once too much water rushed in, the whole ship would flip over, funnels ripping away like tinfoil. It was a silly thought, but then again, the concept of the unsinkable ship sinking was silly.

The entire forward end was beneath water now, all the way up to B deck. He went to his cabin, happy to see that his medical kit was still on the bed where he patched up Byles. Throwing it all into his bag, he left and listened in the hallway—water was rushing up toward him. A slow march, but it was picking up speed.

He turned and headed down the second-class staircase and came upon a large group of third-class passengers lingering on D deck, admiring the carpet and the woodwork. Almost all of them were wearing their lifebelts.

"Why are you all standing around?" he shouted. The room hushed and they turned to look at him.

"We cannot go, sir," said a middle-aged, balding man. He was seated in one of the overstuffed lounge chairs with a small girl on one knee and a small boy on the other. "We're waiting on the staff to tell us where to go." He pointed to a sign hanging above the stairway.

First- and second-class only beyond this point.

Missing the boats for a sign, thought Ben.

"Go!" he told them. "No one is coming to tell you a thing! Get to the boats now!"

Those that spoke English quickly jumped at his voice and rushed up the steps. Those that didn't, followed their counterparts. Ben shook his head in frustration. Most of these people were going to die tonight.

A pair of older ladies required medical attention. One had slipped in the darkness after the ship started to list and bumped her head. The other had a ragged gash across her shoulder but she didn't speak English, so Ben didn't know if it was from a vampire attack or something else. The latter he bandaged up and the former he helped up to A deck until he handed her off to a younger boy, perhaps her grandson.

Down the forward end of each deck was marked by death. He was heartbroken to see so many children—little bodies gripping stuffed bears and cats, their faces pale, lips blue. Without seeing their throats, he couldn't tell if they'd died from vampires or drowning. This late into the disaster, it could be either.

The ship was tilting more—moving toward the aft end was a struggle because he kept sliding across the slick tile. Soon, it would feel like climbing a wall. He'd checked all the decks he could except E deck—but he had low hopes for that one. After making it back across D deck, he continued down the staircase until he heard voices.

". . . may Christ who crucified for you, bring you freedom and peace . . ."

Ben rounded the corner, horrified by what he saw.

"... may Christ who died for you admit you into his garden of paradise."

"Father," said Ben. Byles was leaning against a lattice gate, his arm between the bars. On the other side, so many people reached through that Ben couldn't even see the hall beyond them. Their arms grabbed the priest wherever they could—his legs, his shoulders, handfuls of his clothes, even resting them atop his head.

Byles ignored the doctor.

"May Christ, the true Shepherd, embrace you as one of his flock."

"Father, we have to get this gate open!"

"May he forgive all your sins, and set you among those he has chosen."

"Father!"

"May you see your Redeemer face to face, and enjoy the vision of God, forever."

"Byles!" Ben grabbed him by the shoulder and pushed him against the wall. The priest winced, and that's when Ben saw the tattered mess of his arm. His jacket, two layers of it, was soaked through with blood.

"It's over, Benjamin. This is all I can do for them. I can't save them from the water. I can only save them from the fire."

Ben paid him no attention. He'd lost a lot of blood—and perhaps the will to save himself. The doctor grabbed the bars and rattled them, but knew after one shake they wouldn't come down.

There were at least three children back there, a couple of elderly, but mostly able-bodied men who'd already moved to the front hoping to tear down the gate. Every warm body on the other side had to hold on to someone else, for the list and tilt of the ship was so extreme they feared sliding away.

And then, panic renewed when Ben felt the cold water rushing around his ankles. The men threw themselves against the bars, over and over, the noise deafening in the tight hallway. The children were screaming out, their little hands passing through the legs of their parents. Slowly, the water rose behind them.

"Benjamin," Byles said, almost a whisper. It was so calm that it made him forget the gate for a moment and turn around.

In the hallway just by the staircase stood one of them, her eyes like balls of fire. The light from above passed between her fingers, lighting the claws in which her hands were twisted. She was soaking wet, beads of water dripping off her chin, turning pink as it mixed with the blood from her fangs. And then she threw her head back and rushed Ben and the wounded priest.

LIFEBOAT 11

1:54 A.M.

THE HORRIBLE CREATURE NEVER came back, and the boat continued loading. It picked up more passengers on A deck and by the time it reached the water, it was overburdened with almost seventy people—a few more than the max capacity. It was a tumultuous drop when the ropes cut free and they rowed off on their own power.

Looking over the edge, Reid knew why.

The ruined Lifeboat 13 and all sixty-five of its passengers floated in the water. None of them were alive—all stiff as boards with blue, bloody faces. Reid wasn't sure what killed them—the impact or the freezing water.

"We don't have no light," said a sailor, stepping up to the helm of the boat. "Move out of the way." He pushed aside shivering passengers as he made his way to the front. With the help of another sailor, he brought a match to the end of a thick rope and held it there until it started to burn. Then he placed the flaming end on the edge of the boat.

As they rowed away, everyone stared up at man's greatest creation, soon to be lost forever. The aft end pointed toward the sky. The propellers, dead and still, visible for the first time since drydock. It was all so dark, the electric lights dimmer than they had been an hour ago.

On the front, only the foremast remained above water. The entire forecastle deck and front well deck was consumed, bringing the Atlantic right up to the ship's superstructure. In another few minutes, the bridge would also slip beneath the waves.

Edith Rosenbaum, the socialite who'd been treated for a hangover by Evelyn Marsden (who boarded Lifeboat 16 only thirty minutes earlier), clutched her stuffed pig against her chest. She looked up at the wreck with sad eyes.

"There goes my new Jeanne Paquin dress!" she lamented to anyone who would listen. The sound of her American accent made a scared little girl wail. "Oh, don't cry, sweetheart. I didn't mean to upset you. I'm just . . . lost, is all."

"Yeah," said a sailor with a cigarette in his mouth. He shook out his empty box and tossed it into the water. "We're all lost, miss."

"It's just that . . . the White Star Line wouldn't even let me purchase insurance on my luggage! They said, 'oh, Miss Rosenbaum, that won't be necessary! She's unsinkable, she is!'" Edith reclined back and laughed, tears streaming down her face. She held a hand up to the floundering ship. "Unsinkable!"

Fiona was dozing, steam rising from her pursed lips. As long as Reid could see that, he was happy. It was so cold, but this lifeboat had one advantage over the others—there were so many bodies packed close together that the shared heat made it bearable, at least until the wind blew. Then Reid couldn't feel his fingertips.

He hated he couldn't see through the darkness. The further away the sailors rowed, the less light that fell across the boat. He'd seen the vampires turn to grey smoke. They could fly. It stood to reason they could reach the lifeboats with ease.

That's when he made a startling discovery—he sat up and checked his belt loop—

—the yew stake was gone.

For a moment, he thought he'd lost it in the water, just like he'd lost his father's cross that day on the gangway. But no, he remembered the hug and knew exactly where it was—and it made him smile.

Hopefully, it would protect the doctor the way it had protected Reid.

E DECK

THE VAMPIRE PUSHED HIM against the bars before he could react. Her strength was incredible, but Byles slammed his cross into her head with his good arm, knocking her back long enough for Ben to draw a weapon.

He drove the yew stake into her throat. She knew the weapon well and her body straightened, although she didn't die. Ben kept pushing until it exited the back of her neck, then he gripped both ends. She flailed, attempted to rake her nails across him, but he kept her at an arm's length.

"Through the heart or she won't die," said Byles, resting against the wall.

The water continued to pour into the hallway. It had reached the stairway. Beyond the gate, it was rising high enough for the adults to pick up the children.

"I'm not trying to kill her."

Ben dragged her to the gate, still holding the stake firmly in both hands. She hissed and sputtered and

445

screamed something in a language he couldn't comprehend. The little ones were afraid.

"Back up!" Ben told the group behind the gate. And then, to the vampire: "Pull down this gate or I'll kill you slowly."

She hissed, so he throttled her back and forth, the stake tearing into her flesh. Finally, she settled and placed her hands on the corners of the bars. With a grunt, she ripped the metal right through the wood—it was still too sturdy for even vampire strength, but she moved it aside just wide enough for the trapped passengers to squeeze by. They hurried along, racing up the steps, hoping to secure a lifeboat.

"Hold her still," said Byles.

"No!" Ben said. "I don't want to kill her."

"What?" The doctor pushed her until the stake rested against the wall. Then he stood in front of her, both hands on the tip, ready to rip her head right off if she didn't cooperate. Her eyes were filled with malice—little dancing flames ready to set him on fire. She hissed and spat.

"You're going to deliver a message to your master for me. Tell him I have the stake." Ben jiggled it to make sure he had her full attention. "Tell him if he wants it, meet me on the third-class promenade. Do you understand?"

The vampire made a wet gurgle that he took as an acknowledgement.

He pulled the stake through her throat and she dropped to the ground, then stood and glared at him threateningly. Byles was ready to brandish his high cross, but the vampire hissed, a spray of blood slapping Ben in the chest, then turned to vapor and left toward the rising water. At the far end, the electric lights caught her sifting through a vent.

"What's your plan, Ben?" asked the priest as they climbed the steps up to D deck.

"I don't have one, father." He stopped by the nearest porthole, the waterline not far below them, and found a couple of the lifeboats. It was dark out, but he saw the disturbed water each time they put the oars in.

"The King will kill you."

"Maybe, but don't you see? Once the ship goes down, he'll take out the lifeboats. I don't know how far he can fly, but we have to buy them time." Ben checked the man's arm—it was grisly, but there wasn't anything he could do. It needed cleaned and stitched, neither of which the doctor could manage right now.

"What makes you think the lifeboats will keep rowing away?"

"When the ship goes down, it's likely to drag the boats down with the whirlpool. The sailors will know this. They'll try to put as much distance between themselves and Titanic as possible."

"Why are you doing this, doctor?" But Ben knew it was an over-arching question, not necessarily about the boats.

"Because I've been running for a long time now. I can't run any longer. I have to face what I was called to do. I have to help people."

Byles nodded, that answer good enough for him.

As they entered C deck, Ben looked through the windows of the library and saw the table and chairs all turned over, the shelves dumped of their books. Byles stopped and looked back toward the staircase.

"You coming with me?" Ben said. "I . . . I understand if you don't want to, father."

Byles smiled. "I'll be there. But I'm going to gather my flock first."

And then he turned and hobbled up the stairs.

R.M.S. TITANIC

2:00 A.M.

WITH ONLY TWENTY MINUTES to live, water trickled over the A deck railing. The forward compartments were so waterlogged that it was taking on weight far quicker than before. The portside list, thanks to the dimensions of Scotland Road, forced everything not bolted down to shift to one side, adding more weight to an already unstable ship. Most passengers had already found their way to the upper decks.

Of the twenty boats available on *Titanic*, seventeen had already launched. That left around one thousand five hundred passengers and crew stuck on the ship, most of them driven back to the third-class promenade—the last stand of *Titanic*.

The ship's power continued to decrease. No telegraphs could come or go—*Titanic* was an island unto itself with no way to communicate besides the odd rocket fired from the portside by the bridge.

Captain Smith relieved the two wireless operators, a defeated look on his face that scared both Jack Phillips and Harold Bride. Shortly after, the men would part ways, never to see each other again.

With only smaller, collapsible lifeboats remaining, Officer Lightoller drew his pistol—one of the three that a bewitched captain didn't throw overboard—and fired shots into the air. Many passengers, fearful of both the water and the vampires, tried to overpower him and launch the boat themselves. A blast rattled the night and one man staggered back, his lifebelt blown open, bits of cork and guts splattered across the deck. He fell on his side, his darkening eyes settling on the guide wire for the front mast and the black and white cat walking across with a newborn kitten in her mouth.

Atop the roof of the officers' quarters stood Thomas Andrews, Captain Smith, and Chief Officer Wilde. Using a megaphone, the captain screamed in desperation for the half-full lifeboats to return to the ship and pick up more passengers. This fell on deaf ears, and when a vampire snatched Wilde and dragged him through a window on A deck, the other two men gave up the attempt.

Bruce Ismay, despite his atrocious behavior throughout *Titanic's* maiden voyage, handled the final disaster with aplomb and civility. When no women or children were left, at least on the starboard side, he entered the Collapsible C lifeboat along with forty-two other people. Because the ship was listing so much to portside, the boat rested against *Titanic* and it scraped the hull the entire way down. The sound was maddening.

Below, most of the decks were filled from floor to ceiling with water. Bodies danced slowly in perpetual darkness. Ernest Burr, the first victim aboard *Titanic*, floated out of the surgery, his coffin rotating slowly against the moving water.

Some passengers were caught in rooms, some trapped in watertight compartments. Some died with their hands still gripping the lattice gates. The entire Olsson clan—from Erik to little Jack—floated in the blackness between F and E deck.

The lucky ones who made it topside were hopeful of getting in a boat, although most were realistic. Benjamin Guggenheim and his valet Victor Giglio, who dressed in their finest and pulled up chairs in the first-class entrance, were determined to go down with the ship like gentlemen. But they were forced to move away as water rushed down the steps.

The Strauses, still sitting on a bench on the promenade, also had to move because the shift of *Titanic* was pulling them toward the front.

Many of the passengers watched as the last collapsible boats were pulled down off the roof of the officers' quarters. There was no way to lower them gracefully, so the crew formed ramps from oars. Judging by the flimsiness of the boats, most just turned and moved to the other end.

And this would be *Titanic's* final breath. Its death throes were upon it. A surge of people in white lifebelts, fancy coats and hats, moved like a wave away from the encroaching water. It was a difficult trek toward the aft end of the ship, for this late in the sinking, it was a steep climb.

Ben climbed up the third-class steps, holding the rail to keep himself from sliding back down. Up top, he put his back against the railing and fed his arms through it to keep him in place. He looked down—it was a long way to the propellors, but he chose not to think of that right now.

And then he waited.

Third-Class Promenade

BEN REGRETTED SUGGESTING THE King meet him here. It would be a bloodbath and he wasn't sure which death would be the most preferred—drowning, freezing, or being torn apart.

Crowds were still gathering by the boats, but Ben was certain none remained. It seemed so long ago that he'd discussed the scarcity of them with Fiona. He hoped she and Reid were alright, and that they rowed with haste away from the doomed ship.

More people lingered on the promenade, but many remained on the well deck below and the Boat Deck above. He didn't think there were as many vampires left—they'd all been put to the stake, or the worst-case scenario, ventured out to the lifeboats. Ben turned to the ocean and couldn't see anything. For all he knew, every one of them could be empty by now.

In one hand, he gripped the yew stake. In the other, the crucifix he bought for Reid in Queenstown. That also seemed like an eternity ago. He was shaking now, probably from the cold, but also from

453

the fear. Ben had fought these creatures since they started to make trouble but only tonight did he realize he would die. The good Lord in all his wisdom had stacked so much against the people of *Titanic*. It didn't matter to what class one belonged—death cared not.

He was scanning the crowds for Father Byles when a column of smoke dropped on the promenade deck only thirty feet away. When the King emerged, all nine feet of it, people screamed and dispersed, tripping over one another to get down to the well deck or the general assembly area beneath Ben's feet.

The beast had only two long fangs. The rest were coming in at different intervals, making the lower half of its face appear to be in a perpetual smile. But any hope of humor evaporated at the creature's eyes. They were blazing, like the tips of red-hot pokers. When it opened its mouth, a long, vile tongue slithered out and back in.

"Do you speak?" said Ben, hoping to stall the creature.

"I do," it said, and the accent was odd—like some kind of ancient Gaelic mixed with the rot of the ground.

"Why did you hurt all these people?"

The creature smiled—a real one, fangs turning up in a half-circle. "It's what I am." It took a few steps forward, the robe trailing behind. The gravity from the sloping deck that kept Ben's muscles active seemed not to bother the creature.

"Back!" said Ben, raising the crucifix. The vampire simply turned its head and held up a large, bony hand, as if it were a mere irritation.

"Don't make this unpleasant, child." Its voice was low and gravely. "I can break your neck and suck out your blood straight from your heart, or I can open up every artery in your body and make it last."

"Ship's sinking," said Ben, looking past the creature and feeling a surge of defiance. "I don't think we have time for all that."

The flames in the creature's eyes thinned and it lunged. Ben raised the stake above his head, ready to strike its heart. But then it stopped just short of him, a stake ripping through its stomach from behind. Quickly, it turned around, swinging Father Byles with it.

The stake turned out to be the priest's high cross, and upon seeing the tip poking through, the vampire wailed. Smoke billowed from its robe. Byles let go and reached for something in his pocket, but the creature grabbed him by the shoulders and tossed him.

More people rushed away, heading toward the forward end—and the rising water. The vampire lunged, hidden legs carrying it with great speed and stability. It snatched Byles in one hand just as Ben's feet started moving. Again, he raised the stake.

The King tossed Byles toward him. Ben missed the stake by inches as the priest slammed into him and they both went down on the deck. Ben tasted blood in his mouth from his own bitten lip. Quickly, he pushed Byles aside and raised the cross. The vampire averted its eyes, and in the same gesture, snatched the priest.

Ben scrambled to his feet, raised the yew stake while the creature was lifting Byles in the air and stabbed—

—only to have his forearm caught in the beast's oversized hand. Ben knew he was in trouble and perhaps the chilled air helped when the vampire bent his arm back, cracking the bones so completely that his fingers touched the back of his forearm. He screamed out in red-hot pain as the yew stake clattered to the deck.

The vampire released him and turned its attention to Byles. Ben crashed against the deck, banging his forehead but feeling nothing but the pain in his arm. He cradled it close to his body as he watched the certain death of Father Byles.

But while the creature was snapping Ben's arm, the priest was pulling a vial of holy water from his belt. He smashed it across the monster's face with a satisfying crunch. Water exploded out, filling the air with the smell of charred, rotting flesh. The creature threw its head back and screamed as smoke and flame rose like a halo above it.

Rather than stagger back, it braced itself against the pain and gripped Byles by the shoulders, then bit into him with a mouth large enough to send his head rolling off his shoulders. The monster, flaming fangs and all, chomped down on the stump of a neck and drank from him as if he were nothing more than a flask.

When he tossed the dead man aside, the flames were almost extinguished. It whirled around to face Ben, but that's when the doctor realized the stake was still embedded. The beast couldn't reach behind and remove it, so it gripped the point with both hands and pulled it deeper into its body. A horrifying scream bellowed out of its twisted mouth as smoke wafted off its hands, the holy weapon as good as the water. Its eyes went wide as the cross section entered its back and left through the chest. And then it dropped the high cross atop the dead, headless man.

The beast turned its attention back to Ben, but before it could finish the job, another vial of water exploded upon its face. It hissed and screamed and Ben followed the source of the attack and found Byles's flock—a group of steerage passengers with their arms loaded full of holy water. They tossed them, one after another, driving the beast away from Ben—but they were only bellowing its anger.

In half a heartbeat, it rushed across the deck, carried by unnatural speed. It picked up one burly man and ripped him in half at the shoulders. The spray of blood was enough to send the more squeamish passengers away. A few continued to fight, but those also met a grisly end, as the King had gone into a rage, a quick feeding frenzy that left people in clumps and the deck slick with blood.

Another group came at it from the well deck below. The vampire staggered as many scored enough hits to set it entirely on fire. It took a knee, then rose and raced forward to quell the attack.

"Come quick!" said the monster, speaking in a demonic voice that rose higher than the clamor of passengers. "I need aid!"

Three columns of grey smoke entered the well deck, materializing as two women and the boy, Colin. They picked off a few of the King's attackers but there were still more, hurling vials of water, using crucifixes to redirect it.

Ben got to his feet just in time to see its flaming head moving down the steps to the well deck. He was in so much pain, but he tried to keep his broken arm steady. With his good hand, he snatched the yew stake and followed. At the top of the stairs, he watched the King directly below him pick up a woman and squeeze her throat until she stopped flailing.

And without thinking, Ben jumped, stake leading . . .

The tip sunk into the creature's back and continued through until Ben's fist touched its robe. The doctor spun away, landing painfully on his arm, but he pushed it from his mind. He scrambled to his feet and looked up at the creature. The tip was pouring blood.

It sank to its knees at the same moment the flames burnt out in its eyes. Little wisps of smoke wafted up. Now, only soulless black dots remained. Weak fingers tried to pull the stake on through, but it didn't have the strength. Ben watched it fall over, then raced up the steps as everyone else pushed past him to get back to the rear of the ship.

The water was rising faster. The stern was rising higher. He was about to run past the second-class library when he saw one of the other vampires—it was Minnie Pembroke, one of the first. The flames in her eyes were weak. She approached Ben and tried to scrape him, but he simply sidestepped. She fell to the ground, then quickly got up and ran off.

They lost their connection to the King, he thought. *Just like when we took the fang out of Clarence Clarke. They're mindless now.*

He didn't have time to appreciate this revelation. By the time he reached the Boat Deck, the forward end was almost in the water. The highest deck on *Titanic* was now level with the Atlantic. All the boats were gone—portside and starboard, but he spied one more floating in the water by the bridge. It was one of the collapsibles.

Ben ran counter to everyone else. All the others had abandoned hope. They sought the high ground, even if the high ground was about to go under with everything else. Many people had resigned themselves to die, sitting calmly on benches or with their legs over the railing. The ship's baker was tossing floatable chairs into the water. John Astor stood in a throng of men, each shivering and smoking cigars. The band, now set up just outside the door to the first-class entrance, continued to play, although there was a noticeable staccato to the strings—whether from the cold or the fear, Ben couldn't tell.

"Help me, doctor!" said a voice next to the overturned boat. He thought it was someone gravely injured, but it turned out to be Second Officer Lightoller. When Ben faced him, Lightoller shook his head. "You got a busted arm? Bah, I think I can do it myself."

"Here!" said a young man, wading into the water. "Shite, that's cold!" It was Harold Bride, one of the Marconi men.

A few others surrounded the boat and flipped it over, then began scooping water out before trying to launch it. Ben watched as the Boat Deck went under much faster and knew they needed to get off the ship now.

"Let's go, let's go," he said, and then jumped in after Lightoller. As the men picked up oars, they heard a colossal boom somewhere beneath the ship, followed by what sounded like thunder.

"The boilers are exploding!" said one man.

Bride shook his head. "Nah, boilers are cold by now. That's all the damned China in the lounge!"

The ship was groaning angrily, the list getting better, but the waterline continued to sneak up until it was around the first funnel. Ben had been watching the ship go under, but that's when he saw a lone figure coming toward them.

The King, stake embedded in its heart, trudged forward. It held a hand out toward the boat, but the men saw it and picked up the pace, rowing them out of harm's way. Ben knew the creature was dying, otherwise it would've floated out and killed every man in the boat.

A few of the guidewires for the funnel snapped. Each one slapped the water, sending up a fan ten feet high. After the fourth one ripped away, the funnel groaned, and then shifted. The King who'd lived for so long, who'd killed countless innocents, who'd survived by pure instinct, never saw the funnel coming toward it.

His tall, yet weak body crumbled beneath the metal and the splash sent a wall of water rushing toward Ben's boat. Another boom below the ship. Another groan of metal and wood. Ben didn't hear any of it because his ears were full of water. The wave hit the boat and turned it on its side—and the pain in his arm retreated to the far corners of his mind as a new anguish came like a thousand icy daggers.

LIFEBOAT 11

2:16 A.M.

THE WORST PART WAS the screaming.

The sailors in Lifeboat 11 were confident that when *Titanic* went under, they were far enough away to escape the ensuing whirlpool. Fiona and Reid had been off the ship now for almost an hour and were able to watch each horrifying moment, helpless to do anything.

No one spoke, they only watched and listened. The ship continued to make awful noises that echoed all the way to their boat. Sporadic screams erupted at the rear, followed by flashes of light that Fiona hoped was the quick death of the vampires.

She also hoped that Ben was alright but knew better in her heart. It had been foolish to follow her fantasy so far—to believe that a man of his stature could ever be interested in her. At least she had Reid. After all the tragedies in their life, at least she still had him.

He was currently cradling her in his arms. Anytime she drifted off to sleep, he slapped her face gently with his little fingers. They would talk for a moment, then revert to watching the carnage in front of them.

She was shaken from her thoughts when the lights on the ship blinked. A collective hush fell across the lifeboats as *Titanic's* power failed and the entire world plunged into darkness. They could see the ship's outline because of the star-filled sky. The screams and splashes never stopped, nor did the twisting metal.

Soon after the lights went out, the world was filled with a horrible sound as the ship broke apart. The bow could no longer support the weight of the stern as it continued to rise, so the whole ship snapped right in the middle. As the stern crashed back down, the water displaced rocked the lifeboats a hundred yards away. The rear two funnels fell over—one rolling off the starboard side and the other back across the well deck.

The front of the ship was gone, already plunging down toward the bottom of the ocean. But, unknown to any of those witnessing its death, it was still connected to the keel, so it dragged the stern along with it. The back of the ship rolled toward port, bobbed for a moment, then rose straight into the air. Fiona could still hear the screams of the people perched atop the railing. And then the stern went straight down.

Titanic was gone.

RMS TITANIC

She wasn't sure now which was worse—the screams or the absolute darkness. At least the screams perished—eventually.

She lay back in Reid's arms, eyes closed, listening to the awful sound. More than a thousand people went into the water once there was no place left to stand. Even if every boat rushed back to pick up survivors, it would be too late. The cold would claim them in short order. Fiona remembered the posted letter outside the promenade early yesterday morning that stated the water temperature was around minus two degrees.

One by one, the screams went away. When it began, it was a cacophony of noise. She wanted to plug her ears with her fingers, but she was trying to appear strong for Reid. Instead, *he* made the decision he didn't want her to hear, so he cupped his hands over them.

Within thirty minutes, those in the water were silent. Occasionally, they heard splashes. Voices from the other boats drifted her way. If they were all still seaworthy, nineteen of them lingered nearby, waiting for a rescue that may never come.

There were no other lights on the water, except the one at the front of their boat—the length of rope was still brightly burning. Fiona thought it strange that none of the others had lanterns or lights, but that was because she didn't know the others had already learned to turn them off.

"How are they still splashing around?" asked Walter Brice, one of the crewmen. "How come they ain't freezing?"

Just then, the little girl who'd been holding back a wall of tears the whole night finally lost it. She let out a long, ragged cry that echoed in the near silence. The fancy lady, Edith Rosenbaum, pet her like a dog.

"There, there, sweetie. It'll be okay. Another ship will come to rescue us. Not as nice as Titanic, but I suppose that doesn't matter."

The splashing came closer. The little girl continued to wail. Edith rolled her eyes and presented her with a little stuffed pig. For a moment, the girl's eyes widened as she reached out and took the toy.

"That's right, sweetie. This is Lucky. She'll play music for you if you wind her tail."

The little girl's shaky fingers twisted the metal, and then the night filled with sweet music. It was loud, but that was probably because of the otherwise dead silence.

Except the approaching splash.

Reid shifted uncomfortably. He slipped from beneath Fiona and moved toward the front of the boat. "Quiet the music! And douse the light!"

"What?" said Walter, wondering why Reid had such audacity to demand such things.

"You're leading it right to us!" he said, voice just above a whisper.

The splashing grew closer still, only now they could hear a mindless, coarse moan.

"Oh, shite!" said Walter. "It's one of 'em!"

He backed away just as a pair of pale, stiff hands grabbed the front of the boat. The burning end of the rope illuminated Colin's dead face, only now his eyes matched. There were no more little flames. Now it was pure darkness. He lunged at the nearest woman, who screamed and almost went over the side of the boat. The men stood at once, the boat teetering dangerously.

One of them stabbed with a wooden stake, but the boy dodged it and then smacked the weapon away. It clattered to the basin of the boat.

Two more of them grabbed Colin, and pushed him back but it wasn't enough to get rid of him. He slithered out of their grasp and dropped to the basin. His eyes locked with Reid and he crawled forward, hissing like a rabid dog. Reid backed away, falling into the arms of a passenger.

Colin grabbed his leg and threw back his head, ready to bite down, but Fiona was on him in a flash. In the depths of her being, she found a reserve of energy, picked up the stake, and drove it through his back. He howled in pain, twisted around, then launched himself at her.

And both tumbled out of the boat and into the water. The last thing she remembered was a bright flash of light and a sting like a thousand knives.

PART V

FURTHER PARTICULARS
LATER

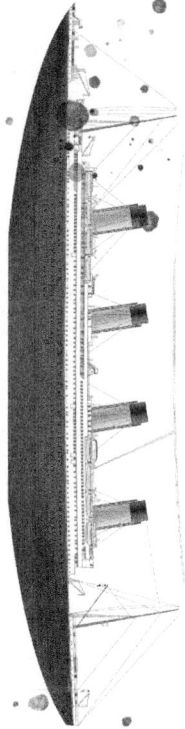

THE DARK

SHE WASN'T SURE WHAT happened after that, but knew nothing but a cold she would never forget. Her body seized as they dragged her back into the boat. And then, strangers were shedding their own clothes hoping to wrap her in enough layers to keep her alive. The lifebelt had saved her. God bless Ben for putting it on her.

After that, her memory was fuzzy. She remembered Reid talking to her, pleading with her to survive. Someone with bad breath was constantly checking her pulse—didn't he know that his fingers on her throat only made her colder?

When the light came, she thought she was dying. She thought she'd go to that big green field where Emmet didn't drink and Erin wasn't covered in fire. Where Reid would one day join. But it wasn't her time yet, and the light was sun. She heard people talking, saw other lifeboats in the water, but worst of all—a sea of floating lifebelts strapped to bodies that they failed to save.

A ship loomed in the distance—not nearly as big as *Titanic*, but that was okay. This single-funneled ship was going to save them. She hoped they'd prop her next to a fire and let her sleep.

And sleep she did. For hours, days, weeks. She had no idea. Voices hung above her, floating ethereally in the air. Some of them were familiar, although she'd sunk so deep into herself that she couldn't place them. Time stood still. Time marched forward. She experienced more cold, more warmth, more light, and more dark. And finally, she woke up and didn't recognize her surroundings.

It was raining and it was dark out. When she opened her eyes, she knew she was no longer on a ship. The floor beneath her was too steady. There was no low droning of engines. She looked through a window directly ahead and saw a brick building just beyond the sheets of falling rain. The window was open, an oil lamp burning in the sill.

Fiona shifted on the bed, feeling her stiff joints attempting to wake. Her throat was dry and her head was pounding. But she was warm—thank God above that she was warm.

A row of beds spread out to her right, each holding a sleeping body.

"Mrs. Lynch?" said a voice to her left. Fiona's heart raced as she rolled over and found a nun sitting at a small table, reading by candlelight. She stood and rushed over, then put a hand to Fiona's brow.

"Where am I?"

"Your husband and son are waiting downstairs. But they can't come in here. Let's go to the common room. Do you think you can walk?"

"I think . . . my husband?"

"Well I suppose that's who he is. Hasn't left the hospital since you all came in." She helped Fiona to her feet—her legs were shaky, and she almost pitched forward, but the nun's strong arms kept her upright. Together they walked through the door at the end of the long infirmary, where she then put Fiona into a chair in the next room. It was dark inside and the rain continued to beat down on the roof above her. The nun excused herself.

Fiona wore a thin gown, her pale legs poking through the ends. This garment made her look tiny and sickly and she couldn't stand it. The thought of being weak bothered her, but if *Titanic* had taught her anything, it was that she was certainly far from weak.

"Mama!" came a voice from the doorway across the hall. She heard Reid's footsteps on the stairs before she even saw him. He rushed her and wrapped his arms around her so tightly they almost turned the chair over. He was holding a book—of course he was—and he clubbed her back accidentally. "How do you feel?"

"I'm fine. I'm thirsty, though."

"Wait here, I'll get the nurse!" And then he left the same way he came, passing by Ben, who stood in the doorway, looking twenty years older than he had the last time she saw him. His arm was in a sling, his skin pale, eyes sunken.

"Oh thank God," she said, and broke down into tears. He rushed over, knelt in front of her, and put his arm around her. She hid her face in her hands, slightly embarrassed.

"You're safe now. It's over. Every bit of it. We killed him and our feet are on solid ground."

"All those people," she said. "So many dead."

"Yeah," Ben said. "It's in all the papers."

"How long have I been here? And where *is* here?"

"You've been under for about five days. We're in New York. Carpathia arrived three days after picking us up. It would've been two days, but this damned storm . . ."

"This is a hospital?"

"Yeah, St. Vincent."

"Your arm . . .," she said, and stroked his jacket.

"It's fine. Or it will be. It sure hasn't stopped them from putting me to work."

"You've been helping?"

Ben nodded. "It's helped me more than them. I've needed to . . . keep my mind busy."

That made her smile. She leaned in and kissed him, and the angle hurt his arm and made her dizzy in the same moment. She fell back against the chair, head swimming.

Reid returned with a glass of water. He handed it to her and as she started drinking, his eyes went wide and he said, "No, wait!" Once she stopped, he added, "Nurse says you gotta drink it slow, okay?"

"Okay," she said, and smiled. Then she drank slow.

He nuzzled up to her until she draped an arm across him. Of the three, Reid seemed to be the only one to escape any trauma—physical trauma, anyway. He couldn't handle much more.

They sat there in silence for a moment. It was the first time life wasn't throwing hardships their way. No vampires. No sinking ship.

"Where did you get that?" she asked Reid, rotating the book so she could see the cover. *The Wonderful Wizard of Oz* by L. Frank Baum.

"The library," he said. "Ben took me."

"The library? Oh, *the* library." She knew at once what he meant. They'd visited the big one here in the city, the one with the lions guarding the front.

Ben said, "We didn't know how long you'd be out and I knew he liked to read so we've spent our days there."

"And where have you been sleeping?"

"Downstairs," said Reid.

Ben nodded. "They have a nice spot for families. There's a lot of them down there." His face darkened a little at this, but she didn't need him to elaborate. She already knew.

"So . . . what will you do now?" Fiona asked him, hating her wording. It wasn't fair to him to assume his plans included her and Reid.

"There's an official inquiry starting tomorrow morning. I've been asked to answer questions. I plan to have strong words with Ismay."

"Oh."

Reid looked up, knowing there was more she wished to pose but couldn't find the strength.

"But after that . . .," Ben said, just as his arm tightened around her shoulder. "I'll go wherever you go."

That made her smile big, and she closed her eyes and squeezed out happy tears on his shirt. His thumb rubbed affectionately across her shoulder.

"Pittsburgh," said Reid. "We're supposed to go to Pittsburgh. For da."

"Yeah," Fiona said.

"Pittsburgh sounds lovely," said Ben.

"You're sure?" she asked him.

He smiled and kissed her forehead. "Pittsburgh is as good a place as any. And the best part?"

Both Reid and Fiona looked at him curiously. She smiled, for she knew the answer. "We don't have to take a ship to get there."

He grinned and nodded, then pulled them both a little closer.

AUTHOR'S NOTE...

FOR AS LONG AS I can remember, I've been fascinated by *Titanic*. Sound familiar? I'm sure it does because everyone who listened to me talk about this project shared their own stories of fascination. Many of us started early, some of us came aboard for James Cameron's blockbuster in 1997—and that's okay. *Titanic* brings us together in a weird way. Some of us like the Edwardian era. Some of us like the architecture, some like the hubris of man, of the greatest technological feat of the time, simply ending in tragedy. When I set out to write this story, I wanted to make sure all lovers of *Titanic* could find something in my words to enjoy.

I am not a *Titanic* purist. I've talked with experts who could tell me the number of rivets on each watertight door. I know people who can quote the timeline from memory. With every new book, I try to become an expert in my subject matter, at least for the time I'm writing it. Despite this, I'm sure there are issues in the ship's layout and timeline. Many of these I changed for artistic value and to make certain elements more exciting. Just know, purists, that this was done with love.

Special thanks to all the people who helped me along the way. My wife and son were paramount to my success. I'm sure they both grew tired of my constant *Titanic* facts or moments of OH MY GOD in the middle of the night when I learned something new and exciting during the research phase. I also want to thank Phillip Hind, the webmaster of *Encyclopedia Titanica*. This site features a database so big that it did a lot of the heavy lifting for me. I urge everyone to check out the site because you won't find a better resource for all things *Titanic*. And lastly, I want to thank the guys over at *Titanic: Honor & Glory*. This team has assembled a virtual *Titanic* that lets the user explore almost every nook and cranny of the ocean liner. It was such a valuable tool for this visual writer. Whenever I was stuck on a route the characters needed to take, I could 'walk' it myself and figure it out. Everyone needs to support these guys. They're doing great work at *THG*.

Finally, I would like to thank all of you, my readers. I think of you for every word I put down. Many of you I've talked with and I envision how you'll feel when you read a part that's important to me. I thank you again for staying with me this long and I look forward to our next adventure together. Perhaps something a little drier this time . . .

Love always,

Hubert L. Mullins

1/22/22 – 7/5/22

PS: If you enjoyed this story, please consider leaving me a review! It helps me and it helps others find my books. Thank you!!

Printed in Dunstable, United Kingdom